# Gitel's Freedom

# Gitel's
# Freedom

A Novel

Iris Mitlin Lav

SHE WRITES PRESS

Published 2025
Printed in the United States of America
Print ISBN: 978-1-64742-858-7
E-ISBN: 978-1-64742-859-4
Library of Congress Control Number: 2024922329

For information, address:
She Writes Press
1569 Solano Ave #546
Berkeley, CA 94707

Interior Design by Kiran Spees

She Writes Press is a division of SparkPoint Studio, LLC.

Company and/or product names that are trade names, logos, trademarks, and/or registered trademarks of third parties are the property of their respective owners and are used in this book for purposes of identification and information only under the Fair Use Doctrine.

For:

Yehuda Leibe Mitlin and Pesha Gershonbein Mitlin

Isser Mitlin and Feige Rokhlin Mitlin

Yaakov Moshe Minkow and Rayzel Cashdan Minkow

Shmuel Hersh Mitlin and Itta Gitel Minkow Mitlin

Phyllis Mitlin Warren

*zikhronam livrakha*

May their memories be for a blessing.

# On Language

Throughout this historical novel, I have attempted to stay true to the language that was used in the specific years covered in the story. At times, that required using language that today would or could be considered offensive. In 1963, the character Ilana worked at a camp for "mentally retarded children." Beginning in the 1990s, the term "mentally retarded" was replaced by "intellectual disability," but it would be jarring and incorrect to use "intellectual disability" in a scene set in 1963. Similar considerations apply to the term "Negro," which was the term by which Black Americans identified themselves from the 1940s until the late 1960s, after which the preferred term became "Black." The issue of the term "Indian" to refer to Indigenous Americans is less clear, nor is the current preference consistent across tribes. "Indian" is only used in the novel to refer to "Indian Village," the common name for an actual group of apartment buildings that were in Hyde Park at the time in which each building was named after a tribe.

This novel uses many Yiddish and Hebrew words throughout, especially in the earlier chapters. The words generally are explained where they appear, and there also is a glossary at the end of the book. Yiddish actually is written in Hebrew letters like this ייִדיש, but the Yiddish words in this novel are presented in transliteration. The spelling of Yiddish terms in this book uses the transliteration standards of the YIVO Institute for Jewish Research. From its website: "YIVO became the acknowledged authority on the Yiddish language and pioneered important linguistic research on Yiddish. The standards YIVO developed for Yiddish orthography, or spelling, and for the transliteration of Yiddish into English are today the most commonly used by publishers and scholars." The YIVO spelling standards may be less familiar to readers than some other spellings. The name of the main character is often spelled Gittle, but here it is spelled Gitel. It rhymes with the word "little." Another example is the word *khutspe* (audacity), which may be more familiar to readers as *chutzpah*. Nevertheless, the YIVO spelling is more appropriate.

However, words that came from Hebrew into Yiddish, such as *shabbes* (the prescribed day of rest from sundown Friday until sundown Saturday), *challah* (the braided bread eaten on shabbes), or *mazel* (luck), are spelled in their more well-known form in which they have passed into English usage. About twenty percent of Yiddish is Hebrew words, often with a slightly different pronunciation.

# 1

Rayzel, a small, slim woman with dark curly hair, who is less than five feet tall, is still wearing her night clothes when she adds wood to the coals in the huge bakery oven. With satisfaction, she looks around at the white walls, the large, scrubbed-clean wooden tables, the bins of flour, and the closed cabinets containing nuts, honey, poppy seeds, raisins, cinnamon, chocolate, and other ingredients. Nothing has been disturbed. It is 4:00 a.m. on Friday, and there is much work to do. She knows that the Jews of Borisov depend on her challah and sweets to make their *shabbes*.

She goes back into the living area attached to the bakery and wakes her five sons and her sister Yokha to help her, all the while nursing her baby daughter, Gitel. The sons tumble into the bakery, the younger ones mixing dough, the older ones kneading it to make the challah. She begins to create sweet dough for filling with poppy seed, and to make rugelach, babka, and raisin cookies. Everyone works with great concentration. The only sound comes when she periodically takes a bit of dough from each batch, says the required blessing, and tosses the bit into the fire.

Rayzel gazes at her children and sister working so well together, and covers with her hand the wide smile she feels developing on her face so she will not distract anyone. The warmth of the bakery is favorable to the dough rising quickly, so by 8:00 a.m. the bakery shelves are lined with many dozens of challahs shining from the egg wash on their crusts or glistening with sesame seeds on top, along with pastries whose fragrance invites eating. She shoos her sons inside, reminding them all to wash their hands and the older ones to *daven* (pray) before doing anything else.

As Rayzel gets dressed for the day, she thinks about her life up until now and where it may be going. *My husband Yankel had been in the Russian army since we were married. He is expert at handling horses, keeping them healthy, and treating them when they are ill. The army felt they needed him, and did not want to let him go. He did get paid, but not that much—and it sometimes was difficult for the pay to reach me. My earnings from the bakery always were very important for the family. The earnings are especially important now, because Yankel has gone to America to avoid the army's insistence that he sign up for another five years. He has had enough of army life, which is especially hard on Jews. But I am not sure what that means for me, the children, or my bakery. I try not to think about that.*

At nine o'clock, she opens the bakery to customers, with baby Gitel settled into a cloth sling close to her body. She does not expect many customers this early, so her eyebrows rise in surprise when the door dings an arrival almost as soon as she has turned the sign to Open.

A woman walks in quickly and without the customary greeting says, "Oy, Rayzel, I have such a problem. I think you are the only one who can help me."

"And *a gut morgn* to you too, Khavele," Rayzel says. "I am well, *Gott's dank*. Now what is your problem and how can I help?"

"This is the third Friday in a row. I go outside to get a goose for our dinner to take to the *shoykhet* to have it slaughtered. I count the geese, and one is missing! Each week! There is no way a goose could have escaped. Someone in this town is a *ganif*! He's stealing from us! We'll be begging for alms soon if this keeps up."

Rayzel leans her elbows on the counter to be closer to Khave. "I see. This is a problem. Have you talked to the rabbi?"

"The rabbi would be sympathetic, but what will he do? Everyone knows that you are good at finding things that are lost. People still talk about how you figured out what happened to Feigel's brooch. And how you cure people of headaches and melancholy. And so many other stories about you. You are famous among the Jews of Borisov. Please help me!"

Rayzel sighs. "Just a moment." She goes to the door of the house and calls Yokha to come into the bakery.

"Yokha, I must go out for a while to help Khave. Could you take care of the bakery?"

"*Gotenyu*, dear God, I just got the older boys off to *kheder* [religious school]. I need to clean the house and start preparing the food for *shabbes*. How can I stand in the bakery all day?"

"Not all day. Just for a couple of hours. *Kheder* ends early today. When Hirsh gets back from *kheder*, he can watch the bakery, and I'll help you get us ready for *shabbes*."

"I guess I can do that. Let me just change from my housecleaning clothes. I'll be right back."

Khave says, "Thanks so much, Yokha. I appreciate it."

"So Khave, do you have a suspicion about who this ganif is?" Rayzel asks.

"No, none at all."

"Then I will just have to start from scratch and see what I can do. Go home for now and take your goose to the shoykhet to be slaughtered."

Yokha comes back into the bakery. Rayzel takes a basket and puts into it six loaves of challah and some pastries, covering them with a kerchief. *Someone in this town who steals a goose must be hungry and too poor to buy one*, she thinks. *And he or she probably has a family, because there are more convenient foods for a single person to steal. A goose requires a lot of preparation.*

It is a clear autumn day. It has not yet snowed to turn the dirt paths into slush, so she makes good time walking past the neighboring houses. Her first stop is at the small, not well-kept house of Mira and Shmuel. Mira answers the door with two small children hiding behind her.

"*A gut morgn, Rayzel*. What brings you here?"

"I wanted to be sure you have what you need for shabbes. I brought along a freshly baked challah and some pastry. Would you like to have it?"

"Thank you. That is so kind."

She hands Mira a challah and a few small pastries, and asks, "What will you be eating tonight?"

"I was able to get several chicken necks from the butcher and am planning on making a hearty chicken soup with beans, potatoes, carrots, turnips, and other vegetables. This challah and the pastries will make it very festive indeed. Again, thank you and *gut shabbes*." Mira closes the door.

Rayzel stops at two more houses, gives out challah and pastries, and has similar conversations. Then she walks a little past the outskirts of her neighborhood to the house of Blume and Mendel. The house is in serious disrepair. When she knocks, Blume comes outside the door and closes it behind her, as if she does not want her to see what is inside.

"*Vos makhstu*, Blume? How are you? I've come to give you a gift for shabbes. Would you like some freshly made challah and pastries?"

"That is very kind of you, but we don't need it. I'm making challah as we speak. It is very strange. For months we haven't had enough money to have a proper shabbes meal. Then three weeks ago, Mendel said he earned some extra money and came home with a goose. What a treat! And he has done it each week since then. Isn't that wonderful?"

"Yes, indeed. Do you know where Mendel is right now? I would like to talk with him. Just a bit of bakery business. I may need to hire him to help move some heavy bins. You know that my husband Yankel went ahead to America to escape from the army."

"Of course. Mendel is studying at the *shul* now."

"Thanks. I will look for him there. *Gut shabbes.*"

"*Gut shabbes.*"

She walks to the *shul*, peeks into the study hall, and sees that Mendel is indeed there. She makes a noise to get the rabbi's attention, and motions for him to come into the hallway to speak to her.

"Rabbi, it has come to my attention that Mendel has not been earning enough lately to properly feed his family. I plan to give him a little work at the bakery, but it will not be enough. Could you encourage some of the other shopkeepers and factory owners to find some work for him? Maybe get him some steady work at the match factory?"

"Thank you so much for telling me, Rayzel. I certainly will do what I can to help."

"And could you ask Mendel to come talk to me for a few minutes now?"

"Sure," the rabbi says, going into the study hall to tap Mendel on the shoulder and point to Rayzel.

She watches Mendel get up and slowly walk toward her, as if he is reluctant to arrive. When he is close enough to talk without being overheard, she says, "I just spoke to Blume, who told me that you brought her a goose to prepare for dinner. In fact, this is the third week in a row that you have done that. That would be great, except one of Khave's geese has gone missing each of the past three Fridays. I believe that is where you got the geese that you brought home."

Mendel looks at his feet. "Rayzel, I haven't had much work to do for a few months. First, I hurt my back and couldn't lift anything, and then I just couldn't find anything. You know, I'm not real smart. I'm shy and I don't speak well, so it is hard for me to ask people to hire me. Blume just kept nagging me, saying we can't even have a proper shabbes. So, I took the geese. I am ashamed. Are you going to tell the Russian police? Or the rabbi?" Mendel doesn't look at Rayzel, but she sees a couple of tears leaking from his eyes.

"Here is what I am going to do, Mendel. I want you to come to the bakery on Sunday. I can give you a little work. I told the rabbi that you needed work, that is all, and he is going to try to help you find some. I will tell Khave that she is not going to lose any more geese. But you need to do enough work to pay for the geese you took. You need to take any job you can get. You can give me the money and I will give it to her, so she will not know who took them."

"Thank you so much, Rayzel. God bless you!"

"And if there is any shabbes for which you do not have enough to make a nice meal, you come to me. I will make sure you have a little meat and challah and pastry."

"I'll never be so stupid again. I promise!"

Heading back to the bakery, Rayzel feels satisfied that she could solve this problem. She decides to take a few more minutes and stop at Khave's nearby house to tell her that she no longer has to worry about her geese, and that she would in the future receive some compensation for the three that were taken.

She sits down in Khave's kitchen. After telling Khave the outcome of her search, she decides she needs to share some of her own worries with her friend.

"Khavele, I am frightened about the idea of moving to America. Yankel expects us to follow him as soon as it is practical. And I certainly do not want to deprive my children of growing up with their father. But I like my life here in Borisov. And I enjoy working in my bakery." Looking down at little Gitel sleeping against her body, she continues, "I felt such joy finally giving birth to a daughter, after having five sons. I love all my children, but Gitel is special."

"She is, indeed," Khave replies. "But I'm surprised that someone as strong as you is frightened of moving to America. We hear only good news from those in the community who have already gone. And in America there is no worry about Cossack raids or pogroms. I'm sure you've heard about the terrible pogroms in Kishinev and Gomel. We haven't had one here, but it certainly could happen, *kholile*, God forbid."

"It could happen, of course, *kholile*. But I wonder if the good news about America is the real story." Rayzel looks down again at Gitel. "I understand why Yankel needed to go to America. The army was very hard for him; the *goyim* tormented him all the time. For all his talents with the horses and the desire of the officers to keep him, his fellow soldiers resented and disliked him and let him know it. And never let him forget that he was different from them. I hope America will be better for him. On the other hand, I really do not want to leave everything here and start over again there. How can I learn such a strange new language at my age? I never was able to learn Russian. How will I fit into a community there, if there even will be a community? I hear that many American Jews are not even *frum*, they are not observant. But what choice do I have?"

Khave just looks at Rayzel. "Oy, Rayzel. You should live and be well. I understand your concerns. Please feel free to come talk to me at any time. I know you wouldn't want the whole community to know how you feel, but I'm careful about not spreading *loshn hora*; I never gossip."

Rayzel thanks Khave and hurries back to the bakery.

It isn't until four years later, in 1911, that Rayzel has to face the reality of the move to America. Yankel has finally earned enough money to cover the trip for her and the six children to join him in South Bend, Indiana, where he has settled. Rayzel receives a letter, written in Yiddish, inviting her to pick up the tickets and funds that Yankel had sent from a bank in Chicago to a bank in Minsk. She arranges to go by horse-drawn coach from Borisov to Minsk, a distance of forty-six miles, the following week. She has been to Minsk a couple of times before with Yankel to visit a cousin, but has never traveled alone. She is fine being independent and resourceful in her own community, but this is a far different situation. By the time she reaches the bank, she is breathing in short, anxious breaths and perspiring.

The bank is in a small red brick building. Judging from the customers already there, it seems to be in the business of helping people who want to emigrate. The staff of the bank seems to be Jewish, and she hears Yiddish being spoken as she walks inside and presents her letter. She thinks, *Vos a relief! I will be able to understand this.* A receptionist asks her to have a seat. Soon after, a man invites her to sit across a desk from him and shows her the packet.

"Here is what your husband sent. You have tickets for yourself and six children on the SS *Volturno*, a ship that operates between Rotterdam and Halifax, Canada. To get to Rotterdam, you have railroad tickets from Minsk, passing through Lithuania, Poland, and Germany to get to the Netherlands. After you get to Halifax, you again have train tickets to take you to South Bend, Indiana, changing trains in Montreal, Canada."

"Oy, that is so complicated. I hope I can manage to do all that. Traveling alone with the children would be difficult enough without all these changes from trains to the ship and back to trains." Rayzel stops speaking and thinks for a minute. "*Antshuldik mir*, excuse me, none of that is your concern. *A dank*, thank you. I will go now." She picks up the tickets and the money, and goes to her cousin's house to spend the night before going back to Borisov the next morning. She is happy to see her cousin, but she lies awake all night with images of all the bad things that could happen on the trip. She imagines being stranded in a place where there are no Jews, losing one of the children while transferring from one thing to another, running out of money for food, the ship sinking, and all sorts of other disasters. She reminds herself to get new amulets for everyone before leaving, lest a *dibuk* or *shed*, an evil spirit, chase them on the trip.

## 2

Rayzel has a great deal to do before the family can travel, so she distracts herself from her fears by being busy. She thinks about how the family can avoid eating *treyf*, food that is not kosher, during the long journey. She bakes lots and lots of what she calls traveling biscuits, ones that won't get stale on the long trip. She knows they will start out hard and get harder as the trip goes on, and that her sons will object to the meager fare, but she cannot figure out anything else to do. She hopes that she can buy some fruits and vegetables, which are always kosher, between segments of the trip to improve their meals.

Yankel has not sent tickets or money for Yokha to travel with the family. Rayzel has to decide the best thing to do for Yokha, who would have to find a place to live and money to support herself after they left—at least until she could find a husband. She does not know what to do, so she asks to speak to the rabbi.

After Rayzel explains her dilemma, the rabbi says, "You are good to have *rakhmones* on your sister, kind to try to provide for her. One idea might be to sell the bakery, which should fetch a good price and give Yokha enough to sustain her for about a year. Maybe she will get married, or maybe you can send for her after that."

"That is a good idea, Rabbi. But do you know who might want to buy the bakery, and who might have enough money to do that?"

"I might. A rabbi in a nearby town asked me if I knew of any opportunities to buy a business here. I will check on it."

"*A groysn dank*, Rabbi. Thank you very much."

The rabbi stops by the bakery to see Rayzel a week later. "I think I have found a buyer who can afford to pay a decent price. I would be happy to help you with the negotiations."

"That would be wonderful, Rabbi. I know how to bargain for my bakery's ingredients, but I have never negotiated something so expensive and consequential."

Within another week, all is settled. The price paid for the bakery easily covers what she wants to give to Yokha and provides ample funds for their trip expenses.

Rayzel speaks to Yokha and tells her of the arrangements. "I guess you are wondering what will happen to you when we leave. Here is what I propose. I have sold the bakery for a good price, and plan to leave you enough money for a place to live and food for a year. Obviously, it would go further if you find another job. After we get settled in America, we will see what happens. Perhaps you will find a husband. Perhaps we will be able to afford to bring you to America if that is what you want."

Yokha begins to cry. "You are so good to me, Rayzel. I couldn't have a better sister. *Ikh vintsh dir ales gut*, I wish you everything good."

The departure day arrives. A family friend who has a horse-drawn wagon drives all of them and their many pieces of luggage and bundles to the train station in Minsk. They settle into a cluster of seats in the third-class carriage for the long ride to Rotterdam. The children sit quietly for most of the trip, fascinated by the strange crops, trees, and towns they see through the windows. At some of the stops along the way, especially in larger towns and cities in Poland and Germany, there are vendors selling food on the platforms. Rayzel sends one or two of the older boys out of the train carriage to the platform, giving them some of the money that she had exchanged to the appropriate currency before they left, and explaining its value. "Go buy some fruits or vegetables or something dairy," she says, flapping her hands nervously. "Be sure to stay near the train and return quickly." Occasionally, she sees through the window that there is someone who is clearly Jewish selling some kosher food. "You can get whatever that man is selling to eat. You can trust him." She saves her biscuits for the ship, when other supplies will not be available.

Rayzel thinks that the children behaved well during the train trip. The strange surroundings, perhaps, may have held down the usual level of bickering among the boys. Four-year-old Gitel, on the other hand, will not let go of her mother. She whines a lot and insists on sitting on Rayzel's lap all the time. *Gitel is a bit annoying*, Rayzel thinks, *but clinging is better than running around on the train. I would be terrified of losing her.*

After nearly two days of traveling, they arrive in Rotterdam and go to the port to look at the SS *Volturno*. The ship is very long and wide, but not high. There is a single deck with a large cylinder that looks like a chimney in the middle, and two masts on each end. As Rayzel soon finds out, the majority of the ship is under the water, where it cannot be seen from the shore.

After finding the Jewish neighborhood in Rotterdam, they spend one night in a Jewish-run hotel and are able to eat in a kosher restaurant. The next day, in a kosher market, they buy some additional provisions for the trip, including dried figs, apples, and preserved meats. The family returns to the port, boards the ship, and descends two sets of ladders to the steerage compartment.

In the steerage section of the ship, Rayzel makes a little area for the family in the large room that contains many families. She uses their many suitcases and bundles to create something of a wall around the bunks that are assigned to them. She promulgates rules for the children.

"You are not allowed outside this wall without permission. If you need to go to one of the communal bathrooms, you need to tell me first so I know where you are. One of you older boys needs to go with Nokhem or Gitel if they need the bathroom. It is important that you watch out for each other. It looks like there are as many as seventy people in this room who are strangers. Who knows if any of them can be trusted."

Rayzel's admonitions work for a short while. But as time goes on, the area in which they are staying becomes increasingly stuffy, and the younger children become increasingly bored and restive. One day, on the second week that they are on the ship, Rayzel notices that Nokhem and Gitel have been gone for a while. They had said that they were going to the bathroom with one of the older boys, but the older boys are all in their places and Nokhem and Gitel are not. Rayzel is about to send her two oldest boys to search for them when they reappear.

"*Oy gevalt*. I was so worried. Where were you?"

"We just went to the bathroom, like we told you," Nokhem says.

"Uh-huh. What took so long?"

"It just took long. Gitel had an upset stomach."

"Is that true, Gitel?"

"Yes, Mama."

"Neither of you is allowed to go to the bathroom without one of your older brothers. Remember what I said when we first got here. That is true even if the two of you go together. I am nervous enough about being in this room with all these strangers, and worrying about how we will manage on the rest of the trip. And what it will be like in South Bend. I do not need to worry about where you children are. *Farshteyt?*"

"Yes, Mama. We understand you," they say in unison.

Two days later, Nokhem and Gitel tell Rayzel that they have to go to the bathroom and that Hirsh, who is already ten years old, will take them. After a reasonable amount of time, Rayzel notices that the three of them still have not come back. She paces around, hoping they will come back soon. She does not want to make a scene if they are just being slow.

Just then, two uniformed employees of the ship come into the steerage compartment, holding tightly to Hirsh, Nokhem, and Gitel. Rayzel rushes to meet them. She asks the employees what happened, but they do not understand her Yiddish. She grabs hold of the children and drags them back to their enclosure.

"The three of you are in big trouble. Who is going to tell me the truth about what happened?"

Hirsh begins to talk. "We thought the air down here smelled so bad, so we wanted to go up to the deck to smell some fresh air. When we went up the stairs, we were sort of blocked by an exhaust fan that by its smell may have come from the kitchen. We carefully walked around the edge of the exhaust, with me helping Gitel, and got to the deck. The sea air smelled wonderful. We saw some chairs facing the sea on the side of the deck, so we went to sit down and stared at the sea. But after a few minutes, those men in uniforms came up to us. They asked us something in a language we didn't understand. Then they grabbed us and took us back down here."

Rayzel is so angry that she slaps each of the three children on their cheeks. Gitel begins to cry.

"Stop crying, Gitel. You need to learn to do what I say. From now on, you tell me when you need the bathroom, and I will go with you."

All three of them slink away, but Rayzel sees them giggling together later. She suspects that they are happy that they had such a nice adventure.

A couple days later, Gitel begins to complain to Rayzel. "I'm itchy," she says. "We haven't had a bath since we left our home."

"Gitel, this is not the time or place to complain. You need to understand that we are really lucky to be able to leave Russia, and that life in America promises to be much better. We will be in America soon."

"What was wrong with our life at home? I was happy there!"

"You are too young to understand. You will someday."

Gitel sulks off to talk to Nokhem.

As the ship nears its destination, Rayzel bustles about gathering up their things, repeatedly counting the children, and assigning each of them what to carry. They all struggle up the ladders from steerage to the deck with their bundles as the ship docks in Halifax, Canada. After they get off the ship, they follow ship's personnel across some railroad tracks and past some sheds with freight, and into a large room on the second floor of a building.

Rayzel keeps a tight hold on Gitel as she looks around, moving this way and then another way, still counting the boys. She is confused about what to do and where to go. She does not understand anything people say to her in the strange language. Then a woman comes up to her and begins speaking to her in Yiddish.

"*Bagrisung tsu ir*, welcome. I am from the Hebrew Immigrant Aid Society, HIAS. I can help you through the immigration process and give you something kosher to eat."

"*Dos volt zeyn vunderlekh*, that would be wonderful," Rayzel replies. "The children have not had much good food since we left Minsk."

The woman from HIAS takes them to a table in another room where other Jews are sitting and eating. They are given hot chicken

soup, herring, and bread—as much as they want. Rayzel feels warmth
flowing through her body. She stops fidgeting with the bundles and
counting the children, who all appear to be happily eating. This is
the first time since they left home that Rayzel feels some hope that
America will be okay.

When they finish eating, the HIAS lady directs them to a line for
the place where immigrants are inspected. She stays with them to
translate for Rayzel. Rayzel is given some papers that the lady says
mean that the family is allowed to stay.

Rayzel once again organizes the luggage and bundles, giving each
child something to carry, and leads the family to the lower level of
the building, following after the HIAS lady. There is a big waiting
room with benches that is very noisy, leading Gitel to burrow into
Rayzel's skirts. The HIAS lady helps Rayzel find the right train. She
also gives Rayzel some packed kosher meals to take on the train.

"You will have to take two different trains, changing trains in a
place called Montreal. Each train will take about a day and a night."
Gitel, hearing what the lady says, starts jumping up and down, pull-
ing on Rayzel's arm, and whining.

"No! I thought we were done traveling. I'm tired! I'm itchy!"

Rayzel just gives her a disgusted look and says, *"Zay shtil,"* be
quiet.

Everyone settles into the seats on the train, and again they stare
out the windows at the scenery. The houses and fields look different from those back in Borisov, and different from what they saw
traveling through Europe. The children doze off for much of the trip,
but Rayzel is carefully watching the family and the strangers that
get off and on the train, and cannot fall asleep at all. When they get
to Montreal, they drag all their stuff into another waiting room and
show their tickets to someone who helps them get on the train that is

headed toward Chicago. Toward the end of the second day of travel, Rayzel tells the children that the train is crossing into the United States at a place called Detroit. But she says they will stay on the train to continue on to South Bend, Indiana. Rayzel had practiced saying "South Bend" before they left home, so she would know when to get off the train. She reminds the children that South Bend is where their father is living.

Finally, Rayzel hears the conductor announce South Bend, so she begins to organize all their stuff. Gitel again hangs on to her skirt while she bustles about. The train stops. There is no platform or building, but the conductor puts down some portable stairs to allow them to get off. There is a man coming toward them, and the boys are all mobbing him. Rayzel is smiling broadly. She says, "Yankel, this is Gitel—your daughter who was born after you left."

Yankel picks up Gitel and swings her around. Gitel screams, "Mama!" so he puts her down. Rayzel says, "She will soon get used to you, and scream, 'Papa!' instead. Just give her a little time."

Yankel has brought a cart with a couple of horses to move all the luggage and bundles. He says to Rayzel, "I bought a house not far from the train stop for us to live in, at 719 West Colfax Avenue. We can walk from here while the horses pull all your stuff."

When Rayzel sees the house, she says, "Oh, Yankel. It looks like you have chosen well. This two-story house appears big enough to fit us all. And I like the porch that wraps around the front and side of the house. It is good to have a place to get out into the fresh air."

Walking in the front door, Yankel says to Rayzel, "The children will have their bedrooms upstairs. Gitel will have her own room, but some of the boys will have to share the other three rooms. There is a bathroom up there. You and I will sleep in a bedroom on the first floor."

"That sounds very nice," Rayzel tells him.

In addition to the bedroom and a bathroom, the first floor has a big front room, a dining room with another room off to the side, and a large kitchen. The kitchen has a door to the backyard, where various trees are growing. Yankel points to one and says, "That is a pear tree. In the summer, we can eat the pears."

Rayzel walks into the kitchen and looks at the coal-burning stove and icebox, which she thinks are barely adequate for their large family. She notices a trapdoor in the floor, and opens it. A ladder leads to a root cellar, which is empty. Despite having praised Yankel for his choice, she worries, *How am I going to manage? Am I going to have to do all the cooking for the family and cleaning of this large house myself? I had imagined that I might set up a bakery here in South Bend. I would rather do that than all this household drudge work. I guess we will have to see what is possible. Maybe Yokha will want to come here to live with us.*

# 3

Gitel has to wait another year until she is old enough to go to school, but she begins to learn English from her brothers. Yankel speaks English well by this time, so he also helps Gitel and the boys learn. She and her brothers tease Rayzel, because she can't speak English at all.

"Mama, why don't you learn to speak English?"

"You annoying children. You know that I tried to go to a class for adults, but I just could not catch on. And I have much too much work in the house, feeding all of you and everything else to be bothered with a class. It is not like I have Yokha here to help me."

After a couple of years, when Gitel is eight years old, she begins to resent the way Rayzel wants her to behave.

"Mama, why do you always pull me away when I want to play with my brothers? They are allowed to play sports in school and after school. They also are allowed to play-fight and wrestle with each other. I'd like to do that too!"

"Gitel, you are a girl. Girls do not do things like that. I have told you before. I was so happy when you were born. I had prayed for a daughter after having had five boys, and then you came. I love your brothers. But you are special to me."

"You want me to be like you were, a girl growing up in Russia long ago, wearing a long skirt and long sleeves and rarely going out of the house. We are living in a new country in a new time. The other girls in my class don't have to follow old rules like I do. They can get together after school, play jump rope and other games, go to the park, do lots of things. You insist that I come right home. And you won't let me go to any other girl's house after school unless you know the mother. But because you don't speak English, you rarely know the other mothers. You won't even let me walk to school alone. You make me walk with one of my brothers. It is embarrassing. It isn't fair!"

"I am trying to keep you safe," Rayzel replies. "Who knows what can happen to a girl in this country. I have heard bad stories about dangerous things. I do not understand this country. I have not yet become comfortable here. Maybe I never will. I just want you to stay safe."

"I'd call it buried, not 'safe.' I've heard my father suggest that you learn English and try to fit in to this country. Just because you can't do either of those things, please don't take it out on me."

"You are too young to understand. Someday you will be a mother, God willing, and then you will look back and realize that I was right."

"No, I won't. I don't want to be that kind of mother. I don't think I ever want to be a mother at all."

On shabbes there are additional restrictions. Gitel can't do anything, not even go outside alone. She can sit on the front porch if the weather is nice and read a book, but otherwise she is stuck doing nothing inside the house. That is also the situation for her brothers, except that they go to shul with their father on shabbes morning to pray. The afternoons are always tense, as the boys grow bored and irritable. It often ends up with a loud fight—verbal or physical— breaking out among them. Their father, who likes to nap on shabbes afternoons, becomes very angry and yells at them to each go into their bedrooms and stay there. Sometimes Gitel will relieve her own boredom by instigating the fight. She'll say something like, "I saw Nokhem wrestling in the schoolyard yesterday. He already beats boys three or four years older than he is. Aisik and Hirsh, I bet Nokhem could beat you both." That might at least bring some excitement as Aisik and Hirsh try to prove her statement wrong.

Gitel is short like her mother and brothers, and like her brothers she likes to exercise. Although she is sure she knows the answer, one day she asks Rayzel if she can wear pants after school, like her brothers.

"After school, I like to go to the playground that is two blocks away. You said I could do that sometimes if one of my brothers goes with me. Could I wear pants when I go there? I like to swing high on the playground swings and climb up to the top of the monkey bars, but those things are difficult to do in a skirt that comes below my knees. Wouldn't it be more modest, as you are always telling me to be, if there was no chance that my skirt would blow up when I swing?"

"Your skirt better not blow up! And you certainly cannot wear pants. Girls wear dresses. The Torah says that boys should not dress as girls and girls should not dress as boys. End of story. God would punish you if you disobeyed."

Gitel sighs. Rayzel's mind would never leave her traditional community in Russia.

When Gitel is nine years old, her father and some of his friends get together to establish a synagogue about a block from their house. They call it the Taylor Street shul. The shul had existed before in an old kosher meat market farther away, but this is the first time it has its own building and a new name. Before that, Gitel's three youngest brothers had gone to kheder (religious school) in the old location. They would sometimes go with Yankel to services, especially on holidays but also most of the time on shabbes. It was a long walk. Rayzel and Gitel never went before it moved to the nearby building, but now Rayzel starts going to the new shul and insists that Gitel come too. They have to climb up to the balcony to sit with the other women and girls.

Gitel has no idea what is going on in the service. She sees that many of the women, including her mother, have their own prayer books in Yiddish. They read from their Yiddish books in quiet voices, each at their own pace, while the service down below proceeds in Hebrew. Her brothers have learned Hebrew and the prayers in kheder, but girls are not allowed to go. Although she speaks Yiddish all the time at home, Gitel has never learned to read Yiddish, as it is written in Hebrew characters. Her father has told her that she should be an American; there is no point to reading Yiddish. Her father feels that they should leave all that behind. All Gitel can do in shul is sit there and fidget, tugging at her mother to explain what is going on. Gitel wonders, *Why does God put so many restrictions on girls? Why can't I learn Hebrew like my brothers? Why can't I wear pants when I play? Why do the women and girls have to sit up here, disconnected from the service going on below? Does God hate girls?*

Gitel often has to listen to the stories Rayzel tells about life back in Russia. Gitel hears all about how, at least in Rayzel's telling, she was so well respected in her neighborhood. Her bakery in Borisov was famous; all the Jews got their challahs and pastries for shabbes from her bakery, and many bought bread every day from her as well. She bemoans that she has not yet found her place in Jewish American society.

"Mama, I know that you are unhappy here, and that you haven't made many friends. Maybe now that you go to shul, you will meet some other women like yourself who speak Yiddish and mostly stay at home. I've made friends at school, and I think my brothers have. You could too."

"*Oy*, Gitel. *Fun dayn moyel tzu gots oyer*, from your mouth to God's ears. You are my special girl."

After a while, Tante (Aunt) Yokha follows the family to South Bend. She moves into the house and begins to do most of the cooking and cleaning. She also takes care of the geese that live in a pen behind the house, which sometimes are slaughtered for shabbes dinner, and she makes wonderful pillows and quilts from their down.

"Mama, why did Tante never marry?" Gitel asks. "And why does she want to live with us and do all that work? It is as if she is a house-keeper or maid. And why is Tante, as everyone calls her rather than saying her name, so nasty to me and my brothers? She doesn't want us around her. And she won't let me in the kitchen when she is cooking."

Rayzel tells Gitel about Yokha's story. "You see, Gitel, Tante had been engaged to be married to someone in Toronto, Canada. She had never met him, but the marriage had been arranged through people from their neighborhood in Borisov who had earlier immigrated to Toronto. When Tante arrived in Toronto, she learned that the man had become ill and died. Not knowing what else to do, she continued on to South Bend to join us."

"That accounts for why Tante has a bitter personality," Gitel replies.

"But couldn't she find someone else to marry and have her own family rather than live with us and be so mean?"

"You will understand when you are older."

"That is always your answer. I want to understand now!"

# 4

Gitel does very well in school as she grows older, although she does sometimes get in trouble, when she passes notes to her girlfriends or reads a novel on top of the textbook she is supposed to be reading. She often is sent to the principal's office.

"Gitel, why do you misbehave in class so often?" the principal demands to know.

"I'm bored in class. The lessons go so slowly. I have trouble just sitting still while other students catch up to what I already understand."

"I appreciate that you are smarter than many other students, and catch on more quickly. But school is for everyone. You must make an effort to not be disruptive."

"Why is it disruptive if I read a book while I am waiting for the class to move on?" Gitel asks.

"Other students notice, and it is a bad example for them. I trust you will behave from now on. You may go back to class now. I will not contact your parents at this time, but I will if your bad behavior continues."

*I can't stop being bored*, Gitel thinks. *I'll do my best, but I guess I will find myself back in the principal's office again.*

Gym classes are Gitel's favorite. She is never bored in gym. For sports, all the girls can take off their skirts and wear bloomers, baggy pants fastened below the knee. She especially likes to play field hockey, which requires nearly constant running. *Running gives me such a feeling of freedom, an escape from the life Mama wants for me,* she thinks.

But that is just in school gym class. Rayzel still won't let her wear pants or play any sports outside of school.

Gitel has a frequently repeated argument with Rayzel.

"Do you want me to just sit around and do nothing after school and on Sunday, Mama? I have a lot of energy and no way to use it."

"You should do girl things, Gitel. You could read or learn to sew or begin to cook and bake."

"I do read a lot, but it gets tiresome after a while. And how could I do any of those other things, Mama? Tante doesn't let me near the kitchen; she doesn't want me around her. And she won't want to teach me to sew or embroider either. You could teach me to bake, but you have let Tante have complete control of the kitchen. Besides, I am good at sports. Sports are good for girls as well as boys."

"No, good Jewish girls don't play sports."

Sometimes, when Rayzel is out of the house and Tante isn't paying attention, Gitel takes a pair of Nokhem's pants, puts them on, and looks at herself in the long mirror in the upstairs hallway. Nokhem is short like she is, so the pants fit pretty well. Sometimes she'll also borrow a shirt and tie to put on. She has long, dark hair with unruly curls that she thinks ruin the picture, so she takes a cap from the pegs in the entrance hall and stuffs her hair under it. *I rather like the way I look*, she thinks. She jumps up and down a bit and tries running in place to feel the freedom of wearing pants. But she can't ever leave the house like that. Neighbors would tell Rayzel.

When Gitel gets to high school, she learns that there is a word, "tomboy," that might describe how she feels. She thinks that she does indeed feel like a tomboy. She tells a couple of her brothers about her discovery of the word. Hirsh tells her, "Little girls can be tomboys, but you are too old for that stuff. You now have to worry about your reputation and your ability to find a husband."

"I'm not interested in getting married, ever! I'd prefer to keep my freedom. I didn't expect you to side with Mama on this. I thought you were on my side!"

Gitel makes friends with a few other girls who resent not having the freedoms their brothers have, and feel they might be happier if they had been born as boys—or at least treated the same as boys. Gitel thinks, *I'm glad that I'm not the only one who feels that way. Even some really pretty girls share these thoughts. I'm less than five feet tall, with long hair that is always messy and a face that would not be called pretty. One of the girls who became my good friend is nearly five foot six, with a short, straight bob haircut. She is thin, although I noticed that she has a nicely rounded bottom. I think she has a pretty face as well.*

There are a few more opportunities to play sports at Central High School, the only one in South Bend. But the girls just play among themselves, nothing competitive. Nokhem does competitive wrestling. His team plays against other schools in Northern Indiana. Hirsh has already finished high school, but he had been on the baseball team that also played other schools.

There is a club for high school girls, sponsored by the shul, that Gitel joins, the stated purpose of which is to conduct charitable activities in the Jewish community and beyond. They also study a bit about Judaism with the rabbi and—together with the sisterhood of adult women—organize some of the holiday celebrations. In her junior year of high school, Gitel is elected president of that club. Rayzel tells her that she is very comfortable with her involvement in this club, a rare vote of approval for her behavior. But that year, for

Purim, Gitel talks all the members into borrowing clothes from their brothers or fathers and dressing up as men. They take a photograph together, which is widely circulated. Rayzel can't complain, because Purim is the one day a year that cross-gender dressing is allowed and even encouraged. On Purim everyone wears costumes; a person is not supposed to be able to distinguish Mordechai, the hero of the Book of Esther, from the villain Haman, or, by extension, a girl from a boy.

Gitel sometimes has a date for a school dance, but she doesn't go out of her way to try and entice boys to ask her out on dates. A lot of the girls in her class work hard at flirting, but her group of close friends does not.

"Don't you think that most of the boys we know are so concerned with being perceived as very masculine that they use vulgar language and try to out-boast or out-muscle each other?" Gitel asks four of her friends over lunch.

"I definitely agree," one of them says, as the others nod their heads.

"I'm used to some of that behavior among my brothers, particularly the wrestling and roughhousing, but the language and the boasting do not appeal to me," Gitel continues. "I prefer to hang out with you girls rather than try to get dates with these thugs."

When Gitel is sixteen, some of the non-Jewish girls from the high school start an after-school softball team. Gitel has heard that girls' softball is becoming popular in Chicago, and South Benders always look to Chicago for the latest trends. Softball is considered better for girls than baseball, because it uses a larger ball and the pitches are made underhand, so they are slower than baseball pitches. Gitel asks to be included on the team. She makes up a lot of excuses for what she is doing after school so she can attend the practices, and secretly brings along a pair of pants that Nokhem had left behind when he went to college, to wear while playing. But it is hard to keep secrets from Rayzel, and she eventually catches on to the fact that Gitel is hiding something.

"Where are you really going after school?" Rayzel demands to know. "Someone I know thought she saw you playing ball in the park with other girls. And wearing pants!"

Gitel has to admit that she is playing softball.

"You are a *vilde khaye*, a wild animal," Rayzel declares. "I don't know what I am going to do with you."

Gitel knows that Rayzel can't do much to stop her. At age sixteen, she feels pretty independent. Rayzel stops talking to her for a while, but Gitel doesn't mind that so much. Gitel overhears her mother complaining to her father, saying that she is out of control, but Yankel tells her that Gitel is just acting like an American girl—which is fine with him. She often hears him suggesting to Rayzel that she get her mind out of Borisov, learn English, and learn more about life in America.

When Gitel is seventeen years old, on Saturday, May 17, 1924, the Ku Klux Klan plans to come to South Bend in huge numbers to rally against the Catholic University of Notre Dame. The impending event has been the talk of the town since it was announced ten days earlier.

At dinner, Gitel listens intently as Yankel explains why this is going to happen and what it means.

"The Klan hates Catholics as much as they hate Jews, or almost as much. Notre Dame, which is considered the best Catholic university in the country, is a tempting target for them. At least that is what I read in the newspaper. The paper noted that Klan sympathizers had taken over Indiana's Republican Party in the last statewide election, and they had also won several offices right here in St. Joseph County. The support for the Klan is widespread in the state and locally, the article said."

Nokhem, who had come home during a break in his classes at the University of Wisconsin, interrupts, "What does that mean for us? Are they just going after the Catholics, or will they turn on us Jews too?"

"It is hard to say," Yankel replies. "The newspaper said that the Klan is planning a parade through town. The South Bend police refused to give them a permit for the parade, but they are likely to have their parade anyway. The male students from Notre Dame have been asked by the school's administration to stay on campus and ignore the Klan activities. I doubt that they will do that, because many or most will feel that it is their obligation to oppose anti-Catholic forces. I think that those who fight against the Klan would be doing the right thing!"

"Shouldn't Jews also oppose the Klan, Dad?" Aisik chimes in.

"You certainly could make that argument," Yankel says.

At this point, Rayzel says that is enough political conversation at the table. Most of it had been in English, although there was enough in Yiddish to worry her. Especially Aisik's comment and Yankel's reply.

As the day approaches, Gitel's brothers Nokhem, Aisik, and Hirsh tell her that they have organized a substantial number of Jewish men to oppose the Klan. They plan to join forces with the Notre Dame students who they anticipate will be happy to face off with the Klan members.

When the day comes, some of the Klansmen are marching in groups around downtown South Bend wearing their white robes and hoods, carrying signs and shouting their slogans of hate. They are promising to make Indiana a place for white men, by which they mean no Catholics or Jews. Gitel's brothers, the young Jewish men that they had organized, and a number of the students confront some of the Klansmen on the corner of Main Street and LaSalle Avenue. The young men overpower the Klansmen, and strip them of their robes and hoods. They forcefully push them out of the center of the city toward Island Park, across the St. Joseph River from the campus, where the main group of Klansmen have gathered to hold a rally.

Earlier in the day, Rayzel notices her sons' absence and asks Gitel if she knows where they are. Deciding to tell the truth, she says, "They went out to fight the Klansmen with a group of young Jewish men they organized."

"*Oy, vey iz mir!* Woe is to me! What if they get killed? What if they get arrested? Why are they so stupid? In Russia, when the Cossacks came to our neighborhood, all the Jews stayed indoors or hid somewhere. Why did your brothers go out to meet trouble?"

Gitel is silent. She knows that her mother does not expect any answer from her.

She looks on as Rayzel puts water on a cloth, lies down on her bed, and puts the cloth over her forehead and eyes, saying, "Oy, such a headache I have!" Tante comes to her bedside and busies herself taking care of Rayzel.

Gitel sees her opportunity, and quietly slips out the front door. She finds her brothers at Island Park by asking people on the street what is happening, and watches the action from a safe distance.

Her brothers, the other Jewish men, and the students are standing on the Jefferson Boulevard Bridge over the St. Joseph River, preventing the Klansmen from crossing over into the Notre Dame campus. Gitel hears them telling the Klansmen that anyone attempting to cross will be thrown into the river. Luckily, a huge rainstorm with high winds begins just as the confrontation is heating up. The Klansmen disperse, using the rain as an excuse, and begin to leave town. Gitel is disappointed; she had hoped to see her brothers throw some of them into the river.

When Gitel returns home, Yankel is there with Rayzel. He is furious. "What if you had been arrested?" he asks Gitel.

"What if I had been?" she replies. "At least it would have been something exciting happening. You think I always need to stay home. I hate the rules you think girls need to follow."

Yankel shrugs, just saying, "What am I ever going to do with you?"

Gitel is about to graduate from high school and is thinking about her future. She tries to talk to Rayzel, who has been suggesting that it is about time to engage a matchmaker.

"Mama, I'm not in a hurry to get married. I don't know if I ever will want to be married. I am hoping I can go to college and become a teacher. Nokhem is studying at the University of Wisconsin. I'd be happy to go there, or to Indiana University, or to some school in Chicago."

"Gitel, as you have just pointed out, there is no college in South Bend, except for Notre Dame and St. Mary's College. Going to a Catholic college is out of the question. Knowing you, you would come home with a Catholic boyfriend just to shock us. Anyway, Jews do not go to those places. And any other college would require you to live away from home. Nice Jewish girls from observant families do not live alone in some faraway place. You would lose your reputation! You say now that you do not want to marry, but you may change your mind in the future. And what nice Jewish man would want to marry a woman who is so independent and does not care about customs Jewish women and girls should follow?"

Gitel just sighs and leaves the room.

Gitel graduates from Central High School, but her parents will not budge on sending her to college in another city. In talking to one of her high school teachers during graduation, she learns that there is a small, new Indiana University outpost in South Bend as an extension of IU Bloomington. The classes meet at the high school, but she has never noticed what is going on in the few classrooms the college occupies. The teacher gives her the contact information for the person who runs the college, with whom she later meets.

"Hello, Gitel. I am glad you are interested in our small beginnings of a college here. I see that your high school grades were very good, so you are welcome to become a student here."

"Thank you. For various reasons, I can't go away to college. I am so happy to learn that there is this opportunity here. I hope to become a teacher someday."

"Unfortunately, we do not have a track for a teaching certificate because this is only a two-year college. We do, however, teach accounting and business management. Is that something that would interest you?"

"Yes, I think it would," Gitel replies. "I took a secretarial skills class for typing and shorthand in high school. I think I would like to learn about bookkeeping and accounting and especially management."

"That is great. We will see you in September when classes start. In the meantime, I will send you a letter that confirms that you have been accepted to study here."

"Thank you very much."

Gitel thinks, *This is not exactly what I want, but it is better than nothing. Maybe after two years I'll be able to transfer to Bloomington and get my teaching certificate. I'd be happy teaching secretarial skills and bookkeeping.*

The transfer never happens. Rayzel still is staunchly opposed to the idea of her living away from home. Gitel does study in South Bend for two years, and then gets a job at the Studebaker Automobile Company in the bookkeeping department. She still lives with her parents, who remain opposed to her living on her own, even in town. Nevertheless, her relationship with her parents changes a bit. She doesn't need their permission if she wants to go out after work with some of the people in the bookkeeping department—although they expect her to come home at a reasonable time. Since she is earning her own money, and contributing to the family's costs, they begin to treat her more as an adult—although still differently than they treat her brothers. Her brothers who still live at home can wear whatever they want and stay out all night without any objections from her parents.

By this time, the three youngest brothers, Hirsh, Aisik, and Nokhem, have opened a men's clothing shop on Michigan Avenue in downtown South Bend. South Bend is a big labor union town, given that the large unionized employers, Studebaker (which makes cars) and Bendix (which makes home appliances such as washing machines), are the major source of jobs in the city. Her brothers make the decision to sell only union-made clothing in their store, to attract the workers from those factories. Alex, the next-oldest brother, who had been apprenticed to a barber before the family left Borisov, has a barber shop on Western Avenue. He moves his shop to the same block as his brothers' store. They all help each other out by watching out for problems and covering for each other if any of them has to be away from their store for a while.

Despite the fact that the Studebaker bookkeeping department is considered management, and thus Gitel cannot be a union member, she becomes very interested in the idea of unions. She reads what she can find about the Workmen's Circle, the Jewish organization that promotes unions and supports other left-wing causes. It has a chapter in Chicago, and she begins traveling to go to some of their meetings.

# 5

One Wednesday evening in the fall of 1930, Gitel takes the South Shore Line train to Chicago from South Bend to attend a Workmen's Circle meeting. Arriving in the large room in their office building, she sees that the seats are arranged in a semicircle around a podium. A sign near the entrance announces that the topic for the evening is workers' rights and welfare.

Gitel sees that a man wearing a cap, introduced as Shmuel, stands and goes to the podium to speak. He is tall and thin, with a dark, neat mustache and delicate-looking hands with which he gestures while he speaks. Gitel thinks, *He certainly is handsome.*

"I work as a pharmacist," he begins. "Many working people who come to the drugstore where I work do not have enough money to afford the medications their doctor prescribes. When I tell them the price, they say, 'Never mind, I won't get that today.' By which they usually mean that they will never get the medicine they need. They often tell me that they cannot both pay for the medicine and put food on the table or heat their apartments. Others do not even have the money to see a doctor, and they ask me if I can illegally prescribe for them—which of course I cannot."

"Wow," exclaims the man leading the meeting. "You really have a sad view of what is happening to people."

"Unfortunately, I do. Ever since the stock market crash last year, more and more people who come into the store tell me that they have lost their jobs. Others still have jobs but ask me whether there is anything I can recommend to help with exhaustion. They say they feel sick because their employers require them to work as much as sixty hours a week. A lot of people tell their woes to their pharmacist."

"So, what do you advocate?" someone in the audience shouts out.

"I think we need federal legislation mandating no more than a six-day workweek of forty-eight hours," Shmuel replies. "You may be aware that Ford Motor Company instituted that policy a few years ago with no ill effects on productivity. We also need Congress to pass a minimum wage, so people who work can afford the necessities of life.

"I know that the problems in Chicago are not as bad as they are in states like Oklahoma and Nebraska, where the severe drought is pushing people off their farms. But I think President Hoover's policies are making everything worse and need to be changed before the whole country is unemployed and poor.

"I know that many of you are not as observant as I am, but we are all Jews nonetheless. Our traditions urge us to take care of those in our midst who, for whatever reason, cannot take care of themselves. As you may know, our word for the charity we as Jews give to provide food, clothing, and shelter to those in need is *tzedakah*. The word *tzedakah* comes from *tzedek*, which means justice. While it is our obligation as Jews to take care of other individuals, I think it is as much our obligation as Jews to be sure that the laws and rules in this country are fair and helpful to all its residents."

Gitel is mesmerized. She stares at Shmuel the entire time he is talking. And she thinks that he seems to be looking at her as he speaks, although she suspects that might be just in her imagination.

After the meeting, when everyone gets up for refreshments, he comes over to talk to her.

"Hello. You seemed very intent on what I was just saying."

"I am very interested. I've been working for a large manufacturing company as a bookkeeper, and I see how hand-to-mouth some of the workers are living, especially those working on the assembly line or who do janitorial jobs. They often try to get an advance on their pay, because there are times that it doesn't last the two weeks until the next paycheck. And these are supposed to be the good jobs in town. There are a lot of people worse off. By the way, my name is Gitel."

"Where is 'town'? Where do you live?"

"I live in South Bend, Indiana, and work for the Studebaker Automobile Company."

"Really! I have never thought about there being Jews in some place like South Bend. I mostly associate it with Notre Dame University."

"There are a few thousand Jewish families," Gitel explains. "Initially most were German Jews, but now more are like my family. From Belorussia. That is where I was born, in Borisov."

"I also was born in Belorussia, in Gomel. I was very young when I was brought to this country by my grandparents. I do not remember anything from back there, but I have been told stories."

"Same for me. I remember a little bit about the sea voyage and trains we took to get to South Bend. I think I probably did quite a bit of whining on the way. I was only four years old. At least that is what my brothers said I did while traveling. I have five older brothers and no sisters."

"Wow. Five older brothers," Shmuel replies. "I have one older sister who never has had much to do with me. Our mother died when she gave birth to me, and I think my sister never stopped blaming me for the loss of our mother. And she never much liked living with our grandparents, who are very religiously observant and tried to control her behavior. As soon as she finished high school, she moved to New York and got a job there."

"That is so sad. I love my brothers, and they are very protective of me. But they also tease me all the time and try to tell me what to do and not do. It is hard to imagine life without them." Gitel pauses. "You said that your grandparents are observant. So are my parents, especially my mother. What about you?"

"Yes, I am observant. I only eat kosher food. I *daven* every day, and I regularly study Gemora, the Talmud, with a group of men. All of that is important to me."

"Interesting. I've always thought that left-leaning Jews are not religious."

"There is so much in Jewish texts that supports a more communal and supportive society," Shmuel explains. "Those who are rejecting that tradition are reinventing the wheel."

"I may have a lot to learn about that. In any case, while I would like to continue this conversation, I have a train to catch back to South Bend. But I'll come to some future meetings."

"I hope to see you again, Gitel."

Meanwhile, Rayzel, her friends, and a couple of matchmakers have been coming up with a variety of men for Gitel to meet. She regularly refuses to meet with any of the suggested men. She tells Rayzel that the South Bend men are narrow-minded and not interested in how to improve the country and the world—which is increasingly a preoccupation of hers. She doesn't want to jump the gun and tell Rayzel yet, but she thinks that this Shmuel might be the ticket into that world. She thinks her parents would probably approve. He has a profession, he is a practicing Orthodox Jew, and, if he studies Gemora, he probably is a scholar. And he speaks excellent Yiddish as well as perfect English.

Gitel and Shmuel both continue to attend Workmen's Circle meetings, and Shmuel invites her to attend a couple of Young People's Socialist League meetings with him. The passion for social justice in these meetings intrigues and excites Gitel.

She tells Shmuel, "My mother Rayzel is extremely charitable. She strongly believes in the personal responsibility for giving tzedakah, but no one in my family and few among my friends talk about or think about the societal and governmental responsibility for alleviating poverty. And while I have heard that Jews have an obligation to treat workers fairly, it again seems to be a personal obligation rather than a societal one."

"You are nearly right about that. But there are communal responsibilities toward the poor as well," Shmuel replies. "In places where Jews controlled their own communities, it was the leaders of the community who made sure every person had a place to live and food to eat."

"I am thrilled that the Socialists also talk about the equality of men and women—something I certainly do not hear in my family. I really like working and being independent. I can't imagine being happy just staying home to clean the house and cook, which is what my family considers the proper role of women, or at least of wives."

"I am in favor of the equality of men and women in the secular sphere of life," Shmuel replies. "But not in shul or Jewish ritual life. In my view, Jewish law does not permit that."

"I'm fine with that," Gitel tells him. She thinks, *I do not care about equality in* shul; *I prefer to not attend* shul *at all—or as little as possible.*

They often talk to each other about their childhoods.

Shmuel tells Gitel, "My *bobe* and *zeyde* told me about my birth and early life. I was born in 1905. My father had gone ahead to America, so my mother, Feige, and my sister Zelda were living with Bobe and

Zeyde, my paternal grandparents, in Gomel. My mother was very sick during her pregnancy, and died when I was just a month old. Bobe said that they had trouble finding a Jewish wet nurse for me close by, so they gave me to a woman who lived on the outskirts of Gomel—several hours away by horse-drawn wagon. Despite paying the woman so she could eat enough food to nurse her own one-year-old and me, and have some funds left over for other uses, she apparently couldn't produce enough milk. They suspected that she fed her son first and then I had what was left. When Bobe and Zeyde came to see me a few months later, they realized that I was malnourished, not thriving. They took me back home with them, fed me as best they could, and made plans to take me and Zelda to America to join our father in Chicago as soon as possible."

"That is so sad for you!" Gitel exclaims.

"I guess it is. Bobe and Zeyde took good care of me, but they already were old and had raised seven children of their own. They were very traditional and observant. I did miss having a mother who might have had more energy for taking care of me. My father was a traveling salesman with a territory in Tennessee, so he was not home much. And while Zeyde was considered a well-off man back in Gomel—he owned a lumber mill and was part owner of the family soap factory—he never worked in the United States. We all had to live on my father's earnings, which sometimes were not very much."

"I guess that I was lucky in that respect. I always had a mother and father, although my father left Borisov just before I was born, and my family didn't follow until about four years later. By that time, my father had built up a good scrap metal business in South Bend, so we always had enough money for our needs. My mother was never happy in this country, and tried to hold on to the customs that were followed in the old country. We fought a lot about that while I was

growing up. I'm curious about how you became such a scholar of
Jewish sources and why you decided to become a pharmacist."

"Those are two long stories. Do you really want to hear them now?"
Shmuel asks.

"Yes, I do want to know more about you."

"Okay. It sounds immodest to say, but I was considered a prodigy
when I was young. People called me an *ilui*. Here is a story that illustrates why people thought that. My first memory was going to shul
with Zeyde to say *kaddish* for my mother on the anniversary of her
death. I think I was about four years old. I had begun to figure out
how to read Hebrew and Yiddish on my own from the books we had
in our apartment, and Zeyde had taught me a number of prayers. He
had practiced the mourner's *kaddish* with me. Until it was time for
that prayer, I read the Hebrew prayers from the prayer book, turning
pages to look for prayers with which I was familiar. Then the service
leader announced *kaddish yatom*, the mourner's prayer, and Zeyde
nodded to me. I stood up and said, in my high but clear childish voice,
'*Yisgadal v'yiskadash shmey rabo . . .*' continuing through till the end
of the mourner's kaddish prayer. I could feel all the other men staring
at me, and heard them whispering to each other, but I just looked at
Zeyde, who smiled and hugged me. After the service, the other men
asked Zeyde if I was really reading the Hebrew. When he told them
I was, they suggested that he enroll me in kheder already. But Zeyde
was worried about me being with older boys, because I was a quiet
child who kept to himself and the older boys might bully me. Zeyde
frequently encouraged me to study and read less, and to go out and
play with the boys in our neighborhood. But I was afraid to do that."

Gitel hears some sadness in Shmuel's voice, so she reaches out,
touches his shoulder, and says, "It must have been difficult for you to
be singled out in that way, rather than to be thought of as a 'normal

boy.' Still, I wish my parents would have encouraged me to go out and play. My brothers certainly did, but my mother insisted that girls had to stay home and certainly shouldn't play sports in public. When I was old enough to be comfortable defying her, I ultimately did play softball with a non-Jewish girls' team. But how did you get to study Gemora?"

"It has always been easy for me to learn things. I did start kheder when I was around six years old. I was moved to a higher class because I already could read and write Hebrew well. The eight- and nine-year-old boys in my class seemed very large to me. I was a bit afraid, but they were mostly nice to me. There was one who called me *der shvakhinker*, the weakling, all the time instead of calling me Shmuel. But since I was small and kind of frail, I did not mind his nickname for me.

"Beyond what we learned in class, I decided to memorize the entire Torah with the cantillation marks and the Rashi commentary—something very few people did," Shmuel continues. "I preferred spending my time on that rather than going out to play. I finished memorizing it when I was ten years old. After that, I was allowed to begin to study Gemora with some post–bar mitzvah boys and men. The Gemora fascinated me. It contains the discussions and arguments back and forth among the early sages about what Jewish law should be on a variety of topics. There are a lot of laws in the Torah, 613 of them, but they often are just described in a general way. The Gemora deals with the details of how the laws are to be interpreted and how people should carry them out. There are also lots of stories about the sages and others in the Gemora that give insight into what life might have been like in the years 200 to 400 of the Common Era [AD], when it was written. Those classes met in the evening, because some of the adults already had jobs during the day. I continued studying Gemora in the evenings through high school and pharmacy school, and now I go to study whenever my work schedule allows. It is a lifetime task to learn Gemora."

"Wow! You are amazing to be so devoted to learning Gemora," Gitel remarks. "I'm not sure I could do something like that. I very much wanted to be a teacher. I could imagine being devoted to doing well as a teacher, but my parents didn't let me go to college. So being a bookkeeper and manager was my second choice. At least I have a skill and can earn a decent amount of money. But I still mourn not being a teacher."

"My career developed in a similar way, as a second choice. I did very well in public school. I skipped a few grades because my teachers understood that I was both bored in class and that I loved chemistry and math. They thought I should get to high school as soon as possible. I went to Crane Technical High School—called Crane Tech. I really liked high school. I was able to take chemistry, organic chemistry, physics, and some advanced math classes. I wondered if I could become a chemistry teacher, or even get a PhD in chemistry and do research. I thought that would be a great life. But as I was graduating from Crane Tech in 1921 at age sixteen, I realized that my grandparents were very old and that my father's business was not doing as well as it had been. People living in rural areas were then able to order anything from clothing to an automobile from the Sears catalog and trust its quality. A traveling salesman had less and less advantage over catalog sales."

Shmuel continues, "My father explained to me that there was no money to pay for college tuition, or even to support me for all the additional years it would take to get a doctorate. He urged me to become a pharmacist, which was only a three-year course after high school. As I was thinking about that choice, I became very sick, spiking a fever of 106 degrees. My father took me to the Mount Sinai Hospital emergency room, where they said that I had meningitis. I was in the hospital for three weeks. I knew someone who had died of meningitis, so I was scared. I started praying Psalm 130: '*Shir hama-lot, mima'amakim koratikha Adoshem*—out of the depths I call on you, God.' The hospital did what it could to bring down the fever by packing ice around me, and tried to make sure I stayed hydrated by giving me a saline solution through an intravenous line. Zeyde and Bobe came to sit in my room and pray.

"When I came home, I was pretty weak. It took me a few months to recover. During that period, I came to terms with the fact that pharmacy was my fate, and that I was lucky to be able to do at least that. I enrolled in the University of Illinois pharmacy school in Rockford, Illinois, which I could get to on a commuter train. That is my story."

Gitel notices a catch in Shmuel's voice as he finishes explaining why he became a pharmacist. Again, she reaches her hand out to him to offer some comfort. She says, "It sounds like you are still sad about having to make that choice. Or, actually, about not having a choice. I certainly can relate to that."

"Yes, if I talk about it, I feel sad. All my life, people told me how smart I am, praised me for how quickly I learn things, and moved me rapidly through both kheder and public school. Yet here I am doing a routine profession, one that has little room to express my intelligence and creativity. I know that it is not right to complain. I could have died when I was an infant if my grandparents had not rescued me. I could have stayed in Belorussia and been conscripted into the army or killed in a pogrom. I could have died from meningitis. I do thank God for protecting me throughout my life. But I feel sad that, as immigrants, neither of us had the opportunity to live up to our potential."

"That is sad for both of us. But you are right that we each have something more than we might have. Our lives certainly aren't terrible."

Gitel and Shmuel continue getting together at meetings and on a few Sundays in between for several months. Gitel thinks that they might be in love with each other, even though she is uncertain about what love might feel like. They eventually talk about what life might be like if they were to marry.

"I dream of having my own neighborhood drugstore," Shmuel says. "I really do not like working for other people, and I especially do not like working in a chain drugstore where the rules and procedures are rigid, as I did as a first job. I learned from that job that I do not like someone constantly telling me what to do and how to do my job. At that job, I often could see better ways to accomplish various tasks, but my opinion was repeatedly rejected. I was considered 'difficult to work with' by management. Now I work at a small neighborhood drugstore, which is much better. If we could have our own drugstore, I imagine that I could handle the prescriptions, and you could use your bookkeeping and management skills to run the other aspects of the store."

"That sounds to me like a pretty good life," Gitel replies with a wide smile. "We both could use our talents."

Gitel decides to tell her parents and brothers about Shmuel. They frequently asked her why she was taking all those trips to Chicago, but she had never answered their questions. She asks Rayzel if she can invite Shmuel to spend a shabbes with the family, and they agree. She says that Shmuel will ask for a weekend off from work toward the end of January. For the sake of propriety, he is going to stay with her brother Hirsh, who already is married and has a house that is just a short walk away from Rayzel and Yankel's house on Colfax Avenue.

When the date comes, the household bustles with preparations all day Friday. On Friday morning Tante takes not just one, but two, geese from the backyard to the shoykhet to be properly slaughtered. At least three of Gitel's brothers and their wives are expected to join the family for dinner. Two different kinds of *kugels* are prepared: a savory *lokshen kugel* (noodle pudding) and a slightly sweet carrot version. Chicken broth had been made the day before, and dough is prepared and rolled out for *kreplakh* (dumplings). The geese are roasted with cut potatoes cooked beneath them in the fat dripping from the geese. Jars of pickles, preserved green beans, beets, and fruit are brought up from the root cellar. Gitel is asked to polish the silver candlesticks and *kiddush* cup.

During dinner Shmuel asks Gitel's father if he could say a few words about the Torah portion that would be read in shul that week on shabbes morning. Talking about the portion at Friday evening dinner is a traditional practice. Yankel smiles and invites Shmuel to go ahead with his comments, asking him to speak in Yiddish so Rayzel can understand.

"The Torah portion for the week is Beshallakh from the book of Shemot [Exodus], which includes the story of the Red Sea parting to allow the Israelites to cross over the sea on dry land and the sea subsequently closing over the pursuing Egyptians and drowning them," Shmuel begins. "The text says that when the Israelites were standing at the sea, knowing the Egyptians were close behind, that God caused an east wind to blow, Moses stretched out his arm while holding his rod, and the sea parted. The Gemora tells a somewhat different story. Rabbi Yehuda says that when they got to the sea before it parted, all the tribes were standing around, none of them wanting to go in first.

Then in jumped Nakhshon ben Amminadav, a prince of the tribe of Judah, accompanied by his entire tribe. As described in Psalm 69, Nakhshon prayed: 'Save me, God, for the waters have come in even unto the soul. I am sunk in deep mire where there is no standing . . . let not the water flood overwhelm me, neither let the deep swallow me up.' The Gemora continues, saying Moses was still standing on the edge of the sea, praying. God said to him, 'Why are you praying when my beloved ones are drowning?' That is where the story ties back to what it says in the Torah text: 'Speak to the children of Israel that they go forward. And you, lift up your rod and stretch out your hand.'"

Shmuel pauses, then continues. "This story suggests that brave, individual action is sometimes necessary to prod our leaders to action. We have a leadership problem in this country. It has been a year and a half since the stock market crash. Some banks are beginning to fail. Millions of people are losing their jobs and their homes, and the shanty towns people call Hoovervilles across the country are filling with desperate families. Maybe we all must take the role of Nakhshon to prod our leaders into action, or even to change our leadership."

Gitel holds her breath. The family normally does not discuss politics at the table, and she wonders how her parents and brothers will react. The campaign for the 1932 presidential election has not yet heated up, but pretty much everyone she knows is grumbling about the terrible job President Hoover is doing. Her father begins to speak, praising Shmuel for his knowledge of Gemora and agreeing that the country is in trouble and something different surely needs to be done.

"Shmuel gave us all something to think about," Yankel says. "We have been helping out people in our community, especially members of our shul, who have lost their jobs or savings. People certainly do not have money to buy cars and washing machines in this economy, so the whole town is suffering. I am going to talk to some people and see what we can do."

The conversation then turns to the amazing marzipan dessert that Tante had made.

Shmuel leads *zemiros* (traditional songs) after dinner in Hebrew and Yiddish, which makes everyone feel festive and happy. Gitel has never realized that Shmuel has a beautiful singing voice, something she and most of her brothers lack.

On shabbes morning Shmuel goes to shul with her father and brothers, and Gitel breaks her semi-boycott of shul to sit in the balcony and watch what happens. As they walk in, Yankel introduces Shmuel to the man greeting people at the door. Since it is their custom to give honors to visitors, the greeter asks Shmuel if he is a Cohen or Levi, who receive the first and second Torah honors, respectively, and Shmuel says he is a Levi. Gitel sees that her father smiles broadly at hearing that. She guesses that he is happy because being a Levi suggests that Shmuel comes from a good lineage. She knows that a Levi is a descendant of the tribe of Jacob's son Levi. They were given the responsibility of serving in the Tabernacle and the Temple in Jerusalem in ancient times.

Shmuel is called to the Torah for the second honor and chants the blessings. All goes very well, and members of the shul, gathering around for *kiddush*, are anxious to find out who this young man is. Gitel overhears Yankel say only that Shmuel is a friend of Gitel's—which makes the congregants even more curious.

After shul, lunch, and a rest period, everyone gathers in the parlor of Gitel's parents' house. Shmuel tells the family about his father and grandparents, about his schooling and studies of Torah and Gemora, about deciding to become a pharmacist and about his current work.

He also mentions that he had earned money for school by chanting Torah in various *shuls* if they did not have a cantor or congregants to do that, or if someone planning to do it got sick at the last minute. Because he had memorized the Torah, and has a good voice, it was something he could easily do. He does not mention anything about his political views. When Gitel asks him about that later, he says that he did not know how his politics would be received. Gitel thinks, *He is so wise and diplomatic to refrain from talking about politics, even though that is a major element in our relationship.*

After Shmuel leaves for Hirsh's house, Rayzel and Yankel take Gitel aside. Rayzel comments that Gitel had been glowing all the time Shmuel was speaking. Gitel blurts out, "I'm in love with him, Mama!"

Rayzel exclaims, "My *vilde khaye* who didn't like any men has chosen a most appropriate man! What more could I ask for in a son-in-law?"

On Sunday morning, before returning to Chicago, Shmuel asks to speak to Gitel's parents. Gitel is pretty sure he wants an official blessing for their engagement. She goes up to her room while they talk. When she comes down, Shmuel is grinning and says simply, "Will you marry me?" Gitel immediately says, "Yes, I'd love to."

Shmuel has to catch his train back to Chicago, so he and Gitel do not have much time to talk after his proposal. But as soon as he leaves, Rayzel starts talking about wedding plans. Since Gitel is the only daughter, this is the first time that Rayzel has an opportunity to plan a wedding. Gitel thinks her mother won't have much competition for the role of wedding planner. Shmuel's grandfather Yehuda Leibe passed away in 1927, and his grandmother Pesha is in her late seventies. His father, Isser, is in his fifties, but is unlikely to get involved in wedding planning. Gitel says, "Mama, I hope that Shmuel and I will have some say in what the wedding will be like!" Rayzel just waves her away.

Gitel goes to Chicago the following Sunday so she and Shmuel can talk in peace about what they want for the wedding. Shmuel says, "So long as it follows Jewish law, I will go along with whatever plans your mother wants to make."

Gitel replies, "Mama will surely be consulting our rabbi. She would care that everything will be perfect in that respect."

They decide on a wedding date of Sunday, August 28, 1932, about seven months in the future. They want a summer wedding to be sure a South Bend snowstorm will not ruin their plans.

During the seven months, Shmuel and Gitel keep going back and forth from Chicago to South Bend, usually just on Sundays because both of them have to work on Saturday. When they are in Chicago, they look at apartments in the Lawndale neighborhood.

Shmuel explains to Gitel, "Jews in Chicago, particularly observant Jews, initially clustered in the Maxwell Street area, famous for its crowded shopping area along the street, its many pushcarts, and the haggling over prices. The Jews began to move to the Lawndale neighborhood—about four or five miles west of Maxwell Street—in the mid-to-late 1920s. Lawndale has the greatest concentration of Jews in the city, as many as a hundred thousand. My grandparents and father also made that move."

They are especially interested in Lawndale because Gitel's father has told them that he will buy them a drugstore, or a place and equipment for a drugstore, as a wedding present. Gitel and Shmuel can barely believe their good fortune. It is the fruition of the dream they had talked about—working together in a pharmacy that is their own. Without Yankel's offer, they do not have enough funds to make that happen. Shmuel has not been able to save much money because he is helping to support his grandmother. Gitel has saved some from her work, but they do not have nearly enough to set up a drugstore on their own. Shmuel is particularly interested in establishing a business in Lawndale, because in such a heavily Jewish neighborhood they could keep it closed on shabbes and holidays. In addition to looking for an apartment, they spend their time on some Sundays going in and out of small neighborhood drugstores in Lawndale and nearby communities, inquiring if anyone is interested in selling to him.

Despite all the joy and anticipation, Gitel has a worry in the back of her mind. Being highly attuned to profit and loss as a bookkeeper, she asks Shmuel if this really is a good time to open a business. "Shmuel, I'm sure you have read that there have been banking panics in several cities, with people losing faith in the security of banks and demanding their cash. The unemployment rate is going up every month, and it already is greater than twenty percent. The newspapers report that the US economy shrunk by more than six percent in 1931. It seems to be continuing to shrink this year."

"I know all that," Shmuel replies, "but I think there is reason to be optimistic. I am sure Hoover is going to lose the presidential election. Surely the Democrats will nominate someone with enough sense to get us out of this. Of course, I would prefer the Socialist candidate, Norman Thomas, but I know that will not happen. And in the past, downturns have never lasted very long. It could all be over by the time we open our store."

Gitel loves his optimism and passion for his dream, and so she goes along with the plan despite her misgivings. They find Lawndale Pharmacy for sale on South Kedzie near Douglas Boulevard, a great location with lots of foot traffic. It seems just right to Shmuel. They also find a one-bedroom apartment not far from the store.

As their wedding day approaches, Shmuel and Gitel talk. "Has your mother told you about the *mikveh* [ritual bath]?" Shmuel asks.

"She hasn't talked to me about it at all. In fact, she has never talked to me about anything having to do with sex during marriage. I really know very little about it, just what some girlfriends whisper about. And what I have read in some novels."

"*Oy vey.* That is not right. The mikveh is very important. I can tell you about the laws of *taharos hamispocha*, the laws of family purity for a woman, but your mother should really be giving you practical advice about it." Shmuel continues with scientific precision to describe the need to wait seven days after the end of a menstrual period and then immerse in the mikveh before sexual activity can be resumed. From the beginning of the menstrual period until after the mikveh, the husband and wife are not even supposed to touch each other or sleep in the same bed. He says that immersion in a mikveh is also required before marriage. "At the mikveh the woman prepares herself by bathing and washing her hair, brushing her teeth, cleaning under her nails, and removing anything that would prevent the water of the mikveh from reaching every part of her clean body. Then she goes in the water and immerses completely and says the prescribed blessing. There usually is a woman there who checks that all has been done right. Then the woman who immersed comes back to a happy husband."

"Why is all this necessary? It seems like a lot of bother."

"The Torah says three times in Vayikra, Leviticus, that a man and a woman should not have sexual relations while the woman is bleeding. This practice has grown up to assure that is followed. It also has practical implications. It means that the husband and wife will have sex at the time of the cycle at which she is most likely to get pregnant. The Torah says, '*P'ru ur'vu,*' be fruitful and multiply."

"Okay. I'll ask Mama how to go to the mikveh. I'm sure she knows. Maybe I can get her to talk about some other things too." Gitel wonders if her brothers' wives had to do all that. She thinks, *I guess having a husband who is very religious has its costs.*

When she asks her mother, Rayzel acknowledges that Gitel will have to go to the mikveh before the wedding and says that she will go with her. That is all she is willing to say, and she changes the subject to the wedding preparations. As Rayzel wants, Gitel is having a very fancy wedding dress made by a seamstress. The silk gown is going to have a lace-trimmed train about five feet long, which is as long as she is tall. There are a lot of fittings. The veil Gitel will wear hangs from a hair covering topped with what looks like a peacock's crown, albeit white. The bridesmaids' dresses will be made of satin. There are to be eight women and eight men, a flower girl, and a ring bearer, who will be attending Gitel and Shmuel at the ceremony. It is to be a huge event. Yankel and Rayzel have rented out a large union hall in which to hold the wedding and the catered meal after the wedding.

The big day finally approaches. Rayzel does take Gitel to the mikveh as she promised, but she still has not said anything about what to expect either there or after the wedding with her husband. Gitel's sister-in-law Elsa, Hirsh's wife, drives them to the mikveh and waits with Rayzel. When Gitel comes out, she asks her how the experience went.

"Truthfully, Elsa, I didn't like the mikveh very much. The mikveh lady was very brusque, ordering me about. After I had bathed and done what I needed to do before immersing, she made me stand naked and poked me in various places. She said she was making sure there were no hairs or anything else on my skin. When I immersed myself in the mikveh, the water was cold. I didn't like getting completely underwater, including my face and hair. I couldn't wait to get out."

"I know what you mean," Elsa replies. "We only have this one mikveh in South Bend, and it isn't very nice. I've heard that others are better. I did go before Hirsh and I were married, but he doesn't care if I continue to go or not. We do refrain from sex during the seven days after my period, but I just bathe at home after that. Maybe Shmuel will agree to something like that? Or maybe Chicago will have a better mikveh?"

"That is helpful to think about. I doubt Shmuel will be flexible about this. He is very observant. But we'll see. Thanks."

Having finished with the mikveh ordeal, the wedding is wonderful. Gitel feels surrounded by a huge amount of love from her parents, brothers, sisters-in-law, and friends. After the ceremony and before the dinner, she and Shmuel have the traditional time alone, which he tells her is called *yichud*, privacy. They have a chance to relax in each other's arms and cuddle for a while. Then they join the wedding dinner. There are several toasts from Gitel's brothers and Shmuel's friends. Then Shmuel gives a brief talk about Jewish marriage, called *kiddushin*, which means sanctification.

"There is a tradition in the Gemora that marriages are made in heaven. Forty days before the formation of a child a *bas kol*, a voice, comes down from heaven and announces, 'This person is to marry so-and-so's daughter.' It is God himself who makes the matches. I give my thanks to God for choosing the wonderful Gitel for me."

They are planning to stay in a hotel for four nights in South Bend after the wedding, and then go to their apartment in Chicago. The night after the wedding, after settling in at the hotel, Shmuel begins to talk to Gitel about sex, citing sources from the Gemora and other religious texts. "Sex is supposed to be pleasurable for the woman," he says, "and it is a husband's duty to be sure that happens." Gitel smiles at him, thinking that could be a good thing. He also says, "Judaism is very liberal about sex, so long as it is with the right person, that is, a man and woman who are married, and is at the right time of month for the woman. The sources permit various positions and almost all forms of sex between the married couple." Gitel has no idea what he means, but she keeps silent. She doesn't know enough to even begin to ask what the meaning of positions and forms is.

Gitel showers and changes clothes in the bathroom, putting on the fancy sheer nightgown that Mama had insisted she buy. Then she gets into bed and waits until Shmuel showers, which he does quickly. He comes out of the bathroom naked. Gitel has never seen a grown man naked before. She begins to look a bit, then turns away. Shmuel gets into bed and begins to stroke her all over and kiss her. She thinks, *That feels nice. I guess that is the pleasurable part Shmuel talked about.* Then he rubs some Vaseline on the part of her body that she thinks of as "down there," and pushes his *shmekel* into her. She gives an involuntary yelp, telling Shmuel that it hurts a lot. She wonders what happened to the idea of pleasurable.

After a while, he withdraws and says something about being finished. She asks him why it hurt. He says, "A woman who has never had sex has something called a hymen, a piece of tissue that covers the opening of the vagina. Sometimes it hurts the first time a woman has sex as it stretches or breaks to allow the man to penetrate, and sometimes there is some blood." Gitel looks down at the sheets, and sees that there indeed is a little bit of blood. Shmuel continues, "The sexual experience should get better over time."

Gitel replies, "I certainly hope so." They both are really tired from the day, so they go to sleep.

For the next three days, they have nothing to do other than to be together. Gitel had resigned from her job in anticipation of moving to Chicago. Shmuel has taken a week's vacation. Each evening, they go to the home of a different relative or friend of Gitel's for dinner and the traditional *sheva brochos* (the seven blessings recited to a bride and groom after dinner for seven days after the day of the marriage). During the day, they have time to talk to each other about many things that they had not discussed during their sometimes brief and rushed encounters over the past several months.

Shmuel again brings up sex, and asks Gitel how she has felt in the couple of days subsequent to that first, uncomfortable time. Gitel wonders if she should tell the truth, ultimately saying, "I still find it uncomfortable and painful. I don't know if something is wrong with me, or if it is something you are doing."

Shmuel says, "Sex is not supposed to be either of those things. I will work harder to make sure it is comfortable and enjoyable for you." Gitel is skeptical but doesn't say any more. That night they have sex again. Shmuel asks her how it was for her. She says, "It only hurt a little bit, but I still don't understand how it could be enjoyable." Shmuel scrunches up his face as if in pain, saying, "I have to figure this out." The next night, he tries using his hand to rub her in the place he calls her "vagina," but nothing much happens for her. She thinks, *I want to have children, so I need to act as if I want him to have sex with me. I don't think I will tell him anymore that it isn't good for me.*

# 6

After the four nights in the South Bend hotel, they move to their apartment in Chicago. Gitel's brother Hirsh, who has a car, drives them there with Gitel's several suitcases. The train is a lot faster than driving, but they need to move her stuff. Shmuel still has a few more days off, and they continue to have dinner and *sheva brochos* with members of Shmuel's family and friends to complete the week.

When Shmuel goes back to work on Monday, Gitel goes to the drugstore they are buying to figure out what they need to do to open it up. She makes lists and consults with Shmuel in the evenings about what they need to order. They purchased it with quite a bit of stock on hand, so they hope to have it open by the end of the following week.

Meanwhile, Gitel realizes that she is responsible for cleaning their apartment and cooking dinner every evening. Because Tante had never let her in the kitchen, she has no idea of how to go about making their dinners or even how to maintain a kosher kitchen. Luckily, there are many kosher restaurants in Lawndale that sell carryout food. She knows that they can't afford to buy prepared food forever, so she asks Shmuel's great-aunt Ida, who lives near them, to teach her how to cook. But before they can get together for lessons, she creates a disaster.

On the first Friday they are going to be alone for dinner, Shmuel brings home a whole chicken for her to cook for shabbes. Gitel has a cookbook someone had given them as a wedding present, so she looks up roast chicken. The book says, *Season the chicken with salt and pepper, put it in a roasting pan, and cook it for about twenty minutes per pound at 350 degrees.* That is exactly what she does. But after it has been roasting for some time, there is an unpleasant smell coming from the oven. Shmuel walks in.

"What is that awful smell? The kitchen smells like a public toilet. Is it the chicken? Did you clean out the intestines and organs from inside the chicken before you put it in the oven?"

"I was carefully following a recipe. The recipe I was using didn't say anything about that. It must have presumed that the butcher had already cleaned it out."

They turn off the oven and throw out the chicken. Luckily, some places are still open for kosher carryout food.

Gitel is very careful after that. They don't have a phone in their apartment, so it is a little difficult to ask for advice. She does spend quite a bit of time with Aunt Ida and begins to get the knack of cooking. She knows that she will never be a great baker and cook like Mama and Tante, but at least she can get the meals on the table. She can always buy challah and sweets at one of the many kosher bakeries in Lawndale. Gitel thinks, *Mama and Tante could have prepared me better for marriage, but perhaps they believed that I would never marry.*

The following week they get the pharmacy open, and Shmuel leaves his job working in a different pharmacy. Having a store is ideal for them. Shmuel mostly likes giving health advice and compounding the prescriptions that customers bring from their doctors. Gitel helps people looking for over-the-counter medicines, which are kept on shelves that are inaccessible to customers, and things like candy, greeting cards, and liquor. She keeps track of the stock and what needs reordering. She also balances the cash in the register at the end of each day, comparing it with what had been sold. And she keeps the books so they know what profit they are making and what taxes have to be remitted. They work well together. Frequently, one of them says to the other, "I'm so happy to be working for ourselves and not for others. What a relief to not have a boss tell me what to do."

Gitel and Shmuel continue to have sex a few times a week when it is permitted. Gitel thinks, *I get a break for twelve days each month when it is not permitted. And at least in our Lawndale neighborhood there are several choices of mikveh, and they are much nicer and better kept than the only one in South Bend. But I still don't like being inspected and poked. And I still can't figure out what there is about sex to enjoy. I am never comfortable with Shmuel's thing inside of me.*

Gitel and Shmuel frequently discuss the news with each other, as they have since they met. The newspapers keep writing about economic problems in the country, calling the situation a depression. Gitel, remembering Shmuel's earlier optimism, asks him, "Are you worried about what will happen?"

Shmuel replies, "A lot of the problems are in rural, agricultural areas of the South and Plains states. That seems far from us, here in highly urban Chicago. It is something like the crash of the stock market in 1929, which did not have anything to do with us. It was something that affected rich capitalists who had money to invest, or folks who gambled by buying stocks on margin with borrowed money, who had to pay up when prices dropped—not ordinary folks like us."

"But what about a few of our customers telling us about their difficulty in getting cash from their bank accounts, or others mentioning that they can't access their savings at all? You know about the June 1931 failure of the Noel State Bank near here. As I understand it, it was known as a 'Jewish' bank, and some of our customers had banked there. What if other banks around here fail?"

"You worry too much, Gitel. These problems will pass."

"I hope you are right, but I think the situation is more serious than that. And I know you are never willing to deny anyone the medicine they need. I understand that you opened some credit accounts for a few customers who can't access their funds, but we need to be careful in case the problems get worse."

Gitel continues, "I still have the concerns about opening a business right now that I had expressed before we were married. Remember that in Chicago there are large numbers of small local banks that don't necessarily have charters or requirements to follow any rules on the types of investments they make with customers' deposits. Each bank is independent, because Illinois does not allow banks to establish local branches. Now, many people are like you, they think the downturn is beginning to be over; they are not alarmed. I disagree. The press is reporting a large number of layoffs each week, and unemployment is high. People without jobs can't buy things, and that pulls the economy down."

The situation is discussed at a Workmen's Circle meeting that Shmuel and Gitel attend that week. The speaker urges members to pressure President Hoover through letter writing and rallies to establish government payments to unemployed individuals. And since Hoover is unlikely to do that, it is most important to support Franklin Delano Roosevelt in the 1932 presidential election. Roosevelt, who is running against Hoover, has been supporting relief payments since

1930, saying it is "a matter of societal duty." Shmuel and Gitel support the election of FDR, although running the store does not leave them much time to engage in politics.

FDR wins the election, but the inauguration will not be until March. Between the November election and March 1933, the federal government seems paralyzed, and the economy deteriorates rapidly.

Gitel says to Shmuel in February 1933, "Did you see in the newspaper that the economy is declining at a rate of nearly thirteen percent a year, and the unemployment rate has surged to nearly twenty-four percent! The American banking system is barely functioning, and some reports suggest that it is teetering on the brink of complete collapse."

"Yes, I read the same article. Another report noted that in Michigan, the governor declared an eight-day banking 'holiday' on February fourteenth to prevent the shaky banks from collapsing. All I hear from customers in the store, congregants in shul, and people we know on the street reflects a sense of impending doom. Some people say they are withdrawing all their bank deposits; some even are demanding payment in gold. I fear all that is just going to make the situation worse."

"Don't you think we should withdraw our money from the bank as well?" Gitel asks Shmuel. "That seems to me to be the prudent thing to do in this situation."

"No, I do not think we should do that. Hiding our working capital for the pharmacy under our mattress just seems like the wrong thing to do. It is a lot of money to just lie around our apartment. But I will think about our options some more."

While they are thinking about it, other states follow Michigan's example. By Inauguration Day banks are shut in thirty-two states, and other states have put limits on withdrawals. No one knows what might happen next, but most are looking forward to FDR's impending inauguration for some solutions.

In the midst of all this worry, Gitel tells Shmuel, "I am feeling sick to my stomach in the mornings. I've even thrown up my breakfast some mornings. I hope I am okay. The last thing we need is for me to be sick."

"I do not think you are sick, Gitel. I think you might be pregnant—at least I hope so."

"Oh, what a time to bring a child into the world! Still, we have been hoping to have a child."

In early February, Gitel goes to a doctor who confirms that she is indeed pregnant, with the baby expected in September 1933. Shmuel and Gitel embrace when she returns from the doctor with her news. They make a little celebration together with some brisket and *kugel* that they buy at one of their favorite kosher carryout stores, and glasses of wine.

Gitel continues to work at the pharmacy; they certainly cannot afford to hire someone to do her work there. There are no problems during the pregnancy, so she is very willing to continue. She can't imagine just staying home and having nothing to do. But knowing they are going to have a baby sharpens even Shmuel's concern about the economy.

Shmuel and Gitel listen on the radio to FDR's inaugural address. He talks about government-financed public works projects to give people jobs, about the government buying excess agricultural products to stabilize markets and put cash into the economy. He advocates strict supervision of all banking and credits and investments, and hints at measures that could combat the deflation that is occurring. He says that if Congress will not act on these policies, he will use wartime-type executive power to accomplish what is needed. The next day, FDR calls a special session of Congress for March 9, halts all transactions in gold, and declares a four-day banking holiday. Gitel and Shmuel hug each other and cheer at the radio. Gitel says, "Finally, a *mentsh*, a good person, is in charge!"

One of the bills at the special session calls for the reopening of banks with federal government supervision. In FDR's first fireside chat, he tells listeners that "it is safer to keep your money in a reopened bank than under the mattress." The banks reopen on March 13, and it is reported that deposits and gold begin to flow back. But Gitel and Shmuel's bank, which held both their personal money and the working capital for their pharmacy, is among those that never do reopen. It was considered too insolvent.

Shmuel and Gitel talk about what they should do, but they do not have any good ideas. Gitel says, "You know I am already four months pregnant, which makes me scared. What kind of world will we be bringing our child into? How will we pay the rent and eat if we lose the store, or if it is not showing a profit because no one else has money to buy the things we sell?"

Shmuel replies with a slightly shaky voice, "We have some extra cash around, as you suggested, and the pharmacy is fully stocked for now. I do not think we have any choice except to just keep going and hope the bank might reopen after some time or that perhaps the government will reimburse us for our losses. FDR is trying to pass a lot of legislation that hopefully could improve the situation."

They hug each other and pat each other's backs. Shmuel says, "Whatever happens, we will weather it together."

Gitel wishes that there was someone in Chicago to whom she could confide her fears. She thinks it is important to sound supportive when she talks to Shmuel, and confident that he can steer them out of their problems. But that is not how she feels.

She wishes she could talk to her mother about her worries and about her pregnancy. She regrets not having learned to read and write Yiddish. Her father wanted her to be American, and while she spoke to them in Yiddish, they thought there was no need for her to read and write in any language other than English. But Mama knows no English, and it would be awkward to have one of my brothers translating a letter for her. Nor could she call her mother. There is a telephone in the pharmacy, but not in their apartment. Telephone service in South Bend is somewhat behind that in Chicago, and her parents' house does not yet have a telephone. Even if some connection could be arranged, long-distance calls are extremely expensive.

Being pregnant does lessen some of the tension between Gitel and Shmuel over sex issues. Gitel no longer has to go to the mikveh, and there no longer are weeks when they cannot touch each other. With everything going on, their worries about their business and the pregnancy, being able to hug whenever they want is helpful. And Gitel is able to say that she is concerned about the growing baby whenever Shmuel suggests active sex.

Gitel and Shmuel pay interested attention to FDR's Hundred Days legislative program. It includes agricultural stabilization policies and government regulation of wages and hours and industrial production, along with the right of collective bargaining for workers, and a significant program of public works to create employment. Congress also passes the Glass-Steagall banking bill, which creates federal insurance for deposits. Reading aloud a newspaper account of the legislation proposed and already enacted, Shmuel comments to Gitel, "All of this is great and will help a lot of people, especially the farmers and workers for whom we have advocated. But little, if any, of FDR's program will help us, as self-employed people with a store. And the federal bank deposit insurance is forward-looking; it will not reimburse prior losses. At best, it might help some of our customers pay for their needs—although most of the policies are not direct enough to help most of our customers, many of whom are also small business owners or people who work in small businesses."

Gitel replies, holding back a few tears, "I agree. It does look as if nothing will help us."

Shmuel answers, "I guess the only thing we can do is pray that FDR's actions turn the economy around quickly. And that it will be soon enough for us."

Gitel goes into the bathroom so Shmuel cannot see her, and lets her tears flow. Should she have been more forceful in pushing her concerns about the economic situation before they bought the store? Or argued harder to convince Shmuel to withdraw their savings from the bank while they still could? She was trying to be a supportive wife, but maybe averting disaster would have been more supportive and appropriate. She does not know.

Gitel decides to pay a visit to South Bend. She cannot be as optimistic as Shmuel, or rely on prayer to save them. She needs to be with her family and discuss options with them. She wants to find out if there is any possibility of her parents helping them out, or whether—if worse comes to worse—she and the baby can stay with them. She thinks Shmuel can manage the store alone for a few days. She knows that he doesn't much like selling greeting cards or toothpaste, but she sees no reason why he couldn't do that for the little while she will be gone. On the next Monday, she takes a bus downtown to the Randolph Street station and the South Shore Line to South Bend.

Sitting on the train, she tries to think through her options. It is clear to her that the store will not survive much longer if they don't have the working capital to reorder their dwindling stock. They are barely making enough for rent and food, especially since Shmuel extends credit to anyone who needs medicine but can't pay for it. Gitel doubts that anyone will hire a pregnant woman as a bookkeeper, especially with so many men out of work. That is not an option. She also is unclear if Shmuel could find a job somewhere in Chicago. He keeps hoping he won't have to do that, so he hasn't tried to look for a job. She wonders if it might make sense for her to move back in with her parents in South Bend; she isn't sure what her parents' financial situation might be, but she will try to ask. If she moves to South Bend, perhaps they can give up their apartment. She wonders if Shmuel could move in temporarily with one of his relatives, or perhaps come to South Bend with her. It is not clear if there is anyone with whom he could live in Chicago. His grandfather had already died some six years before, and his father and grandmother Pesha had decided to go to New York to live with Pesha's daughter Sara and her family. There isn't any work for a traveling salesman anymore. Either people buy what they need from the Sears catalog, which often has lower prices than Isser could offer, or people just don't have the money to buy anything. Her father-in-law looked for other work, but he couldn't find anything. Their only option was to go to New York, where the relatives are doing a bit better than in Chicago. *Oy*, what choices! None of them are good!

Rayzel and Yankel are very happy to see Gitel. Rayzel immediately makes her lie down and rest from the trip, even though she says that she feels fine. *Maybe my worries show in my face or body language*, she thinks. *I guess a mother always knows. I hope I will be that kind of mother.*

After a meal, the three of them sit down and talk. Gitel tells them, "I'm concerned about losing the store. Our working capital was in a failed bank that didn't reopen, so we can't replenish our stocks, our customers don't have much money to buy the things we sell, and

Shmuel keeps giving people their needed medicine even if they can't pay. I don't know what Shmuel and I will do if we can't keep the store going. I don't see any source of funds that would save our ability to keep the store."

Yankel says, "We have enough to keep ourselves going for quite a while during the Depression, but I can't invest any more in the pharmacy."

Gitel quickly tells him that she certainly doesn't expect him to do that. "My main worry," Gitel says, "is how I will be able to take care of the baby I will be having before too long. And I'm also worried about having enough to eat during my pregnancy so that the baby will grow properly."

Yankel looks at Rayzel and immediately says, "You are always welcome to stay with us. Tante has planted a very large vegetable garden behind the house, and is keeping some chickens along with the geese. We have our own food as well as enough money to buy food. And with some of the plans for public construction Congress recently passed, the scrap metal business might start doing reasonably well. We also have begun to rent some of the upstairs rooms to Notre Dame students. That is also extra money coming in."

"Thank you so much. That relieves a lot of my worries," Gitel says. "Shmuel and I have to continue operating the store as long as possible and then try to find a buyer who will pay a fair price. I will discuss your invitation with Shmuel and see what he thinks." She asks carefully whether it would work if Shmuel also came to stay with them, but they sound hesitant. They explain that with tenants occupying the upstairs rooms, there isn't that much space in the house, and Gitel understands what they are saying. It would be okay for her and the baby to stay, but they are less comfortable with Shmuel also staying.

Gitel remains in South Bend a few days to visit with her brothers and some friends, and then returns to Chicago on Thursday. She doesn't want to leave Shmuel alone for shabbes. Her parents gave her a little money while she was there, so she is able to buy a nice chicken, some vegetables, noodles and eggs for a *kugel*, and bakery challah. After they finish eating on Friday evening, they talk.

Shmuel asks her, "How long do you think we can keep operating the store?" He knows that she constantly checks the stock and the sales to figure out how they are doing.

"Not long. We no longer have stock for some of the most common items people buy, such as aspirin or tissues, so folks will probably have to start going to a different pharmacy for at least those items. And once they start doing that . . . well, you know, they won't come back. What about the stock for prescriptions?"

"A similar problem. Some of them I just cannot fill."

"I think we need to start looking for a buyer for the store," Gitel says. "There must be people who have not lost their capital who would like to buy it. It is in a great location. Can you put an ad in the pharmacy magazine you get each month? And maybe we should put an ad in a couple of the newspapers."

"I guess you are right. It will be worth less if we wait until most of our customers have gone elsewhere. But what will we do then?"

"Let's take it one step at a time."

# 7

It takes three months to find a buyer for the pharmacy. The buyer is a Jewish pharmacist who has fared better in the Depression than Shmuel and Gitel have. By the time the sale goes through, Shmuel is literally eating on the charity of the Jewish community and his family. Gitel is staying in South Bend, because she is worried about the health of the baby. She receives a letter from Shmuel with a status update.

> *Dear Gitel,*
>
> *I hope you are well and that the doctor says your pregnancy is going well.*
>
> *We have a good buyer for the store, and all the papers have been signed. Of course, we received a lot less than your father paid for it. I briefly thought that the money should go back to him, but I realized that we need it to survive. I have arranged to give up our apartment and put our furniture in storage. I am planning to live temporarily with my uncle Yeyna and aunt Ida. But I know they are elderly and do not have much themselves. I cannot stay with them for long unless I can contribute to their rent and food. I am going to try to find some kind of job here in Chicago. I am making a little money reading Torah for some shuls, like I used to do before we were*

*married, but the shuls don't have much with which to pay me.*
*At least I am not that far from South Bend. I miss you.*
  *Love, Shmuel*


Before Gitel can answer the letter, their baby girl is born on September 19, 1933, in South Bend. Gitel asks her father to call Shmuel, and he comes to South Bend as soon as he hears. The next shabbes he names her at the same shul where they had their joyous *aufruf* (the Saturday before the wedding when the groom is called to the Torah reading and the couple receives a blessing) a little more than a year ago. They call her Faye in English, and Feygel (little bird) in Yiddish, after Shmuel's mother, Feyge. The next day, as Shmuel is saying goodbye to Gitel before returning to Chicago, Gitel sees that he has tears in his eyes and is struggling not to begin sobbing. Gitel hugs him, but she doesn't know what else to do to comfort him. *Being apart is necessary but so sad*, she thinks.

A few days later, Gitel receives another letter from Shmuel. She isn't anxious to open it, fearing that it holds bad news, or at least an outpouring of Shmuel's unhappiness. She is already feeling overwhelmed by Faye demanding to be breastfed at least every two hours or even more often, the need to keep soaking and washing the many used diapers, and her lack of sleep. She isn't sure she can manage to make emotional space for Shmuel's issues. She lets the letter sit for a day, and then opens it.


  *Dear Gitel:*

  *How are you? Are you managing well? I am so sad that I can't be there with you and baby Feygel, to help you and just to be with you. I will try to visit again when I can afford the train fare, but I never feel welcome to stay any length of time.*

*I have been wondering what I have done to deserve all this tsuris, all these problems. All my life, I did what I was supposed to do. I studied and observed Jewish law—halacha—as best as I possibly could. We even closed our store on shabbes, even though one could argue for an exemption for medical needs. I became a pharmacist because that was as close as I could come to becoming a chemist. I was obedient to my bobe and zeyde and always thanked them for taking such good care of me.*

*We worked together to realize our dream in the store, and it all turned to ashes. Now I am cut off from you and our baby girl, without a job, and I am incredibly lonely. I feel so guilty to not be able to take care of my family. And so sad. Why did all this happen to me?*

*I know there is no answer. You know the common expression, der mentsh trakht un got lakht, man plans and God laughs. Good Jews throughout history have been subject to pogroms and persecution, good Jews have died young from disease or poverty, and so on.*

*In the Gemora, some of the rabbis believed that the arrangement of the stars and constellations determined people's fate or mazel, and that in turn God controlled the stars. In tractate Moed Katan, Rava said: "Lifespan, children, and income are not contingent upon merit, but they are contingent on mazel. For look at Raba and Rav Hisda, both of whom were righteous men. When either of them prayed, the rains came. Rav Hisda lived to be ninety-two. Raba lived to be forty. . . ." (28a)*

*We allude to that in the evening prayer we pray every day, where it says that "God arranges the stars in the sky according to his will." I do not believe in astrology as some of the ancient rabbis did, but it is hard to not want an explanation of what is happening to me that goes beyond human actions. My young life was so promising. I was gifted with a high intelligence; people even called me an ilui. Why is my mazel so bad now? I felt that the explanation might have something to do with what I should do next. Maybe I need to change something in my life?*

*Sorry to burden you. I just had to tell you how I feel. I hope to see you and the little one soon.*

*Love, Shmuel*

Gitel begins to cry, not for the first time since Faye was born. *I'm so tired*, she thinks, *but I have to support Shmuel. He seems so unhappy. I wish we could be together. I never fully understand when he starts quoting Gemora, but the letter certainly radiates his pain.* She thinks about what to do for a day, then writes back to him.

*Dearest Shmuel,*

*I certainly think you are an ilui. I have never met anyone so smart as you—so knowledgeable, so concerned about people and involved in what is happening in this country and the world. You are my treasure, but also a treasure for the Jewish people. You should not doubt yourself just because the Depression has been so hard on us. We are not the only people suffering. We have places to live, even if they are not ideal. We are eating, if not the best or most preferred food. That is far more than millions of Americans have right now. And we have been blessed with Faye.*

*Take heart. All will be well. Looking forward to seeing you*
*the next time you come.*
*All my love, Gitel*

Reviewing the letter before sending it, Gitel realizes that she has flipped their roles. Shmuel had been the optimist, the visionary, and she had been the practical, clear-eyed one. Caring for Faye, she has to be optimistic about the future. She hopes they have not brought a child into the world only to have her suffer.

Gitel receives another letter from Shmuel. This one is long, but has better news and a much better tone than the last one. She smiles as she reads it, feeling glad that she had written what she had back to Shmuel.

*Dear Gitel:*

*I hope you and Faye continue to be well. I received your wonderful letter a few days ago. Thank you. It did make me feel better. On the same day, I received a letter from my father. The letter said, in part, "My sister Sara was asking how you and Gitel are doing. I told her about Faye. And about the loss of your working capital for the store and that you had to sell it. Sara said that the economy in New York has begun to recover a bit." She suggested that maybe I would be better off in New York. The state had established a public works program some months before FDR created his as part of the Hundred Days laws. And New York is managing to provide some relief payments. My father says they are crowded there with Sara and Abe, but he wonders if I should ask my uncle Joe if they have room for me. "What do you think? Should I ask them about it?"*

I wrote back to Isser saying that it couldn't hurt to ask. "But in truth," I wrote to him, "I would rather stay in Chicago if I can. At least from here it is about three hours on the bus and train to get to South Bend. That is difficult, but it would be impossible to see Gitel and Faye at all if I moved to New York."

I recently have redoubled my efforts to find some paying work in Chicago. As much as I disliked working at the chain store Pharmall as a pharmacy assistant before I could be licensed, I cannot afford to be picky. Pharmall has just opened four stores on the grounds of the Century of Progress World's Fair on the Near South Side along the lakefront. The fairgrounds opened in late May 1933. I applied to all of them. One had an opening for a pharmacist to work twelve hours on Sundays. The manager there hired me. I hope he will eventually give me more shifts as well. The drugstore is a long way from Lawndale, but Chicago's transit system works well. I can take the "L," the Douglas branch from Kedzie, and transfer to the Lake Street branch at Ashland. The Lake Street branch goes through the Near South Side close to the lake. I will get off at the Bronzeville stop and catch a bus or the World's Fair shuttle from there.

I also talked to the pharmacist who bought our store. He is not particularly religious, and the neighborhood is starting to have more non-Jews living in it, so he decided to stay open on Saturdays. That means he is trying to do everything in the store himself seven days a week. He told me he would like a day off, and asked if I would take care of the store and make the prescriptions on Wednesdays. I agreed to do that. With these jobs, I can contribute to my uncle Yeyna's rent and food, afford the train fare to South Bend at least once a

*month, and give you some spending money. You were right*
*in your last letter. We are better off than a lot of people, and*
*there is reason for optimism. Or at least I try to tell myself*
*that is the case.*

    *Zay gezunt, be well,*
    *Love, Shmuel*

At the end of 1933, the *South Bend Tribune* reported that the unemployment rate was nearly 25 percent. Gitel doesn't know a lot about economics, but she understands that if all those unemployed people do not have funds to buy anything, it will be hard for the economy to improve. Still, some of the Hundred Days programs are said in the press to be beginning to work, so she has some hope going into 1934. If people have jobs or relief payments, their medicines will probably be among the first things they'll buy. Ideally, if Shmuel could hang on until he got a full-time job as a pharmacist in Chicago, Faye and Gitel could come back so they could all live together again.

Gitel talks to her father about her thoughts, lingering at the table after dinner one evening. Yankel points out that 1934 will be an election year for Congress, so policymakers have every incentive to try to improve the situation. He tells her that he has read about a lot of unrest among the population—rural and urban. "You can even see it here in South Bend," he says. "All the laid-off Studebaker and Bendix factory workers, and the workers from the parts suppliers to those big companies, do not have anything much on which to spend their time. Anyone walking into a bar or union hall in a working-class neighborhood would hear a lot of talk about violence or even revolution. I think there are some politicians and other people whipping up those sentiments."

Gitel writes to Shmuel to ask him what he thinks about what her father has told her. Shmuel writes back.

*Dear Gitel,*

*Those are good questions. I still occasionally attend Workmen's Circle meetings, and there is talk there about the working classes revolting in some way. The Socialists at the meetings favor bringing about the end of capitalism, while stopping what they see as government policy favoring big business and Wall Street. They are happy about the growing movement of labor organizing and strikes. I can see the value of the labor organizing, and changing policy to stop favoring big business, but ending capitalism is pie in the sky, in my opinion.*

*Your father is right that some opinion leaders may be manipulating the working class, although all those unemployed workers have reason enough to be radicalized on their own. Radical change is espoused by some politicians and intellectuals well beyond those who are active Socialists, such as the League for Independent Political Action founded by University of Chicago economist Paul H. Douglas and the philosopher John Dewey. The novelist Upton Sinclair ran for governor of California on a platform of confiscation of unutilized private property and the creation of farmer and worker cooperatives, with the ultimate intention of abolishing private ownership and ending poverty. Father Coughlin and Huey Long are beginning to garner huge radio and in-person audiences for each of their brands of populism, and Coughlin's is mixed with a large dose of anti-Semitism. Neither worries about whether their calls for redistribution are possible or would work; they just play on the anxieties, fears, and real poverty and exhaustion of major segments of the populace. There is a widespread feeling that the New Deal has failed to end the Depression. What I see in my pharmacy customers, however, is more apathy and resignation than fighting spirit among the unemployed, but who knows what might happen if the situation remains so intolerable. If FDR cannot use the two-thirds majority in Congress that the 1934 elections gave him to make the economy a lot better, I fear for what might happen. I wish we could be together so we could discuss all this, rather than writing letters. But letters are better than nothing.*

*Be well! Love, Shmuel*

Gitel is interested in everything Shmuel has written. She is worried about the anti-Semitism overtly embedded in Coughlin's screeds. She thinks, *I am somewhat sympathetic to the idea of redistribution of wealth, even though I understand that taking all the wealth away from millionaires would only yield a few hundred dollars apiece for everyone else. I am more interested in a strong pro-employment policy with fair wages and hours. If people have good jobs, they won't be so vulnerable to the schemes of demagogues such as Coughlin and Long.*

After the 1934 elections, FDR has freedom to push through more radical programs and reforms. They include the Works Progress Administration (WPA), intended to create jobs and increase support for the arts, writers, and the Federal Theatre Project. Other parts of his successful agenda include the Banking Act, the Wagner National Labor Relations Act, the Public Utility Holding Company Act, the Social Security Act, and the Wealth Tax Act.

Gitel receives yet another letter from Shmuel, discussing these developments. She doesn't have much time to write back because of all the work taking care of Faye, but she is happy to receive his letters.

*Dear Gitel,*

*I hope you are doing well. Are you following all the new legislation that FDR has pushed through? I'm wondering if any of it could help me earn a better living. I certainly am not strong enough to do physical labor for public works under the WPA, but perhaps there could be something in the areas of arts and theater. Just as I was mulling this over, I received a new letter from Uncle Joe in New York, talking about all the jobs opening up in New York City, especially in the theater project. He wrote that a friend of his said that he could get me a job as a ticket taker at a theater. They are looking for educated people to take those kinds of jobs. The jobs are full-time and pay a little less than the private sector but significantly more than I am earning now. And I am worried that the Pharmall at which I am working will close or consolidate with another one nearby now that the World's Fair closed a few months ago. I think, sadly, that I have no choice but to agree to go to New York and live with my father's family there. I am so sorry that I will not be able to see you and Faye every month like I have been. But we really need a decent income, and this is a good opportunity.*

*My aunt Sara and her husband, where my father and bobe Pesha are staying, live in the Brooklyn neighborhood of Flatbush. So do my uncle Joe and aunt Fannie. It is crowded at both apartments. At Uncle Joe's, there are his wife and their two sons, and the wife of one of his sons, along with my sister Zelda, who is not yet married. I will be the seventh person*

*to move into a two-bedroom apartment that has very small*
*rooms.*

    *I will write to you again when I get there and tell you all*
*about the job and how I am doing. I know I will miss you so*
*much. I love you, and hope we can get through this soon and*
*be together again.*
    *Shmuel*

Gitel reads the letter and begins to cry large tears that drop freely
onto her skirt. She thinks New York is at the other end of the world,
big, dirty, and dangerous—at least according to the local news
reports in South Bend. And it could be years before she might see
Shmuel again. Faye is growing up without a father, and there is nothing that Gitel can do about that.

The next letter she receives from Shmuel is even more distressing.
She wrings her hands and again weeps. She knows that his difficult
early life, and his long recovery from meningitis, have taken a toll
on him and make him vulnerable to catching colds and other minor
illnesses.

    *Dear Gitel,*
    *Our living conditions are not ideal. There are cots around*
*the edges of the dining room and some in the living room. It*
*is hard not to be constantly bumping into or tripping over the*
*other inhabitants of the apartment. Joe and Zelda have jobs*
*with the state and city government, respectively, so there is*
*some money to feed all these people—although not the best*
*food.*
    *I applied and did get the job as a ticket taker and general*
*manager at a theater just off Broadway. I am not licensed to*

be a pharmacist in New York, so I have to hold on to that WPA job. I take the subway from Flatbush to Midtown Manhattan every day and return that way late at night. I work on Friday evenings, Saturday matinee, Saturday evenings, and four evenings during the week. There is no possibility of my observing shabbes. But at least I am earning enough money to contribute to the rent and food here and send some to you so you can contribute to your and Faye's upkeep. For myself, I have no time to spend money on anything other than a few personal necessities.

My work schedule creates a problem for me and for the other people living in the apartment. On the evenings the theater is open, I am required to stay at the theater until all the patrons have left and the floors are swept before I can lock up. That means I usually get back to the Flatbush apartment at one in the morning or even later. My cot is in a corner of the living room. During the day it is folded up and slid under the couch. I must take it out, take the bedding out of the closet, and set it up. It is hard to do that quietly enough to avoid waking other residents. I often am a bit hungry when I come home and want a snack from the kitchen. That means tiptoeing through the dining room where people are sleeping and trying to be very quiet while I take some bread and cheese or a similar snack. Unfortunately, it is not unusual for someone to wake up while I am setting up and getting a snack.

In the morning, the apartment bustles with life at 6:30 or 7:00. The teenagers need to get to school, and Zelda and Uncle Joe need to leave for work. Aunt Fannie gets up early to make them breakfast before they leave. With people moving around *and breakfast dishes clanking, I have no choice but to wake up. I regularly only get about five hours sleep those nights. It is wearing me down. I hope I can continue this schedule.*

*Love, Shmuel*

## 8

Gitel smiles at Faye, thinking that she is growing well. Rayzel and Tante make sure she has the best, most nutritious food. And she is beginning to chatter happily in Yiddish. Gitel makes a point of talking to her in English, but she has picked up that the language of the household is Yiddish. If Gitel is asking her to do something—such as come to the table or put away her toys—in English, she often has to repeat her request in Yiddish before Faye will do it.

Gitel finally writes back to Shmuel:

> Dear Shmuel,
>
> Please take care of yourself. I understand that you are in a difficult situation with your living arrangements. Perhaps you could nap a bit after others leave for work and school. You really need to get your sleep so you don't get sick. I do appreciate all the effort you are putting in to keep us afloat.
>
> Life is pretty boring here. Faye seems content, but I am a bit restless. I have nothing to do other than care for Faye, to play with her and do our laundry. Tante continues to do all the cooking and general housekeeping. Shmuel, I hate to say it, but it is boring to watch a toddler all day. And Mama watches everything I do with Faye. She never criticizes me out loud, but I do see her frowning sometimes, and that undermines my

*confidence. Having been the youngest child, I never had any experience caring for a child. I wonder if I could ask Mama to just tell me what I could do better, but that direct approach probably won't work. That is not how Mama does things.*

*I wish I could work. I know I can't, even in the unlikely event that I could find a job, because I have to take care of Faye. But working, and feeling confident that I'm doing a good job, is what makes me feel good. It is hard to get that type of satisfaction from taking care of a toddler.*

*I know I should be grateful to have a refuge for myself and Faye. I'm certainly living under better conditions than you are. I just hope that some of the actions being taken by the government will end this Depression and that you and I can get on with our lives, together.*

*Love, Gitel*

Gitel does admit to herself that there are a few good features related to her living in South Bend, away from Shmuel. She is away from Shmuel's pressure to go to the mikveh and then have sex with him. Even when he lived in Chicago and visited, they agreed it was too awkward to have sex in her parents' house. Her bedroom there was not really that private, and Faye was there too. Besides, the last thing they need in their circumstances is another child.

Time goes by. Faye has her fourth birthday in September 1937. Shortly thereafter, Gitel receives an official-looking letter from the New York State Department of Health.

*Dear Madam:*

*Your husband Shmuel is sick with lung disease. It probably is tuberculosis. We understand that he was living in an overcrowded apartment, and his work schedule led him to have a constant lack of sufficient sleep. These factors undoubtedly contributed to his illness, although it is likely that he contracted the disease from someone at the theater where he worked because no one else in the apartment is ill. The public health authorities are looking into that. As he was admitted to the hospital, he was gravely ill with weakness, a fever, difficulty breathing, and he was coughing up blood. He is now at the New York State* Hospital for Incipient Pulmonary Tuberculosis, commonly called Ray Brook Hospital, in the Adirondack Mountains. It is a state-supported hospital, so there will be no charge for his treatment. The prognosis for him is guarded, but there is hope that he will recover with the good air and good food at the sanatorium. Please let us know if you have any questions.

Sincerely,

Infectious Disease staff, NY Department of Health

Reading the letter, Gitel starts breathing rapidly. The room looks fuzzy and is moving around her. She has to sit down. She has never heard of any such thing as a sanatorium for tuberculosis. She takes Faye and goes to the office of her parents' family doctor, and asks to speak briefly to him. He explains, "Tuberculosis is a very serious disease and very contagious—especially when people are living in close quarters. There is no medicine for tuberculosis, but it is thought that rest, lack of stress, good food, and mountain air can cure it. In any case, it is good to isolate those with tuberculosis from their usual surroundings. Otherwise, a whole family or household could become ill."

"So, New York is doing the right thing by putting him in the sanatorium?"

"Yes, definitely the right thing. You should not worry. This is all for the best. Your husband likely will get well soon."

"Thank you, Doctor. You've been so helpful."

Somewhat assured on that front, Gitel begins to worry about their finances. Although Shmuel had not been able to send a lot of money, what he sent had been needed. Faye grows out of her clothes and shoes and needs new ones, she has regular medical checkups that have to be paid for, and Gitel feels that she has to contribute to the food they are eating—especially for all the milk and other special food Faye eats. Without money from Shmuel, she will be even more of a burden on her parents.

She writes a letter to Shmuel's uncle Joe and sends it special delivery.

> *Dear Uncle Joe and Aunt Fannie:*
>
> *I hope everyone else in your household is well, given Shmuel's illness. I thank you so much for letting Shmuel stay with you and taking care of him until now. I hate to ask this favor of you, but I wonder if there is any chance that I could get a job if Faye and I came to New York, and if so, would you be willing to host us? We really can't get along without Shmuel's income, and I'm quite sure that a job in South Bend would be impossible. There are no WPA projects here that do not require manual labor. Even if I were strong enough to do that, so many men from Studebaker and Bendix are out of work. They certainly would be given preference over a woman.*
>
> *Please send me your answer as soon as possible.*
>
> Love, Gitel

She also writes to Shmuel at the Ray Brook Hospital. She tries to keep her letter cheerful, saying that she is sure he will be well soon, and how glad she is that the state has a place to take care of him. She has no idea whether he will be able to answer, but feels that she would be relieved if she did hear from him. Gitel paces back and forth in the house, goes out on the porch, and comes back in again. Then she goes into the backyard and stares at the geese and chickens. She does not know what to do with herself. Faye tugs on her skirt and demands to know what she is doing, but she doesn't want to upset Faye by trying to explain. She imagines that the situation is even more upsetting to Shmuel, who must be lying sick in bed worrying about how the family is going to get along with him laid up.

She thinks a lot about mazel, about luck, not for the first time in her life. *Shmuel certainly has had some bad luck all his life*, she muses. *The death of his mother just after his birth, being malnourished as a baby and being frail throughout his life, being recognized as a kind of genius when he was young but not having the opportunity to do much with that great mind of his, getting sick with meningitis just after high school, having our working capital in one of the few banks that never reopened and therefore losing our store, and now this—having tuberculosis. Shmuel is such a good man, and that is far more bad luck than any one person should have.*

*And now I will again suffer from his bad luck. I don't really want to move to New York. It seems like such a far-off, strange place to me. And I don't want to subject Faye to that crowded apartment. What if she were to get sick? All this is so unfair. I feel angry, but I don't know where to direct my anger. It isn't very satisfying to be angry at* mazel *or fate.*

After about a week, Gitel receives letters from Uncle Joe and from Shmuel. Joe says that if she comes very soon, she could take over Shmuel's WPA job at the theater. That sounds good to her. She thinks she could sell tickets and manage the theater at least as well as he did. The switch has been approved by the authorities, Joe writes. And Fannie adds an addendum to the letter saying, "I would be glad to take care of Faye while you are working. It will be fun to take care of a little girl after having raised two boys."

Shmuel writes that he is doing as well as can be expected. The care at the sanatorium is excellent. He had heard from Joe about the idea of her taking over his job, and he thinks that is a great idea. He acknowledges that the accommodations at Joe's are not very comfortable, but he hopes she can put up with that. He says they need the money. He has been so worried about how they will manage.

Gitel feels her heart pounding at everything that is happening so quickly. *It certainly will break the boredom of South Bend*, she thinks. But she has never traveled farther than Chicago before. New York seems so scary to her. Apparently, it also seems scary to her mother, who undoubtedly would like to tell her not to go but instead is lying in bed with a damp handkerchief on her forehead.

She asks her father, "Could I could borrow enough money for coach train fare to New York, and a little more beyond that to manage in New York until I begin to get paid? I don't want to show up penniless at Shmuel's relatives' apartment."

Yankel says, "I will give you enough to book a sleeper; it will be too hard to travel that far in coach with Faye." He gives her the money, with a generous amount for her to use for her initial expenses.

She makes their reservations and finishes packing. Three days later, they are on the South Shore Line to Chicago where they will change to the overnight train to New York, arriving mid-afternoon the following day. They will have to take a cab to Brooklyn. She hates spending that much money, but she doesn't think she can manage their luggage and Faye on the subway. She will eventually have to learn how to take the subway to the theater where she will be work-ing, but for now she is glad they can take a cab.

They are warmly welcomed by Shmuel's family. The boys have agreed to give up their bedroom so she and Faye can have a more private place to sleep. That is a big help, because Faye still goes to sleep around 7:00 p.m., when the rest of the family is still awake and making noises.

Gitel explains to Faye that she will be going to work, starting the next day, and that Aunt Fannie will take care of her while she is working. She tells her that she will need to work several evenings a week, so Faye has to be good when Aunt Fannie wants her to go to bed. Faye says that she understands that her father is sick and that her mother needs to work. She promises to be good.

Joe is worrying about Gitel walking back from the subway at 1:00 a.m., and so is she. But there is nothing else to do. He gives her a whistle that makes a particularly loud noise when she blows on it. He says that she should hold it in her hand while she is walking, and blow it if anyone begins to bother her. Hopefully, someone will hear it and summon help.

All that taken care of, she wants a bath and a good night's sleep before starting work the next day. After all the traveling, she falls asleep quickly.

With the family's instructions in hand, she manages to find the theater the next day. It is a day without a matinee, so she understands that she has to get there around 3:00 p.m. when the box office is sup-posed to open. She arrives around 2:30 and finds the caretaker to let her in.

"You will have to learn the prices of the various kinds of tick-ets and the layout of the theater. The owner of the theater will be here around three for you to sign employment papers and get more instructions on the scope of the job." In the meantime, the caretaker gives her a tour of backstage. Returning to the box office, Gitel tries to memorize the prices, to figure out where they put the cash and how it is reconciled with the ticket sales at the end of the day, and waits for the owner.

She feels fidgety having to wait to start doing the job, picking up and putting down again the various bits of equipment in the box office. After four years of just looking after Faye, she is thrilled to be back in the business world. When the owner arrives, he asks her about her background. She tells him about her bookkeeping skills, her job at Studebaker, and about how she managed their drugstore until they lost it. He seems to her to be impressed.

"There have been some problems reconciling the cash and the ticket sales, especially after Shmuel was taken to the hospital. I am hoping that you will be able to put in a good system to make sure all the cash gets recorded."

"I would be happy to do that," Gitel replies. "That is certainly within my competency."

He shows her the system that had been used, and explains the duties she has to perform other than selling tickets. She has to supervise the ushers and the people who clean up after a performance. He cautions her to lock up the box office anytime she is in another part of the theater, and to lock it from the inside while she is selling tickets. "Some people are desperate enough for money to try to rob the theater," he comments. And then he leaves the theater with some encouraging words for her. She is alone with the job.

She writes Shmuel a letter.

> *Dear Shmuel,*
> *I hope your recovery is going well. I am managing well*

*enough. I do like the job. I find it interesting interacting with the theater patrons. I try to make them feel welcome. And it is even more interesting to get to know the actors, who are quite a nice group of people. I'm sure you know all that, but you had never written anything about the actors in your letters to me. I was scared the first few times I walked from the subway to the apartment late at night, but then I got used to it. Joe gave me a whistle that makes a loud noise, just in case someone bothers me. But no one has. It is somewhat pleasant walking from the subway to the apartment in the dark, with the shops closed and the streets largely quiet.*

*I am leery of getting worn down by the work schedule, as you had. I try to eat a decent meal before leaving for the theater, and to bring a sandwich and a piece of fruit to eat at my evening break. Once all the patrons are seated, including those who came late and were seated at the end of the first act, there is some free time. At that time, I eat something and sit and rest for a while. Then I reconcile the day's ticket sales and cash, and there is little to do until it is time to close the theater for the night. I make sure that I rest well in those time periods when I have no duties, or even take a nap, given that I must get up with Faye early the next morning. Still, it is a difficult schedule, and I understand why you became sick.*

*Get well soon,*

*Love, Gitel*

Gitel settles into the routine and keeps the job for the next two years. She is often tired, because she tries to give Faye the attention she deserves in the mornings before she leaves for work. She is able to save a fair bit of money because she is only paying a small amount of rent. Other than rent, she buys food, and clothes and shoes for Faye when she needs them. She tries not to spend any extra money because who knows what the future will bring.

Shmuel writes that he is now feeling better and is allowed to have visitors. She travels to visit him a couple of times but doesn't bring Faye because children are not allowed. They talk during those visits about what they want to do when he gets well.

"I have been writing letters to several of my pharmacist friends in Chicago to ask about any job openings, but nothing has turned up yet. I want to work in a small neighborhood pharmacy if possible."

"I'd be very happy to move back to Chicago," Gitel says. "I want to be closer to my parents and brothers in South Bend. The money I've been saving could give us a small cushion for making the transition back to Chicago, but once we start to pay rent on an apartment it isn't going to last that long. It would be great if you have a job offer before we move."

Shmuel finally is released from the sanatorium and comes back to the Flatbush apartment in mid-1939. Gitel feels that it would be a terrible idea for him to stay there again in the overcrowded conditions. They have to either get their own apartment in New York or go back to Chicago. Both of them want to do the latter.

Finally, Shmuel has some good *mazel*. A man named Lou who had been in his pharmacy school class is opening a drugstore on the South Side of Chicago. He remembered how smart Shmuel is, and has been asking around to try to find him. Lou ends up asking someone Shmuel is corresponding with, and Lou sends Shmuel a letter offering him the 3:00 p.m. to midnight shift in the store, which is planned to be on the corner of West Forty-Third Street and South Wentworth Avenue. It would be a do-everything-in-the-store job, from compounding prescriptions to making ice cream sundaes.

Shmuel immediately writes back accepting the job, and they begin making plans to return to Chicago. The timing is good. Faye will be six years old in September, and will need to start first grade. With the move, she can do that in Chicago.

Shmuel and Gitel debate where in Chicago they want to live. Their first thought, of course, is to go back to the old neighborhood of Lawndale. But Shmuel's father and grandparents are no longer there. One of Shmuel's uncles, Yeyna, does still live in Lawndale, but that is all the family he has there.

"If we move back to Lawndale, you would have a long commute to work."

"I do not mind that," Shmuel insists. "I would rather live where there is a good Jewish community, where I feel comfortable."

Gitel has been thinking differently, that living on the South Side might be nice. *When I took the South Shore Line train to South Bend from the Randolph Street station in downtown Chicago, I noticed that it made a stop in the Hyde Park neighborhood at Fifty-Third Street. It would be so much easier and faster to get to South Bend and back if we lived in Hyde Park. But I don't know much about that neighborhood. I'll be sure to check it out once we get back to Chicago.*

Aloud she says, "Okay, we can go back to living in Lawndale, at least for now. Let's see how the commute works out for you."

# 9

They find a small apartment at 117 South St. Louis Avenue, which they think they can afford. It is just east of Garfield Park. It has one bedroom, and a pull-down Murphy bed in the living room. There is a separate dining room, so they are able to rescue their large dining table set that they had put into storage along with the rest of their furniture when they gave up their apartment in 1933.

Shmuel begins his job, and tells Gitel all about it.

"I am thankful to be working as a pharmacist again. It feels right. The store is small, but there are shelves for everything people buy in drugstores, including over-the-counter medicines and things such as toothbrushes and hairbrushes. There is also a counter to serve ice cream treats such as sundaes and malteds. I am there by myself most of the time. It is a low-income neighborhood in which a lot of people are reluctant to spend money on doctors, so many come into the store to tell me their symptoms and ask my opinion on what they should do. I wear a white coat in the store, so lots of people call me 'Doc.' That rather tickles me."

"So how do you know what to tell them?" Gitel asks. "I know you made some recommendations when we had our own store, but this sounds like it goes beyond what you did before."

"I try to first suggest home remedies if possible, such as tea with lemon and honey, or ginger tea for a cough, inhaling steam for a head cold, or an oatmeal bath for sunburn or skin irritation. If there are some over-the-counter remedies I can suggest, such as a laxative for constipation, I do that. Even if I am pretty sure about what prescription drugs would help someone, I cannot offer them. But there is a retired doctor living in an apartment over the store who I can sometimes call on. He is retired because he is too fond of alcohol, something of a drunk. When he is coherent, I can tell him the symptoms and my suggested medication. He trusts my judgment and writes the prescription."

"Is that a good idea?" Gitel asks. "Couldn't you get in trouble doing that?"

"I doubt it. The doctor still has his license. He just does not practice. Who is going to notice? I am helping people get what they need without paying out money that they do not have."

"I guess that is okay. I know you care a lot about the customers and want to help them."

"Your question about getting in trouble reminds me of something that happened a few days ago. My pharmacist friend Morrie, who had given my contact information to Lou, stopped into the drugstore to see how I was doing. He was not familiar with this part of Chicago, so I explained that the store sits on the border between two distinct Chicago neighborhoods, with South Wentworth Avenue forming the east/west border. To the west is Canaryville, a largely Irish Catholic, working-class neighborhood. Canaryville is close to the massive Union Stockyards, and many of its residents work in the meatpacking plants. To the east is Bronzeville, also called 'Black Metropolis,' which was settled when large numbers of Negroes migrated to Chicago from Mississippi and other southern states early in the twentieth century to work in Chicago's industries. Negro families are concentrated in Bronzeville because they face segregation in trying to move to other parts of the city, I explained to Morrie. Morrie said something like, 'Isn't that a road map for trouble?' I assured him that it is not. Even though Wentworth Avenue is a place where two very different and sometimes hostile cultures meet to shop or drink in the abundant taverns on the street, it is quite peaceful. It makes life in the drugstore interesting. I am happy to serve residents of both areas, and relations in the store are generally friendly. Morrie responded, 'More power to you! That would make me pretty nervous.' I just smiled at him and he left."

Gitel and Shmuel often talk to each other about events in Europe, where it is very clear that Jews are in danger. They have been talking about it since 1933, when Hitler was elected chancellor of Germany. But now their worst fears about what he has planned are becoming reality. In January 1939, Hitler makes a speech to the Reichstag, the German parliament, declaring war in Europe and clearly stating the intention to exterminate all the Jews living there and in the rest of Europe. He characterizes Jews as Communist subversives, war profiteers, and hoarders, and as a danger to internal security because of their inherent disloyalty and opposition to Germany.

Gitel and Shmuel know that Jews have been seriously persecuted in Germany since the Nuremberg Laws, enacted in September 1935, stripped Jews of German citizenship. And that the attacks on Jews intensified in 1938. In November 1938, "Kristallnacht" took place. It was an attack on Jewish businesses in Germany, consisting of mobs breaking windows and looting stores, followed immediately by the passage of a law completely excluding Jews from the German economy, banning them from owning businesses or selling goods. Then in March 1939, Germany invades Czechoslovakia, followed by the invasion of Poland in September. It now appears that Germany is headed toward invasion of the Soviet Union.

As far as Gitel and Shmuel know, all of Shmuel's close family had already fled from Gomel in the early part of the twentieth century. But Shmuel does not know anything about his mother's family, or even if he might have some more distant cousins on his father's side still living in Gomel. Gitel's family home, Borisov, is much farther west than Gomel and more threatened. She thinks there are still some cousins from her family living there. But beyond personal concerns, it is hard for them to imagine all that evil falling on innocent Jews—just because they are Jewish.

The United Kingdom and France have declared war on Germany, but reports suggest that their involvement is primarily for self-defense. The United States seems determined to stay out of the war.

Gitel says, "I don't think the world cares what happens to Jews, who have no country to call their own. I'm not sure what we can do to help right now. I'll check around to see if there are any organizations taking useful actions."

Shmuel tells Gitel that even though he is happy to be working as a pharmacist again, he has reservations about his schedule. "My schedule makes my practice of Judaism nearly impossible. I close the store at midnight, arrive home around one in the morning, and rarely fall asleep before two. I am mindful of not getting run-down again, so I try to sleep until ten a.m. or later to get eight hours of sleep. I had been hoping to go back to laying my *tefillin*, *davening*, and saying the *She'ma* every morning, but for most of the year ten a.m. is too late to do that under Jewish law. I also have to work on Friday evening, so I cannot bring in shabbes properly with the family. If I want to go to shul on shabbes morning, I have to get up early—but I still have to leave for my Saturday evening shift by two p.m. That makes it a long day, too long for me most weeks. The only day I do not work is Sunday, when the good Irish Catholic leadership of our city requires just about all businesses to be closed. I feel very guilty about all that lack of observance, because I cannot give Faye the experience of a proper Jewish home."

"She did have that experience when we were living with my parents," Gitel responds.

"Yes, but she was young then. Now she would understand it better."

"Please don't beat yourself up over this, Shmuel. At least we are all alive and well. We have a roof over our heads and food to eat. Given what we have been through, we can't take any of that for granted. Of course, key to our good fortune is your job. That your ability to be observant is a casualty of the job is something we need to live with. Unless you think you can find a job with better hours, of course."

"You do not understand, Gitel, how important Jewish observance is to me. I have had to let it go with all our troubles since we lost our store, but I really want to get back to it. I worry that my lack of observance is affecting our *mazel*. Maybe that is why I got tuberculosis. *Ver veyst?* Who knows?"

"Oh, Shmuel. Between observance and eating, I choose eating."

Shmuel does not respond.

# 10

Gitel isn't that happy living in the hyper-Jewish neighborhood of Lawndale again. Every time she passes the drugstore that was once theirs, she gets a pain in her heart and sheds a few tears. Some of the people in the neighborhood remember their family's problems, and do not hesitate to mention them to her. Gitel still thinks about getting a fresh start elsewhere, preferably in Hyde Park.

Living in New York had been a revelation. Shmuel's relatives do not keep kosher. They don't eat pork or shellfish, but they also don't keep two sets of dishes and pans or carefully separate eating meat from eating dairy. Gitel ate with them, as well as with some of her non-Jewish coworkers at the theater, and no lightning came down to strike her. As she unpacks the boxes they had left in storage and puts the dishes and pots in the cabinets and shelves, she finds that some of their dishes are broken, and a couple of boxes are missing. She wonders, *Maybe that is a sign that we should give up our strict kosher practice, like the New York cousins did.*

On a morning not long after settling in, she takes Faye to school and then makes Shmuel a nice breakfast. After he eats, she asks if they can talk.

"As I was unpacking our goods from storage yesterday, I realized that some of our kosher dishes were broken and some pots and pans and other equipment were missing. I have been thinking about that. We could buy new dishes and pots when we can find some extra money. But I think there is an alternative."

"I am listening."

"The family we stayed with in New York doesn't keep kosher. I assume you ate with them anyway. At least Faye and I did. And what about the sanatorium? Did you just eat vegetables? Or did you go along with what they served you? I'm sure you didn't have any choice. I'm not criticizing at all. I just wonder if we have to be so strict ourselves. Sadly, your father and grandparents are no longer in this world. My parents are, but they are unlikely to come visit us here. Do you think we could relax our practice a bit?"

"It is true that I ate what I was served in New York, although at the sanatorium I told them that I cannot eat pork or shellfish. While I did violate Jewish law eating non-kosher chicken and beef, I told myself that it was more important that I live and get well. It is permissible to violate Jewish law to save a life, in this case mine.

"But *oy vey*! What you ask!" Shmuel continues. "It makes me feel that we are on some kind of slippery slope. My job hours keep me from observing shabbes properly, about which I feel bad. Now you do not want to keep kosher anymore. I know cooking and housework are not your favorite things, and that *kashrus* makes it all more complicated, but I do not know what to say. I certainly do not want to eat *trayf* [food forbidden by Jewish law]. I'll never eat pork or shellfish and probably never eat a cheeseburger. But maybe we could compromise?"

"What are you thinking?"

"What if we continue to buy kosher meat, but the rest of it would just be kosher style? You would not have to worry about keeping the dishes and pots separate. We need kosher meat because the requirement not to eat the blood of the meat comes from the Torah, which is why we—or nowadays the butcher—soak and salt the meat to draw out the blood. And I could agree so long as we do not cook the kosher meat together with milk products because the Torah prohibits 'cooking a kid in its mother's milk.' The rest of the rules are what the rabbis made up to 'put a fence around the Torah,' so people do not make inadvertent mistakes. I am less concerned about the rabbinical rules than those that come directly from the Torah."

Gitel thinks about what Shmuel said for a few moments. She realizes that he is going as far as he possibly can, given his upbringing.

"That sounds fair enough. Thank you for your flexibility."

Gitel wants to talk to Shmuel about the mikveh as well, but feels that she has pushed as far as she can right now. She will take her victory.

Staying home all day is making Gitel feel grumpy and fidgety. She moves around the small apartment from room to room, not knowing what to do with herself. She has very little interest in cooking and cleaning the apartment; she does only the minimum required. Faye is in school for most of the day, so Gitel has long periods of time alone. She knows she would be much happier if she could work, especially if she could work as a bookkeeper. *But*, she thinks, *I would be willing to do any reasonable job; I was happy to work at the theater in New York.*

If she could work, she tells herself, they could get a larger and better apartment, better food, and perhaps even occasionally afford a babysitter and go to some entertainment (although Shmuel's work hours make the latter difficult). But the Chicago Public Schools make it very difficult for mothers to work. Eating lunch at school buildings is prohibited. Children have to go home for lunch and then go back to school for the afternoon classes. *That seems so silly*, Gitel thinks, *as compared to allowing the children to bring a sandwich with them to school. The lunch break is just one hour. We live about a fifteen-minute walk from the school at the pace of a six-year-old, so when Faye reaches home, she has to hurry to eat in order to get back in time. In the winter, when leggings, coats, hats, and mittens have to be removed and then put back on, there is little time left to eat.*

Shmuel has made it clear that he wants her to be home for Faye, which, added to the school schedule, makes her realize that working outside the home is a pipe dream at this time. She starts wondering if she can do some bookkeeping at home for some small businesses. That would be less pleasant than working in an office with other people, but it could bring in some money and keep her mind occupied. On the other hand, she is hoping to leave Lawndale and move to Hyde Park. *Maybe it isn't such a great idea to develop business in this neighborhood if we are only going to leave. I really need to talk to Shmuel about all this,* she thinks. *But his schedule makes him so tired all the time, I feel bad even asking him to talk.*

# 11

One afternoon in the fall of 1940, Shmuel receives an official-looking letter in the mail with a return address that reads, *Selective Service Board*. Gitel is anxious to know what the letter says, but doesn't want to open a letter addressed to him. She worries about it while trying to fall asleep, and gets up when Shmuel comes home from work around 1:00 a.m.

"Shmuel, you have an official-looking letter. Could you open it so we can see what it says?"

Shmuel opens the letter and reads what it says out loud. "It says that I am required to register for the draft. It says that all men between the ages of twenty-one and forty-five must register. Since I am thirty-five, I guess I must do that. I cannot imagine that the government would want to draft me to fight. I certainly would not make much of a soldier, with my frail health."

When Shmuel comes back from his appointment at the draft board, he tells Gitel that the draft board had come to the only reasonable conclusion. "They told me that I am not soldier material. But they said that if we are fighting in the war, there will be other things I can do. They said I could replace a pharmacist who was drafted to fight, since the civilian population would still need access to medications. They classified me II-A, 'deferred in support of national health, safety, or interest.' They said that meant I was deferred for now, but in

case of war I would have to work under the direction of the government doing whatever they said in whatever location they said. I told
them that I understood, and that the classification seemed fair to me.
I certainly want to do whatever I can for the war effort. I mentioned
to them that I was very upset about what was going on in Europe."

"Of course. That all makes sense. Anything we can do to help
defeat Hitler is all to the good," Gitel agrees.

Gitel and Shmuel follow the war closely over the next year. In
May of 1940, Germany invades France, and by the fall of 1940 Vichy
France enacts a law on the status of Jews that defines as Jewish
anyone with a Jewish grandparent. That marks the beginning of
a range of anti-Semitic actions there. Then in mid-1941, Germany
invades Russia. A lot of rumors circulate in the Jewish community
about what is happening over there, although no one knows for sure.
There are rumors of a mass shooting of Jews near Kiev, and of camps
being built to kill Jews. It seems as if that madman Hitler is going to
take over the world and wipe out all the Jews, as he has made clear
that he wants to do. The United States still is sitting on the sidelines,
certainly a frustrating situation for Shmuel and Gitel and all their
friends who are paying attention to what Hitler is doing, and particularly for the fate of European Jewry.

FDR might personally want to help the Europeans fight the Nazis,
but there is a strong sentiment of isolationism in Congress—fueled in
part by the sense that the sacrifices made in World War I had not been
worth it. In 1935, Congress had pushed through a series of Neutrality
Acts that prevented the export of arms and ammunition and also
prevented American ships and citizens from becoming entangled
in outside conflicts. In 1939, these strict bans began to be gradually
lifted, especially with the enactment of the Lend-Lease Act in March
1941, which gave President Roosevelt virtually unlimited authority to

direct material aid such as ammunition, tanks, airplanes, trucks, and food to the war effort in Europe without violating the nation's official position of neutrality. But it was not until the Japanese bombed Pearl Harbor in December 1941 that the Neutrality Acts became irrelevant.

With the United States' entry into the war after Pearl Harbor, the drafting of men to fight goes into high gear. Shmuel is called to report to the Selective Service Board for assignment on the home front. A new, very large Pharmall drugstore had opened in 1940 in downtown Chicago, but it is losing the staff it needs to operate because of the draft. Whether because of political influence or some other reason, staffing the downtown Pharmall is considered more important than staffing a neighborhood drugstore. Shmuel is assigned to work there as a pharmacist.

Gitel asks Shmuel, "Does that mean that you have to leave your current job?"

"Yes, I told my boss Lou about the Selective Service order. He was upset, but there is nothing he or I can do about it. He said he would have no choice but to cut the hours that the store is open, perhaps keep it open from ten a.m. to eight p.m. or something like that. He certainly cannot work both shifts himself."

"What will your hours be at Pharmall?" Gitel asks.

"That is the only good thing about the assignment. It is a regular day shift, eight a.m. to five p.m. most days, with a later finishing time on Thursdays. I will have to work six days, including Saturday, but at least I will be home for Shabbat dinner on Friday night. So maybe this is not so bad."

Gitel knows that Shmuel doesn't like working for Pharmall. He had that experience when he worked at their store during the Century of Progress World's Fair. He kept talking about how he thought the organization of the prescription drugs could be improved and better managed, although his suggestions were not appreciated. But at least he will be working close by, and he won't have to physically fight in the war.

Shmuel now comes home for dinner every evening, and he and Gitel go to bed at the same time. Gitel feels pressured to resume going to the mikveh at the appropriate time, and then to have sex with him.

"Gitel, I want more than one child. It is not good to have an only child. Just think about how much you care for your brothers and they care for you. I only had the one sister, who pretty much hated me, but I would have loved to have more siblings."

"Shmuel, I agree with you in principle. But I feel that it would be a mistake to bring another child into this war-torn, uncertain world. And we would have trouble affording another child."

"Okay, I see your point. I could use a condom. But I still want to have sex. It was difficult to find a time when I worked nights, but this new schedule is great. I really want you to understand that sex is normal and natural. It is a part of marriage. I want to make you feel good and satisfied."

Gitel feels trapped. She certainly didn't know that she would dislike sex with her husband before she married. *If I had, I might have chosen not to marry*, she thinks. *But then I wouldn't have Faye, who I dearly love. And I also love Shmuel, even though I don't like sex with him. And I certainly didn't know how much I would hate the mikveh until I went right before my wedding.*

"Shmuel, I don't know what to say. I know you are not going to want to hear this, but truthfully, I find the mikveh disgusting. I don't like a strange woman poking and prodding at me, and staring at my naked body. And the idea of going naked into the water that so many other women have just been in upsets me. I am convinced that it is full of germs that will enter my naked body."

Shmuel is silent for a while. Gitel just waits. She imagines that he is going to come up with some quotation from the Talmud.

Finally, he says, "Okay. Just so we do not have sex while you are bleeding, and you bathe at home after your bleeding is finished, I can live with that. I can understand not wanting to go to the mikveh if you think it is not completely sanitary. It should be kept very clean, but maybe it is not. What do you think about this compromise?"

"Thank you for your understanding. That is fine."

Gitel is totally surprised. *Shmuel seems to be moving away from his upbringing,* she thinks. *And I can feel how much he loves me. He wants me to be happy. I need to make an effort to be willing to have sex with him. I'm not sure I can overcome my distaste for sex, but I will try. But I will hold him to his offer of using a condom. I definitely don't want another child right now.*

Gitel starts thinking again about the idea of their moving to Hyde Park. The Illinois Central Railroad operates a fast electric commuter train between Hyde Park and downtown. It would only be a fifteen-minute commute for Shmuel to the Pharmall job. He wouldn't have to stand on street corners in bad weather to transfer buses, at least while the war lasts. The train station has a sheltered room in which to wait.

She keeps looking at the apartments-available listings in the *Sun-Times* and *Daily News* to figure out what they might be able to afford. Since Shmuel is working at the orders of the government, Pharmall does not have to pay him as much as they normally would pay a senior pharmacist. He is making a little less than his boss Lou had been paying him. In fact, it was getting difficult to afford their one-bedroom apartment in Lawndale.

A couple of weeks after their conversation about the mikveh, Gitel broaches the subject of Hyde Park with Shmuel. He is in a pretty good mood. He is enjoying his new schedule, including the evenings at home and a couple of nice Friday evening shabbes dinners that she had worked hard to make. They've even had sex a couple of evenings before going to sleep.

"Shmuel, have you given any more thought to our moving to Hyde Park? It looks like rents might be a little less expensive on the South Side."

"I really do not want to move," Shmuel responds. "There are lots of advantages to living here. When you do not feel like cooking there are inexpensive kosher restaurants nearby. And while I do not get to shul that often because of work, I do feel comfortable in the one near here when I can get there. Especially when I take off during holidays. And we live close to my uncle Yeyna and family. At least we have some family nearby."

"Could we just explore Hyde Park? Maybe it would be nice there too?"

"Not now! I'm having enough trouble adjusting to working at Pharmall. And we have moved around so much. I would like to stay put, and I think Faye deserves to stay in the same school for a while. She seems to be doing well there."

Gitel realizes that Shmuel is not going to agree right now. She tells herself that she will try again at some later time.

Life continues as well as it could during wartime. They are managing on Shmuel's salary because there is very little to buy. After mid-1942, everything is rationed. People need stamps to buy meat, dairy, cooking oil, butter, sugar, canned milk, and coffee, as well as various items of clothing and shoes. Since Faye is growing, all of their clothing and shoe stamps are used for her. And Gitel and Shmuel agree with each other to eat a little less so that Faye has enough to eat. They eat a lot of macaroni and cheese, since that requires few stamps and is filling.

Gitel begins to be very active in the American Jewish Congress (AJC), writing copy for newsletters and drafts of letters to editors for members to submit. She also does some fundraising, organizing women members to pull together meetings of their friends to discuss what is happening in Europe and give what they can to the effort.

Since 1933, the AJC had been organizing anti-Nazi protests to raise the knowledge and understanding of the American public about the dangers. It organized a boycott of German goods, long before the US entered the war. And it continues to lobby the US government on issues relating to the rescue of European Jews, cooperating with the World Jewish Congress that it had helped to establish. In 1942, the AJC received definitive word of what had been rumor up to that point—through what became known as the Riegner Telegram, it was verified that Jews were being murdered in the Auschwitz-Birkenau camp. The lobbying efforts became more urgent, but unfortunately had little effect on FDR's failure to take action to save the Jews.

Shmuel tells Gitel, "I am so pleased that you are trying to do something about the situation. I had promised myself that I would take some action, but work is absorbing all my limited energy."

Life continues the same for them until disaster strikes at the end of 1943.

# 12

It is a week before Christmas. "The Pharmall store is packed with customers, especially at the noon hour when downtown workers have a lunch break, and from around four thirty in the afternoon to closing. All the staff are required to work extra hours and skip breaks to manage the workload," Shmuel explains to Gitel when he comes home in the evening. "I hope I don't get overtired. This hectic work environment is taking a toll on me. A lot of things people want to buy for Christmas gifts or for their homes are kept on the tall shelves behind the counter in the prescription area. When customers ask for those things, I have to climb up a ladder and get what they want for them. If they change their mind, or only buy one of two things I have brought down, I have to climb the ladder again and put the merchandise back. All that is a lot harder for me, as you can imagine, than just compounding prescriptions. And sometimes I have to go down through a trapdoor into the basement, located behind the prescription counter, where extra supplies that do not fit on the shelves are kept."

"Please be really careful," Gitel admonishes. "All that sounds like a bad situation for you."

"I am being as careful as I can. But there also is pressure to do everything quickly. Customers are often impatient because they need to get back to their work. And the store management is just generally impatient."

The very next day, a messenger shows up at Gitel's door around 5:00 p.m. The messenger says that he is delivering a note from the manager of the Pharmall store. Gitel gives the messenger a tip as he leaves. She sits down to read the message, thinking that Shmuel might have to work late into the evening and wants her to know. What she reads is quite different.

> *I am so sorry to tell you this, but there has been an accident. Shmuel has fallen off a ladder. The trapdoor was somehow open behind him, and he fell hard on his back onto the cement floor of the basement. He was not able to get up on his own. We called the fire department, and they have taken him by ambulance to Michael Reese Hospital.*

Gitel gasps. As upset as she is, her strong organizing skills kick in. She quickly gives Faye something to eat for dinner, and runs to a neighbor whose daughter is in Faye's class. After she explains, the neighbor agrees that Faye can stay with them until Gitel returns from the hospital, or all night if necessary. Gitel brings Faye over with nightclothes and everything the girl will need for school in the morning, in case she does not get back from the hospital in time.

Gitel decides that she has enough money to take a taxi to the hospital. It is already dark, and she is too nervous to have the patience to take the "L" and a bus. When she gets to the hospital, she finds that Shmuel has already been transferred from the emergency department to a room. He is able to talk a bit, but cannot move.

"I really don't know how it happened, Gitel. Someone must have gone to the basement for supplies and left the trapdoor open. I was up on the ladder when someone called my name. I turned around, must have lost my grip on the ladder, and fell all the way through the trapdoor to the basement. I could hear people yelling, but I could not get up. I think I avoided hitting my head, or at least I was still conscious. But I could not sit up or properly move my arms and legs—so I just lay there waiting for something to happen. My back hurt a lot. After a bit, some firemen came down the stairs to the basement with some equipment. They put me on some kind of board and carried me up to an ambulance, which brought me here."

Just then, a doctor comes into the room. He says, "We have the results of your X-ray. You have cracks and chipped bones in three vertebrae in your lower back. We are going to wrap you in a brace that has hard vertical stays all around it. The brace will go from below your bottom to close to the top of your body, so you will not be able to sit up. We will keep you in the hospital for a few weeks to determine whether the vertebrae are going to heal or whether you might need some sort of surgery. If at the end of that period the vertebrae have begun to heal, we probably will be able to give you a different brace that would allow you to sit up. But while you are in the hospital, I do not want you to put any strain on your back. You will have to stay in bed."

Gitel thinks, *Oy, not again. Did I have to marry such a* shlimazel, *someone with such bad luck? Is he going to get paid while he recovers? How will we get by if he isn't?*

Gitel asks the doctor, "What is likely to happen when or if he has a different brace? Will he be able to come home? Will he be able to work? How about climbing stairs? We live on the third floor in a building without an elevator."

The doctor thinks for a bit. "I am not sure how to answer your questions now. We will have to see how things progress. But I do think it will be a long time before your husband is comfortable climbing stairs, particularly three flights of stairs. You might think about moving to some place with a ground-floor entrance or to a building with an elevator, if that would be possible for you."

"Thank you for your advice, Doctor."

When the doctor leaves the room, Gitel asks Shmuel to again go over the details of what had occurred. Shmuel says, "I am not sure how it happened. One moment I was up on the ladder. The next I was lying in the basement. If someone had not left the trapdoor open, it probably would not have been so bad. I would have fallen on the wooden floor behind the counter, not the concrete floor in the basement. And I am not sure who distracted me while I was up on the ladder."

Gitel thinks, but does not say, *Somebody has to take responsibility for this. It doesn't seem like it was Shmuel's fault.* Gitel makes sure that Shmuel is comfortable and has everything he needs in his limited reach. She tells him that she will come back in the morning after Faye goes to school to make sure he is okay.

# 13

As soon as Gitel can, she goes to the Selective Service Board to ask whether the government or Pharmall is responsible for paying Shmuel's salary while he is recovering. She certainly hopes one of them will be. Wouldn't his situation be considered a disability acquired in the line of service?

The Selective Service Board sends her to speak to someone who tells her that large employers in Illinois such as Pharmall are required to carry Workmen's Compensation insurance, which pays injured employees two-thirds of their wages and reimburses all medical costs.

She responds, trying to remain calm, "How can we get by on two-thirds of his wages? He already is paid less than a pharmacist would otherwise earn, because you classified him as an essential worker and told him he had to work at Pharmall. Under your rules he does not have to be paid equal wages for doing a full job—one that is difficult for him. Two-thirds of those lower wages will not cover our rent and food."

She continues, "I'd be happy to get a job and supplement our income, but our young daughter is in public school and is required to come home for lunch every day. I must be home for her. There is no one else to take care of her."

Her protestations fall on deaf ears. All they say is, "Sorry, lady. Those are the rules." She leaves the office thinking about what she could possibly do. She feels so exhausted that she can barely put one foot in front of the other to walk. How could they have had yet another bout of bad luck? Is Shmuel truly a *shlimazel*?

After going home and thinking about the problem, she decides to try to talk to Pharmall's management. *Wasn't the employee who left the trapdoor open negligent?* she thinks. *What about his supervisor? Shouldn't the supervisor have been more vigilant?*

Pharmall corporate headquarters are in a suburb to the north of Chicago, not conveniently reachable by public transportation. She cannot just take a chance on going there without an appointment. Instead, Gitel goes to the downtown Chicago store where Shmuel worked and asks the manager to tell her the appropriate person at Pharmall headquarters to whom she could write a letter about the situation. The manager is a bit defensive—but he also liked Shmuel and wants to help him. After some hesitation, he gives her the information. He also tells her that the employee who left the trapdoor open has been fired. Not much consolation in that, but maybe it is something of an admission of guilt.

She sits down to compose a strong letter to Pharmall's management. She wants it to be respectful but insistent.

> Dear Sirs:
>
> *My husband, Samuel Mushkin, a pharmacist, was assigned by the Selective Service Board to work at your downtown Chicago store. On December 20, 1943, my husband was on a ladder reaching for some medications that were stored on a high shelf. He was distracted by another employee asking him something, and lost his grip on the ladder. He fell not to the floor of the store but through a trapdoor to the basement that was supposed to never be left open. He suffered damage to*

*three vertebrae in his lower back, and has to wear a brace that prevents him from even sitting up. He will have to wear it for an extended period of time. It is unclear when he will be able to return to work. I was informed that Workmen's Compensation insurance would cover his medical costs and provide two-thirds of his salary. Our family cannot manage on two-thirds of his salary. Since you paid him less than a pharmacist who was not assigned by the Selective Service, we already were having difficulty affording our rent and other—modest— expenditures. We have a young child who comes home from school for lunch each day, making it difficult for me to find employment. Since I think there must have been some negligent employee and/or supervisor that resulted in the open trapdoor, I respectfully ask your company to supplement the Workmen's Compensation payment to restore his full salary.*

The next thing Gitel needs to do is to find an apartment they can afford in a building with an elevator. Not an easy task, since rent tends to be higher in elevator buildings. She needs to be careful not to take on too much rent. She has no idea if she will be successful in her plea to Pharmall or whether they will have to consider a lawsuit. The latter could take a long time to be resolved.

She has her heart set on a place in Hyde Park. Michael Reese Hospital is not that far from Hyde Park, so after visiting Shmuel in the morning she takes the bus from the hospital to Hyde Park. She wants to walk up and down the streets to get a better feel for the neighborhood, and to inquire at buildings that might not have advertised a vacancy in the city newspapers. She discovers that there is a local weekly newspaper called the *Hyde Park Herald*, which has classified ads as well as news stories. Perhaps something will be advertised there.

She first looks at areas of Hyde Park that are close to the Illinois Central Railroad (IC) tracks, which are also used by the South Shore Line to go to South Bend and the commuter trains to go to the Loop. When Shmuel fully recovers, assuming that he will, he could take the IC to get downtown quickly. But the platforms at Fifty-Fifth and Fifty-Third Streets are accessed by sets of steep stairs, which would be a drawback for a while.

Cornell Avenue is the first street east of the tracks at Fifty-Fifth Street, so she decides to look there. The apartments on that block are largely traditional three-story walk-ups, punctuated by a few private homes. When she gets to Fifty-Sixth Street, there is a hotel of about twelve stories called the Windermere. Then she realizes that there are actually *two* hotels, one on either side of Cornell, called Windermere West and Windermere East. She goes into the Windermere West to ask if they are strictly a hotel or perhaps have any apartments for rent. She finds that the hotel does have apartments, but alas, the rent is far above what they can afford. It is considered a luxury building, the desk clerk tells her. She thinks it is nevertheless a good sign that she might find an apartment in a building with an elevator.

Gitel walks a little farther west toward the train tracks on Fifty-Sixth Street, and sees that there is a nice-looking elementary school called Bret Harte. She keeps that in mind as a place for Faye as she continues her search. *It would be good to try to find something reasonably close to the school*, she thinks. She turns back east and walks to Hyde Park Boulevard, the next street over, and heads toward Fifty-Fifth Street. *I'm finding nothing promising here either*, she thinks. She is out of time for this day, and has to catch a bus to return home in time to give Faye her lunch.

She goes back to Hyde Park on two subsequent days to continue her search. On the third day, she finds a possibility. On Cornell Avenue near Fifty-Fourth Street there is a small apartment hotel called The Aragon Hotel. It is nine stories with an elevator. The drawback is that the apartments are quite small. The vacant one is one room with an alcove that contains a pull-down bed, a small kitchen with a stove, refrigerator, and sink, and a bathroom. *It will be close quarters for the three of us*, she thinks, *but we could manage—at least until Shmuel is able to walk stairs again.* It is furnished, but they can bring the studio couch for Faye to sleep on, while she and Shmuel sleep on the pull-down bed. They would have to put the rest of their furniture, including their large dining table and chairs, into storage again. The rent is within their budget, so she agrees to take it. At least they will have a place to which Shmuel can come home from the hospital.

She goes back home to negotiate with their current landlord, to ask him to let them out of their lease. And to break the news to Faye, who would have to adjust again to a new school. Gitel wants to move at the end of January, because the Chicago Public Schools have a two-term-per-year system, with the second term starting at the beginning of February. Faye will be entering grade 5b, the second half of the fifth grade.

The next day, when she goes to the hospital, she tells Shmuel what she has done. He says in a surprised and slightly annoyed tone, "You did all that on your own? Uprooting the family and renting an apartment far from our current one? And forcing Faye to change schools? You could have consulted me!"

"I had no choice. I know you wanted to stay in Lawndale, but we will need to live in an apartment with an elevator for quite a while, until you fully recover. Rents are cheaper in Hyde Park than in Lawndale, and anyway, I know of no suitable building in Lawndale. I needed to get all of this done sooner rather than later, for your sake and the sake of our family. I did what was necessary! Frankly, you have no right to complain. It is your accident that we have to accommodate," Gitel says far more sharply than she normally speaks to Shmuel. Shmuel does not respond.

Faye tells Gitel that she is not very happy at the news. But once Shmuel had his accident, she says she suspected that there would have to be some changes in her life. Gitel says, "I feel so sorry that your father and I cannot give you a more stable life. I understand that taking you to South Bend and then to New York and back to Chicago was unfair to you. And now moving you again to a new school. There is nothing I can do except apologize to you."

"It's okay, Mom. I know you are doing the best that you can."

Gitel looks back on her own young life. She realizes how stable it had been for her once they arrived in South Bend from Borisov. From the age of five until she married, she had lived in a house with her two parents and her brothers. *That was a lot of security I haven't been able to give Faye*, she thinks. *Faye seemed quiet and sad when I gave her the news, but she didn't argue with me. She never does.*

As Gitel is getting the family ready to move, she receives a reply letter from Pharmall. They are willing to supplement Shmuel's Workmen's Compensation if he and she both agree to not sue them for additional funds. The letter includes a statement for them to sign and notarize to that effect. Gitel gives it a little thought, but concludes that they are better off with the immediate income now rather than trusting their luck in a lawsuit. They do not seem to be having a lot of luck these days.

With everything as settled as it can be, Gitel and Faye move to Hyde Park while Shmuel is still in the hospital. Gitel enrolls Faye at Bret Harte Elementary School. And she begins to make a list of small businesses in the neighborhood that might be interested in having a local part-time bookkeeper.

# 14

Shmuel comes home to the apartment in Hyde Park a few weeks after they move in. Twenty-four hours a day, he has to wear a brace that goes around his body from his shoulders to the middle of his *tukhes* (butt). It will be a while until he can go back to work, but at least he can go outside and walk around a bit. The doctors recommend walking, so long as he does not overdo it. When he first comes home, he mostly just walks up and down their block. He is afraid to get too far away, in case he feels tired or experiences some pain in his back.

Gitel continues walking all over the neighborhood to get used to it and to find the stores and other places they will need. On Fifty-Fifth Street, just east of the IC tracks, there is a kosher butcher shop, the only one in the neighborhood. That is very different from Lawndale, where there were several kosher shops. The one in Hyde Park has no competition, so its prices are much higher than she is used to paying. Among the family, she nicknames the butcher "*der ganif*," the thief.

Gitel develops a Friday routine. She stops at the Lake Park poultry store, on the west side of the tracks, to order a chicken. She has to choose a live chicken from the ones in cages in the front of the store, which the employees then take into the back and slaughter. Kosher slaughter costs extra. They mostly sell unplucked birds, but will pluck them for an extra fee. Gitel thinks, *I would much rather have asked a butcher for a chicken and receive a paper-wrapped plucked chicken. I have no need for seeing it alive first, and I certainly do not enjoy plucking the feathers.* But at times when they are somewhat short of funds, she does do the plucking.

While the chicken is being prepared, she walks to Jesselson's fish store on Fifty-Fifth Street, a couple blocks west of the tracks. She usually buys some whitefish, but sometimes some other kind of fish that looks good. Then she returns to pick up the chicken. On the way home she stops by a Jewel grocery, where she can get whatever else they need—although she often goes there on a different day because it is difficult to carry everything at once.

Along Fifty-Third Street both east and west of the IC tracks there are all sorts of shops and facilities. The Hyde Park Bank has a large fancy building of several stories. The banking level boasts lots of marble and wood and a vaulted ceiling. Gitel changes their bank accounts to there from the bank in Lawndale. On the higher floors of the bank building are many doctors' offices and the offices of other services such as accounting and insurance. Along the street are clothing and shoe stores, specialty food stores, a five-and-dime, and a variety of restaurants.

Gitel sees a large stone church on the northeast corner of Fifty-Third and Blackstone. Walking north on Blackstone, she sees a house next to the church that is set back a bit from the street. A sign on the house reads, HYDE PARK HEBREW CENTER. She is curious, so she walks up the few stairs, tries the door, and goes in. She sees that most of the first floor of the house has been converted to a synagogue, with seats facing the ark and the *bima* (altar), which is in the front of the room. There is a room near the front door that has a couple of tables and lots of shelves with books. Opposite the room is a stairway leading to the second floor. As she is looking around, a middle-aged man comes to greet her and asks her what she is looking for. He says his name is Clay, and he is the *shamus*, the person who takes care of the synagogue. She tells him that they have just moved into the neighborhood, and will be looking for a shul to join. He asks her to wait and goes to call the rabbi, who after a short while comes down the stairs. She notices that the rabbi is young, probably in his late twenties or early thirties.

He introduces himself as Rabbi Fishman, and asks what he can do for her. She explains that she and her husband and daughter recently moved to the neighborhood. "My husband is recovering from an injury, but he should soon be well enough to attend shul. He is Orthodox and has a yeshiva background. I'd like to know what this shul is like, so I can tell my husband and, if it is to his liking, perhaps join."

The rabbi explains, "This is an Orthodox congregation, with one exception. We have mixed seating. Some people call us 'traditional' rather than Orthodox. When we took over this building, there was not a good way to separate the women and the men, so the board decided on open seating. We are Orthodox in every other way. Given your husband's background, he might like to know that there are several members who study Gemora together after the daily *Mincha* service. He might like to join them if he has time in the afternoon."

"Thank you for explaining. I will talk to my husband."

Gitel goes home and tells Shmuel about the shul. "It is not that far from here. We could walk there together on shabbes morning."

"I think that would be a bit too much for me. Even if I could walk that far, my back still hurts when I sit for a long time. The three hours of a shabbes service is probably still too much for me."

"The rabbi said that after weekday *Mincha* services in the afternoon, a group of men learn Gemora. Would you want to walk over
one afternoon to see what it is like? You would have to climb a few
steps to get into the shul."

"I probably am sufficiently recovered to do that, especially with the
incentive of studying Gemora."

One afternoon the following week Gitel says to Shmuel that it is
time to try to walk to the shul together. He agrees, and they set out.
She helps Shmuel up the stairs, walks into the shul with him, and
introduces him to the rabbi. Then Gitel leaves Shmuel there to *daven*
(pray) and study. She goes to a café on the corner to have a coffee and
read a magazine. Faye has already made a friend at school and has
arranged to go to the friend's house after school, so there is no rush
to get home.

As they walk home, Shmuel tries to explain to Gitel what they
had studied after *Mincha*. "The group is learning the third chapter
of tractate *Ta'anit*, which means times of fasting. I remembered the
main ideas of the tractate from when I studied it as a teenager. It is
largely about what to do in times of drought. It was thought that God
withheld rain—critical for survival in a largely agricultural society—because the community, or people in the community, had done
something wrong. Fasting was one way to indicate repentance and
influence God to open the heavens for rain. Most of the third chapter is a collection of stories about how righteous people prayed and
averted drought or other problems, some of whom were common
people not generally recognized as special or even devout, but in
the stories they had all quietly done especially good deeds such as
giving food and wine to the poor so they could celebrate shabbes
or teaching children in an effective way. The rabbi asked me to read
these stories from the Gemora and Rashi's commentary that went

with it. I was happy to do so. The rabbi and the other men at the table were impressed, and asked where I had learned. I explained my background, that I had begun studying Gemora when I was ten years old, and they were even more impressed."

"I'm so glad that you had a good experience," Gitel says. "I can understand that you have missed learning Gemora with other men."

"Indeed. I felt happier and better about myself than I have any time since the accident. I also told the men there that I was recovering from an injury, so I am not back at work yet. Until I go back to work, I would enjoy meeting with them most days."

"Do you think you could walk here from the apartment alone?"

"Yes. I think I can," Shmuel replies. "But I also want to talk to you about something else that is on my mind, that studying *Ta'anit* has brought up for me."

"Sure, what is it?"

"The theme that runs through tractate *Ta'anit* is that misfortune [such as lack of rain] and bad luck is punishment for doing something wrong, for displeasing God. That concept is also reflected in the liturgy, in the *She'ma Yisroel* prayer we say every day. I wonder if that has anything to do with my personal bad luck? We made some compromises about the mikveh and *kashrus*. Could that be why I fell off the ladder? It has been a long time since I put on my *tefillin* and prayed every morning. Could that be why I got TB and more recently fell off the ladder? When I was young, I believed that God controlled what happens in the world, but do I believe that now? I don't think so, but it is hard for me to definitively not believe it."

"Oh, Shmuel. You can't think like that. Yes, we have had more than our share of bad luck. But when we lost our store, we were closing the shop on shabbes, you were going to shul on shabbes, and we were carefully observing *kashrus* in our home and other commandments.

I think *mazel* is just *mazel*. It happens. Please don't beat yourself up over the way we live."

"I hear what you are saying. But I need to think about this some more."

# 15

After that first day, Shmuel is able to walk to the shul on his own in the afternoon. His mood improves with his ability to socialize and study. Gitel observes that he even begins praying at home in the mornings, something he has not done in a long time. She is happy for him. Now she needs to figure out what she wants to do with her time while Faye is still in elementary school, and what she wants to do for the rest of her life as Faye becomes more independent.

*In just over three years, Faye will be in high school and will no longer come home for lunch in the middle of the day. And she will be old enough to do what she wants after school, to join activities or visit with friends. I won't necessarily need to be home for her. Could I revive my dream of becoming a teacher? But how would we manage to pay tuition for me to go to college? We will soon need to pay for Faye to go to college, although if I could get a teaching certificate and a job, maybe that could pay for her college? More realistically, I could get a job as a bookkeeper. That would be fine with me. I do like doing that kind of work. If Shmuel objects, I could just push aside his objections, saying that we need money so Faye can go to college. It would be hard for him to say no to that, given that lack of money in his family kept him from realizing his dream to be a chemist. Surely, he would want Faye to be able to study whatever she wants.*

More immediately, Gitel wants to meet people in Hyde Park. She is especially hoping to find some other women with whom she could be friends. She starts with joining the PTA at the Bret Harte School where Faye is enrolled. At the first meeting, she asks what she can do to help. She joins a committee that arranges for field trips and chaperones the children on the trips.

She reads in the *Hyde Park Herald* about a new organization that is just forming in the city, called the Independent Voters of Illinois, or IVI for short. It is a nonpartisan political organization that will support candidates that are anti-corruption and who espouse socially responsible policies. That sounds interesting to her. The organization's main office is downtown, but they just opened a temporary office in a storefront on Fifty-Fifth Street to prepare for the next election, so she goes there to volunteer. A woman sitting at a table near the front says, "There is lots to do to get the word out about the new organization and to research the records of various politicians and candidates. Your volunteer efforts would be very welcome. Is research something you can do?"

"Certainly. Just put me to work. My daughter still comes home from school for lunch, but I could work in either the morning or the afternoon."

One of the women who enthusiastically greets her at the IVI office is called Sophie. She is a thin, petite woman with short, well-groomed hair, wearing a tailored skirt and blouse. Her eyes are bright, as if she might be smart and interesting; Gitel thinks she is very attractive. She looks to Gitel as if she might be Jewish. Gitel makes a point of introducing herself to Sophie as a new resident of the neighborhood, and says she hopes that they will run into each other again. Sophie suggests that they have coffee together the following day, an offer Gitel readily accepts.

Sophie suggests a casual restaurant called Linde's near the

northwest corner of Fifty-Third Street and Hyde Park Boulevard. They meet there at ten thirty in the morning. Gitel just orders coffee, but Sophie apparently has not eaten breakfast, and orders some eggs and an English muffin. She tells Gitel, "My husband is a waiter at a fancy restaurant in the Loop, so he is out in the evenings. He usually gets home around ten p.m., often bringing some pastry or other treat from the restaurant. We usually stay up and talk for a while, not going to bed until midnight or one a.m. As a result, we sleep late in the mornings. I have just gotten up and have not yet had breakfast. Are you married? And if so, what does your husband do?"

"My husband, Shmuel, is a pharmacist. He isn't working right now because the Selective Service Board had assigned him to Pharmall downtown, he had an accident there, and his back was severely hurt. He is recovering. We don't know yet whether he will have to go back to work at Pharmall or whether he can return to his previous job. We have one daughter who is in sixth grade at Bret Harte."

"We have one son who is just in first grade at Murray Elementary, on Fifty-Third and Kenwood Streets," Sophie replies. "I don't work because I want to be home for him, but I do a lot of volunteer work."

Sophie brings up the war and her concerns for the Jews in Europe. "I am working hard with the American Jewish Congress to encourage the US and other countries to rescue more Jews, and with the related Zionist Organization of America to establish a Jewish homeland in Palestine. As you probably know, it is now controlled by the British who are refusing to let Jews escaping Europe go there to live."

"It is great that you are doing that," Gitel says. "I'm already doing some fundraising work with the AJC, but I could be interested in getting further involved."

"There is a South Side Women's Division of the organization that meets in various members' homes," Sophie tells Gitel. "I would be happy to invite you to the next meeting and go to it with you."

"That would be lovely, thank you."

Shmuel tells Gitel that he has just learned that he is required to go back to work at Pharmall downtown. "Despite still wearing the brace, I am able to climb stairs now without too much difficulty. I will take the Illinois Central train downtown. The store is only a couple of blocks from the Randolph Street station. I certainly can make prescriptions, but I hope to avoid climbing on any more ladders."

"I certainly am happy that you are back at work, and sorry that it is at Pharmall rather than with Lou—which I am sure you would prefer." To herself Gitel thinks, *But that also means that now I will have to be home each weekday when Faye comes home for lunch.* When Shmuel had been staying home to recover, he gave her lunch.

Gitel decides it is time to activate her idea of doing some bookkeeping at home for small businesses. She feels good about her involvement in the PTA, the IVI, and the AJC, but she feels that she still has extra energy. Finding some work seems to her to be the best thing to do. If she does it at home, she can be available at lunch and after school for Faye. Shmuel probably won't object—or at least not that much.

Gitel begins her search by walking west along Fifty-Fifth Street from South Shore Drive. Small stores occupy the lowest level of some of the three-story apartment buildings that front on Fifty-Fifth Street. Their windows sit at street level, but the doors to the shops are a few steps down. On the south side of the street between an alley and Everett Street there is a shoemaker, a candy store called Meta's, and a small grocery store/delicatessen called Sam's. She often buys fresh Rosen's rye bread and cold cuts at that deli, so the owner recognizes her. But he says he already has an accountant who takes care of his needs. The owner of the candy store, who is Swedish, seems interested but wants to think about it. She asks Gitel to come back the following week. On the next block, between Everett and Hyde Park Boulevard, there is a beauty shop. The owner there is very interested; she wants Gitel to come back with a written proposal and price for the work. Gitel asks her a few questions to gauge how difficult the work would be, and says she will return within the week with the proposal. Most of the other stores are somewhat larger, and Gitel wants to start small. If she can get the candy store and beauty shop, that would be a good start. Both sign up the following week, so she is in business.

Gitel begins to see a lot of Sophie. They see each other at the IVI office and at AJC meetings. Sophie often invites Gitel to her apartment for coffee after lunch, especially on days that her husband works at the restaurant during lunch rather than dinner. Gitel finds it easy to talk with Sophie, who listens carefully to whatever Gitel says, sometimes responding and sometimes just nodding. Sophie also talks about herself. "My husband and I are members of the Communist Party. We were drawn to the party because of its opposition to fascism in the Spanish Civil War, and remain interested in the party's ideology and policies. We are Jewish, although not religious, so fighting fascism anywhere it shows up is important to us. This is more complicated to explain, but we also are freethinkers, not necessarily bound by society's traditions."

Gitel isn't quite sure what "freethinkers" means, but it sounds interesting to her. *Could I be more free?* she wonders. *Could I choose to not be a traditional wife? Could I choose not to have sex with Shmuel?*

Sophie always hugs Gitel when she arrives and when she leaves. Somehow, that makes Gitel feel tingles in her middle, rising to her head and going down her legs. *Why don't I feel that way when Shmuel hugs me?* she wonders.

Winter is turning into spring. On April 12, 1945, President Roosevelt dies of a cerebral hemorrhage and Harry Truman becomes president. No one Gitel and Shmuel know is sure about whether Truman is qualified to step into FDR's shoes. Could a haberdasher from Missouri guide this complicated war in which the US is embroiled? The war in Europe seems to be going fairly well, but Japan seems far from conquered. Then on the last day of April, Adolf Hitler commits suicide and Germany begins to surrender. Victory in Europe Day is declared on May 8, 1945. Lots of people go out into the street to celebrate, with strangers hugging each other and yelling and singing. People know that the war is not yet over, but it is good to have something to celebrate. Gitel cannot stop smiling. She repeatedly takes deep breaths; she feels as if she has been holding her breath for a long time. Combined with Shmuel's almost full recovery, she hopes that life can return to normal—without rationing or fear—soon. Shmuel is even able to talk her into having sex that evening. They had not had sex since well before his ladder accident.

# 16

School is almost out for the summer, and Gitel wonders what could keep Faye occupied while school is out. They cannot afford to send her to camp, which is where many of her girlfriends go during the summer, first as campers and now as junior counselors. She wonders if Faye could find some volunteer work to do, which would be good experience for her.

It turns out that Faye is ahead of Gitel in thinking about the summer. "I read in the *Hyde Park Herald* about the Hyde Park Neighborhood Club on Fifty-Sixth and Dorchester. It seems like a good place, with summer programs similar to a day camp for children. I wanted to go talk to someone there," Faye tells Gitel, "but I was reluctant to walk past all those taverns on Fifty-Fifth Street west of Lake Park. I decided that I would walk to Fifty-Sixth Street on Everett, then go west on Fifty-Sixth past Bret Harte and under the train tracks to Dorchester, which seems safe to me. I did that one day after school. I didn't tell you what I was planning to do because I didn't want to start a discussion over whether I could volunteer there unless it was a realistic possibility."

"Okay, so you went there. What happened?"

"The meeting with the person in charge went pretty well. I look older than I am, and I think I came across as a serious person. They said that they had been planning to find a teenage volunteer to help with the various activities for young children in their summer day camp, such as artwork and field trips, and that they would be happy to have my help. I said that I had to clear my participation with my parents, but that I was sure it would be okay. I wrote down the information for the person who had interviewed me, and said that I would drop a note confirming my participation in the mail. Camp will start after school is out, near the end of June, and go through July and August. Ideally, I would work from nine to five every weekday, but she said that I could ask for time off if I had something else that I had to do. I said that was fine."

"If it is fine with you, it is fine with me," Gitel says. "Good for you for thinking ahead and figuring all this out. But do avoid walking on Fifty-Fifth Street west of the tracks. I'm glad you didn't do that."

One day in the middle of August, Faye is late coming home. Shmuel has come home early, and he and Gitel are waiting for Faye. Their radio is on, and through the open windows of other apartments they can hear other radios blaring. There are many people on the street outside, smiling and hugging each other. As Faye comes in the door, Gitel says, "We have great news for you."

Faye replies, "I've already heard the news. As I walked across Fifty-Sixth Street, people seemed to be excited. It is a hot day, so I could hear the radio news coming through open apartment windows and shop doorways. I stopped to listen, and realized what was being said. Japan has surrendered. The war is totally over."

Shmuel smiles and says, "That is not what we mean. We have personal good news."

Gitel breaks in. "I'm pregnant! If all is well, you will have a little sister or brother."

"Wow! That's great! I've always wanted a sister or brother. But Mom, you told me that you couldn't have any more children. What changed?"

Gitel just smiles, and doesn't answer.

# 17

Gitel realizes that they need a new apartment. Faye is getting older and could use some privacy. It is not right to continue to live in one room. And they no longer have to live in a building with an elevator, so she can look at more options. Shmuel is planning on leaving Pharmall and going back to his old job. He tells her that Lou is happy to have him back; they will be able, once again, to expand the hours the store is open. It is the type of pharmacy where Shmuel prefers to work. But the salary is not great. They cannot commit to paying much more rent than they already pay, especially with the expenses of a baby coming soon.

With the war over and service members coming home, however, there is a lot of competition for apartments. Their wives may have been living with parents or with roommates to save money during the war, so now there is a pent-up demand for apartments. That is pushing up rent levels.

Gitel finds a two-room apartment on the south side of Fifty-Fifth Street between Everett and South Shore Drive. It is on the second floor of a three-story apartment building that has several entrances with six apartments each. The apartment has a living room with a pull-down bed, a dining room, and a small kitchen. She thinks they can rescue their dining room table and chairs from storage, and put a bed against the wall in the dining room for Faye. Once the baby comes, they can also put a crib at the end of the room; it is a pretty big room. There is also a hallway with a few closets and a bathroom. Not ideal, but the sixty dollars per month rent is probably the most they can afford. The landlord belongs to the Hyde Park Hebrew Center and has met Shmuel, so he is happy to rent the apartment to them.

Gitel ticks off the advantages and disadvantages in her mind. The apartment is still within the Bret Harte school district. It is a little longer walk, but Faye only has one more year there before she starts high school. There is a southbound bus that stops a block away, at Fifty-Fifth and Hyde Park Boulevard, and in front of the high school. That seems convenient for Faye. It won't be as convenient for Shmuel, who will need to take a bus going north on Hyde Park Boulevard and transfer at Forty-Third Street, or walk three blocks to take a bus across Fifty-Fifth Street and transfer on Wentworth. Neither is easy, but there is no other way if he wants to work with Lou.

The baby is due in February 1946. Gitel's doctors are quite worried about a woman who is thirty-nine years old being pregnant. At her most recent prenatal checkup, her doctor tells her, "There is a high chance of the baby having a defect, such as retardation or malformations. There is also a risk of premature birth. I think you should consider having an abortion now."

"There is no way I would have an abortion," Gitel replies. "This baby is wanted and will be loved no matter what. I'll just have to hope for the best."

In fact, becoming pregnant has derailed her secret plans and dreams. With the war over and Faye old enough to take care of herself during the day, Gitel had been hoping to go back to school to get a teaching degree, or if that is not possible, to find a good job as a bookkeeper. *It certainly would be nice to have some additional income coming in*, she thinks. *I would very much like to be able to rent a two-bedroom apartment, and maybe even be able to buy a car so Shmuel could get to work without waiting for buses, and we could drive when we go to South Bend. I am tired of trying to make every penny go further, and of going without many things that I would like. Now all of that is out of the question. Once the baby is born, it might even be difficult initially to keep up with the work for my bookkeeping clients.* Gitel feels her eyes tear up. She was telling the truth when she told her doctor that the new baby is wanted, but her disappointment is also true. And she has to keep the latter to herself. Maybe she can share her thoughts with Sophie, who will not be judgmental.

They move to the new apartment on a cold, snowy January day. They had arranged for some things they had in storage to also be delivered and moved in, including their living room furniture, the dining room set, and an upright piano that Gitel had used as a child. The living room has to be arranged so the bed can fold down at night, but there is enough room for everything. The dining room is crowded, but it is usable for both eating and for Faye to sleep between the table and the wall. The apartment is a small improvement over the cramped conditions at the Aragon, but less comfortable than the one-bedroom on St. Louis in Lawndale. Gitel hopes they will be able to afford a better apartment in the future.

On Monday, February 11, Gitel gives birth to a daughter. When Gitel goes into labor at about 8:00 p.m., she calls Shmuel at work. Shmuel says he will call Lou at his house and tell him he has to close the store and go to be with Gitel. When Shmuel gets to the hospital, he tells Gitel, "When I called Lou, he asked me to keep the store open until the normal time for closing. I told him that my priority was to be with you and that if he insisted that I stay, I quit. I think I said it quite loudly and emphatically. I hung up the phone—you could say that I slammed it down—and I closed the store and came to the hospital."

Gitel starts crying. "You have to call Lou immediately and apologize. The four of us need to eat and have a place to live, and you need to work to make that happen." Shmuel does call Lou again to apologize. Lou tells him that he is sorry he asked him to stay tonight, and that he hopes Shmuel will be back at work the next day.

Gitel thinks about the incident. In addition to Shmuel's *shlekht mazel*, his bad luck, he does occasionally have trouble controlling his temper. His outbursts are never aimed at her or Faye, but come on when he feels that someone, a boss, a salesperson, or the world in general, is being unfair to him. Unfortunately, that happens fairly frequently. One reason Shmuel likes working for Lou is that Lou puts up with the outbursts when they occur.

They have to choose a name for the baby girl. Shmuel wants to name her Ilana, after his father Isser. In Hebrew, as in English, Ilana begins with the same letter as Isser, an *alef*. Faye weighs in on their conversation, saying she thinks that Ilana is not a pretty name. She wants an interesting or unusual name, perhaps Ivory. Gitel wants to name her after her own father Jacob, perhaps calling her Jean or Joan. She argues that Shmuel chose Faye's name, to name her after his mother. It should be her turn to choose a name. But Shmuel insists that he needs to name her after his father, because there is no one else to name a child after Isser. He says Gitel can choose a middle name for her. After much back and forth, they decide on Ilana Joan.

Gitel decides that she will try to call her by both her first and middle name. From the beginning, Gitel calls her Ilana-Joanie and encourages Shmuel and Faye to do so as well. When Ilana begins to talk, she hears her name as Dodi, and calls herself by that name. The family picks up on the name Dodi, which in Hebrew means "my dearest," as Ilana's nickname. That only lasts until Ilana is old enough to attend school, at which point she insists to her parents and to neighboring children that are her friends that her name is Ilana and not Dodi.

Faye tells Gitel that she loves taking care of Dodi. Before the baby was born, Faye often went to a friend's house after school rather than return to their cramped apartment. But now Faye is coming home most afternoons so she can play with and take care of Dodi. Gitel continues to nurse the baby, but Faye wants to do everything else with her. She loves to take Ilana out in her carriage and walk all over the neighborhood with her. Gitel thinks that Faye likes it when people stop them and admire the baby. That makes Gitel extremely nervous about the possibility of the "evil eye," something she thought she didn't believe in but which rises up from her early life as part of her maternal feelings. When she suggests that Faye say, "*Kaynehora*" (no evil eye), if anyone says, "What a beautiful baby" or any similar comment, Faye just laughs at her.

"You always claim to not be superstitious like Bobe," Faye taunts. Gitel knows it is a lost cause to convince Faye to say *kaynehora*. She just has to hope for the best. At least she has some time to work on the bookkeeping while they are out of the house.

Gitel stops nursing the baby in July. Faye is out of school for the summer, and wants to take care of Dodi rather than work at the neighborhood club. Gitel becomes relatively free to resume going to meetings of the organizations she cares about. And she finds a couple more bookkeeping clients. A baby's needs are expensive, and Shmuel's salary won't easily stretch for that without depriving Faye. Faye is good about not asking for things, but Gitel knows she wants nice clothes and a little spending money to at least get a Coke or something when she is with her friends.

Gitel asks Faye where she goes with Dodi for most of the day. "I get together with my friends at the Point," she says. Gitel knows that the Promontory Point is an area in Jackson Park on Lake Michigan with a large meadow and huge limestone rocks creating three or four levels going down to the lake. There is also a field house that looks a bit like a castle, where the bathrooms are located, and a fancy marble drinking fountain—both of which had been WPA projects. It is a very short walk from their apartment. When Gitel occasionally walks by there in the summer, she sees that a lot of young people, mostly high school students, congregate there to sunbathe, flirt, and just mingle.

"Dodi has become sort of a mascot to the group. She is a big hit. She has a lovely smile and is willing to play with anyone who wants to play with her. Having her around actually has made me more popular, since everyone wants to know about her and why she is with me. A few people may suspect that she is my child, but most know that isn't true."

Faye tells Gitel that she is looking forward to starting at Hyde Park High School in the fall. For the past couple of years, she has been mentioning that classes are boring, with a lot of review and not much new material to learn. "The worst thing is having to come home every day for lunch, walking back and forth from school twice each day and having to quickly eat something so I can get back to class on time. I've heard that the high school has a cafeteria and that students are not allowed to leave at lunchtime. Exactly opposite of the elementary school. *Gey veys!* Go figure!"

# 18

Gitel wants Shmuel to ask Lou for a pay raise. "Shmuel, wouldn't you prefer to have a bigger, better apartment? The kitchen in this one is so tiny. It is hard to cook good meals. And as Faye gets older, sleeping in the dining room is not so nice. She never invites friends over. She probably is ashamed of how we live. Lou isn't paying you very much, given your talent and experience. Couldn't you ask him for a pay raise?"

"It is true, Gitel, that he is not paying me that much for someone of my experience and expertise. But I know he isn't making that much money from the store. He does own a house in South Shore and a car, but he isn't living the high life. I can see how much money we are taking in on my shift. I have to balance the cash register before I go home. It seems like a fair bit, but Lou said the rent and especially the insurance costs are high. Insurance is high because the store is subject to being robbed. It is in a neighborhood that generally is middle class to working class, but there are always a few people who are alcoholics or drug addicts for whom the contents of a drugstore is a tempting target. Since I work the three p.m. to midnight shift, any robberies are likely to occur on my watch. There have not been any since I came back to work, but I am always a bit on edge about the potential. Lou thinks that I should just give any robber what he wants—money or drugs—rather than risk getting hurt if I refuse."

"Lou is the owner," Gitel replies. "If there are losses from robberies, that should be his problem and not yours. I agree you should give the robbers whatever they want. Lou probably gets at least some reimbursement from the expensive insurance he has told you about. He nevertheless should be paying you fair wages. Or maybe you could find a better job?"

"It is not easy for me to be back at work. The commute is difficult. I always wear long underwear in the winter, but the Chicago wind cuts through any layers of clothing. And once at work, I must stand anytime someone is in the store, whenever I have to make a prescription, and when I check the shelves or put away deliveries of inventory. I find it difficult to stand so much of the time; my back frequently still hurts."

"I'm sorry. I didn't realize how difficult working still is for you. I guess I should have known. Maybe you could find a better situation, although I imagine that would be difficult to do."

"I probably should look around to see if I could get a better-paid job, or one closer to home, but I am afraid to do that," Shmuel says. "Lou knows me and puts up with the way I like to do things. Another reason I stay is that Lou is aware of my precarious health. Other employers might not be willing to take a chance on me. Lou is patient if I take a few days off to recover from a cold or other minor problem. In other settings, I might be forced to go to work no matter what and a cold could turn into pneumonia. And Lou puts up with my quirks and occasional outbursts of temper. The bottom line is that I feel stuck working for Lou."

Gitel sighs. Not for the first time, she wishes she could just go to work and not be so dependent on Shmuel's salary. She thinks back on the night Ilana was conceived, the night that derailed all her plans. *After Faye was born, I told Shmuel that my "tubes were stopped up" and that I was unlikely to be able to conceive again. The doctor never told me that. It was something I had read in a women's magazine. I didn't even know what tubes the article was talking about. Saying that to Shmuel took some of the pressure off his desire to have sex, and his desire to have another child. He, apparently, knew what tubes were in question. When we had sex to celebrate the end of the war, he must have thought there was no chance of pregnancy. And I was so happy that the war was over that I wasn't paying attention to the risk. So now we have Ilana, who is a wonderful child and I love her. But we don't have enough money to manage.*

# 19

The first two years of Dodi's life go by in a blur for Gitel. *Taking care of a toddler is more than a full-time job*, she thinks. Gitel had help from her mother and Tante when Faye was that age. She hadn't realized how hard it is to be alone all day with a toddler who has to constantly be watched. While Faye is a big help during the summer, she isn't home much during the school year. The only time Gitel can do her bookkeeping is when Dodi naps in the afternoon, and she doesn't always do that. And—in Gitel's experience, mothers don't like to admit this—watching a toddler is so boring. Gitel tries to find places to go and people to see as much as possible. Since there is no way they can afford babysitters, she just takes Dodi along with her to wherever she is going.

The Women's Division American Jewish Congress meetings are usually at someone's home. Gitel never asks permission ahead of time; she just brings Dodi along with her to the meetings. Since Gitel had been elected the president of the South Side Women's Division, she chairs the meetings. Some other woman usually volunteers to keep an eye on Dodi. Dodi seems to be fascinated by the people and the different settings, and spends a lot of time just seeming to take in what is happening. There is a lot of excitement at the meetings, with hope in the air that Israel will soon become a state. They know that once refugees are able to immigrate to Israel, they will need a lot of support. The women are making plans to increase their fundraising for that purpose.

While Gitel likes to keep busy, she is beginning to have some problems that are slowing her down. She feels sick to her stomach a lot, and often vomits up whatever she eats for dinner. She knows that she certainly is not pregnant again, so she worries about what might be causing her nausea. She also has pains in her stomach and sometimes in her back. She begins to imagine the worst, that she has cancer. She doesn't want to tell anyone how she feels. It somehow seems trivial compared to the big things happening in the world, and compared to the need to take care of Dodi. She especially doesn't want to tell Shmuel, who clearly has enough struggles of his own.

Gitel schedules a meeting with her regular doctor. He says that she probably has gallstones, and that it will require surgery to remove her gallbladder. He assures her that she will be fine after the surgery. There will be no long-term consequences or additional treatment necessary.

She is afraid to have surgery. *Being put to sleep with a chemical and having someone cut into me—it seems like something that should be avoided. I don't want it. In addition, the doctor says that I will have to be in the hospital for about a week and then take it easy for six more weeks. I will not be allowed to lift up or carry Dodi during that time.*

She can't imagine how they will manage. Even though she is feeling terrible, she decides to wait for the surgery until early July, when school is out and Faye can help. She finally discusses the situation with Shmuel, who urges her to go ahead with the surgery.

"I think your plan to wait until July is wise. I am fairly sure that I could get a couple of weeks off work to help take care of you at that time of year. I will give Lou plenty of notice so he can find someone to fill in if that is what he wants to do. I think it is too much to ask Faye to take complete care of you and Dodi."

"Thank you," Gitel says. "That makes me feel a lot better about how we will manage. But I still dread the surgery."

# 20

Dodi is two years old when Gitel comes home from the hospital after her surgery. Shmuel and Faye have managed as best they can with Dodi and the apartment while she is gone. One or the other of them regularly visits Gitel at the University of Chicago Hospital and reports on what is happening at home.

Shmuel tells Gitel that he has been at home as much as possible. "I've even cooked eggs in the kitchen for our lunch or dinner. Faye remarked that she had never seen me cooking before. I informed her that I had some experience as a short-order cook before she was born. You should know, however, that Faye has been wonderful. She has been taking care of Dodi, cooking, doing laundry, and cleaning the house a bit. And she has a surprise for you when you come back home."

Gitel seems to be in pain and isn't reacting well to Shmuel's words. Finally, she asks, "What surprise? Something good, I hope."

"You will have to wait and see."

After a week, Shmuel goes to the hospital to bring Gitel home in a cab. Dodi and Faye are waiting to greet her. Faye had encouraged Dodi to make a big deal of the homecoming. Gitel is greeted with signs on which Dodi had drawn in crayon and Faye had written, WELCOME HOME. When Gitel comes in, she kisses Dodi and Faye and says she likes the signs, but then says that she has to lie down right away.

Gitel seems unwell and unhappy. She lies on the couch with a damp rag on her forehead, sort of asleep but not really. She periodically asks Faye or Dodi to bring her things to drink, and sometimes sits up and eats a little. She otherwise doesn't talk much to Faye or Dodi, but she does talk to Shmuel about her experience.

"Shmuel, I had a bad time during the surgery. I'm pretty sure that something went wrong. I didn't understand what was happening at the time. I think I woke up at the wrong time during the surgery, while it was still going on. I could hear the doctors talking, but I couldn't move or talk. It was so frightening."

"That is surprising, but it is all behind you now, Gitel. I hope you can begin to get up and resume your normal life, at least as much as possible. I know it will be hard for you to take care of Dodi with your lifting restriction and the need to rest more than usual, but the sooner you get back to doing your regular activities, the better you will feel."

"Easy for you to say. Right now, I feel awful."

Faye understands that Gitel is having a hard time. She takes Dodi out of the apartment as much as possible, so that she won't pester Gitel for attention. That summer Faye and Dodi again spend a lot of time sitting on the grass in the field at the Point, or sitting on the huge limestone rocks at the waterfront of Lake Michigan. Dodi tells Gitel that the rocks look like stairs for giants. She asks Gitel and Faye if giants come to use them when people aren't in the park.

One day when they come back from the Point, Gitel asks Faye how it is working for her to be taking care of Dodi so much.

Faye tells Gitel, "My friends from school are usually in the park as much as we are. I think Dodi resents that I often pay more attention to my friends than to her. Whenever she wants my attention, she says that she needs a drink of water from the big marble fountain, or that she needs to go to the bathroom in the field house. I have no choice but to take her. She also seems to decide that she likes some of my friends more than others, particularly the guys. She acts distracting and obnoxious if she doesn't like a guy who is trying to pay attention to me. Sometimes she even calls me 'Mama,' which makes the guys she doesn't like do a double take. I suspect that Dodi somehow knows exactly what calling me 'Mama' implies, even at her young age. I pretend to be exasperated with her, but in truth I rather enjoy her antics. I'm happy to take care of her."

Gitel keeps cautioning Faye about the need to protect Dodi from polio, which is just beginning to make the news. It is mostly affecting young children, causing paralysis, and seems to be able to be passed from child to child. Despite Dodi's protestations, Faye follows Gitel's advice and doesn't allow her to play in the playground or anywhere there is a gathering of young children. Faye reports to Gitel, "I make Dodi stay around me and my friends. She plays by herself in the grassy field, often picking dandelions or digging up the dirt. She has a small shovel I bought her and tries to make a deep hole. She says she wants to dig to China. She often says that she is bored and lonely playing by herself, but I assure her that the threat of polio is real and we must be careful. I tell her we are lucky to live just a block from the park, rather than being stuck in the apartment."

Gitel feels bad that Dodi has to continue to sleep in a crib, because there is no place in the tiny apartment to put a regular bed for her. The crib is next to the dining room table and chairs that take up most of the room. Dodi often stands in the crib, pulls over a dining room chair, and climbs out of the crib onto the chair and then onto the floor. Luckily, she never falls; she is good at climbing. Gitel knows that as Dodi grows, they will have to find another solution. But she has no idea how they might afford a bigger apartment.

# 21

Dodi goes with Gitel to the various meetings of the organizations with which Gitel is involved. These are often at other people's apartments or homes, especially the meetings for the American Jewish Congress. Some of these homes are in South Shore, a neighborhood where people tend to be better off. Dodi tells Gitel, "I like seeing how other people live. Not everyone lives pushed together as we do."

Gitel tells her, "It is fine if you look around, so long as you sit quietly and amuse yourself with a coloring book."

Dodi thinks, *It isn't fun to be here with my mother. I feel dragged along.*

Dodi sometimes passes the time by listening to what is going on at the meeting, trying to understand. Especially when Gitel is the one leading the meeting, which she usually is. One day, when Dodi is four years old, they are at a large house in South Shore. Dodi has to use the bathroom, but she has no idea where to find it. Gitel is busy conducting the meeting, calling on other women to speak on some subject. Dodi remembers hearing how the women sometimes are able to get the attention of the person leading the meeting, so she stands up and says loudly, "Point of personal privilege." Everyone begins to laugh. When they stop, she asks Gitel where she can find the bathroom.

A lot of Sundays, Shmuel takes Dodi to the Museum of Science and Industry. It is only about three blocks from their apartment, so they walk there. It is free to go in. Dodi loves the museum because there are lots of levers and dials that make things happen, like balls bouncing in a display or pictures of different things popping up. There is a model farm with some live farm animals, including chickens and an incubator that hatches chicken eggs. Dodi loves watching the newly hatched chickens and would stand there for a long time observing how they stumble around. Living on a busy street in the city, that is her only experience of animals. And the exhibit teaches her a lot about where food comes from. There is also a model train in the museum that runs on a large layout, with little houses and stations and trees. And the museum has a theater where different people explain different science things. Dodi especially likes the one called "Electric Theater," where a light bulb is used to pop popcorn. There are so many different areas and displays at the museum that she never gets tired of going there. She thinks Shmuel, who always tells her how important it is to understand science, enjoys their trips there as much as she does. And since she rarely sees much of Shmuel during the week because of his work schedule, she loves having his attention on Sundays.

At their apartment, the family does not have children's books—or own very many books at all. Dodi owns just one book, about a Navajo child who learns to weave rugs. She doesn't remember where it came from, but Gitel tells her that someone gave it to her. Her parents do like to read, and are fans of the public library. They regularly go to the Blackstone Library on Forty-Ninth and Lake Park Avenue. It is a bit of a walk, but they go every two weeks or so. Dodi is allowed to take out three or four books at a time, and sometimes her mother or father or Faye take out books for themselves. Dodi feels that it is an adventure to go there, to walk in through the huge marble columns that she is told are modeled after the Greek Acropolis and into the cool, vaulted rooms with impressive paintings near the ceiling. She imagines that she is walking into a castle or an ancient temple that she had seen in a book. As soon as they get back home, she is always anxious for someone to read the books to her, although by the time she is four or five she can read some of them herself.

Faye goes to college at Navy Pier, which is a branch of the University of Illinois. Dodi goes with Gitel one time to Navy Pier while Faye is in school there, to watch Faye play in a badminton game. She doesn't understand much of what is going on in the game, but is happy to see where Faye goes each day. The buildings, which look rather shabby, are indeed stretched out along a pier jutting into Lake Michigan. Gitel tells her that the buildings were intended to be temporary, to be used during the war. But now they are being put to another use.

Faye has less time for Dodi while she is in college and even less time when she starts at John Marshall Law School after two years at Navy Pier. She has a lot of studying to do, and she also has a part-time job to afford tuition, help with the family's finances, and have some spending money for herself. But if Dodi really needs her, like if something is making her unhappy, Faye always manages to be there for her. Faye has a beautiful voice, and Dodi is always after her to sing to her when it is time to go to sleep. Dodi will plead, "Sing 'Drink to Me Only with Thine Eyes,'" something Dodi knows Faye likes to sing. Her pleas often work, and Faye will sing to her.

Dodi finally turns five years old and is ready to start half-day kindergarten at Bret Harte School. She really wants to go to school and be with other children. The first thing she does is insist that her name is Ilana, not Dodi. She thinks Dodi sounds too much like "doody," which is a word some children use for what happens in the bathroom. Although it is mostly family who call her Dodi, a few children her age who live near them have picked up that name, as have a few children who go to the same shul. She speaks to each of them and asks them to only call her Ilana at school. The only person she allows to continue to call her Dodi is Faye. Faye likes the name, and Ilana is willing to let Faye do what she wants. She so loves Faye.

When school begins, Ilana makes a surprising discovery. The language they speak at home is not entirely English. It is a mixture of English and Yiddish. Foods, body parts, some feelings, and other things are mostly in Yiddish. She learns which words are Yiddish when other children do not understand what she is saying. Some of the other Jewish children do, but not all. And the non-Jewish children just look at her as if she is strange. That first year of school, she works hard on switching her vocabulary to all English, at least for use in public. She is fairly successful, but sometimes there are English words she has never heard, so she doesn't recognize them or know how to use them.

One day Gitel can't be home for her at lunchtime. She asks another mother who lives a half block away if Ilana can go home with her daughter Mary, who is in the same class, and have lunch at her house. When Mary and Ilana get to Mary's house, her mother says, "I have several different kinds of soup in cans. Ilana, what kind of soup do you like to eat?"

Ilana says, "*Lokshen* soup."

"I have never heard of *lokshen*. Could you explain what it is?"

After thinking for a bit, Ilana says, "It is something that is put into chicken soup. It is sort of flat and thin."

From Mary's mother, Ilana learns the word "noodle." Mary's mother gives her chicken noodle soup to eat.

Around this time, Shmuel receives a small increase in pay. Gitel and Shmuel call Ilana and Faye to the living room to talk to them. Gitel says, "There is a one-bedroom apartment in the next entrance of this building that we think we can manage to afford. That way the two of you can have a bedroom to share, and a little more privacy. There is still a pull-down bed in the living room for me and your father. The only drawback is that the apartment is on the third floor."

Faye asks, "Is that going to be okay for Dad, and what about when you have to carry up groceries?"

Ilana pipes up, "I can help Mama carry."

"Thank you, Ilana. I think we will be fine," Gitel replies, smiling.

# 22

One Sunday when Ilana is walking home from the museum with her father, Shmuel says to her, "I want you to learn how to be a good Jew. I always felt bad that I was not with Faye when she was young. I should have been teaching her. A man is required to teach the commandments and the blessings to his child—boy or girl. But Faye was with Gitel in South Bend and then living with my cousins in New York at the time it would have been best to teach her. Your *bobe* could have taught her some while they were living in South Bend, but probably did not because she would not have wanted to interfere with your mother's wishes. And your mother probably was not interested in Faye learning and did not encourage it. Faye grew up without learning any Hebrew and without much understanding of Jewish observance at all. By the time I was able to live with the family, she did not want to learn. I do not want to make that same mistake with you. I want to make sure you know what a good Jew should know."

"That is fine, Daddy. I'm happy to learn. You know I like to learn new things," Ilana replies. "And you already started to teach me. You taught me to say the *She'ma* at bedtime when I was just three years old. I do say it every night. But I don't know what the Hebrew means. Could you teach me that?"

"Of course. I should have already done so. It is hard, because I am not home when you go to sleep. If I were, we could pray together.

The beginning of it means, 'Hear O Israel, Adonai is our God, God is One.' It means that we accept the one God and God's commandments and that we don't believe in any other or different gods. There are people in this country and in the world who follow other religions, and some of them believe that there is more than one god, but Jews believe in the one God. An observant Jew says the *She'ma* twice a day, although for now it is fine for you just to say it at bedtime. I will teach you what the rest of it means when we have a chance to sit down together. In general, the second paragraph means that good things happen to people who obey God's commandments and bad things happen to those who do not. But it is written in a way that speaks to the Jewish people as a whole, not to individual people. Bad things sometimes do happen to good people."

Ilana doesn't fully understand what her father is saying, so she changes the subject. "Will you teach me to read Hebrew? I can already read English, but Hebrew looks so different."

"When you are about seven years old, you can start Hebrew school at the shul," Shmuel says. "That is a good time to learn to read Hebrew. But if we have time, I can teach you some before that. For right now, I would like you to learn some additional prayers and blessings so you can say them at the right time."

"Okay."

"Let's start with the prayer on getting up in the morning, *modah ani.*" They reach their apartment, and they sit in the living room to continue their conversation. "That prayer says, 'Thank you, God, for returning my soul to me.' Your soul is what makes you alive." Shmuel says the Hebrew words slowly, and Ilana repeats after him. By the following Sunday when they work on it again, Ilana has memorized it. Shmuel gradually teaches her the blessings to say over different kinds of food and over washing before eating.

"I'm so proud of you," Shmuel tells Ilana. "You are just five years old, and you know how to say all these prayers and blessings correctly. I hope you continue to say them."

Ilana thinks, *I know that Mama and Faye do not say these blessings and prayers. At dinner they just start eating. They never wash with the blessing before eating or say the correct blessing over the type of food we are eating. But I want to please Daddy, so I continue to say them. It seems to make him happy that I do it.*

When Ilana is seven years old, she starts Hebrew school at the Hyde Park Hebrew Center, the mostly Orthodox synagogue to which the family belongs. That year, she learns to read Hebrew and write Hebrew script. She already knows most of the prayers and blessings they teach in that first-year class. At the end of the year, Rabbi Fishman explains to the class that they will begin learning Torah, the five books of Moses, in the fall.

Ilana raises her hand. "What will the learning be like?"

The rabbi looks at her as if he had forgotten that she was in the class.

"Oh, the girls—you and Ruthie—will have a different class to learn about keeping kosher and running a Jewish home."

Ilana opens her mouth to object, but realizes that is hopeless. Nothing she can say will change what the rabbi is planning. She wonders if she can transfer to the conservative synagogue in the neighborhood, where a lot of her friends from school go. They say that boys and girls study together there.

She talks to her father. He says that he does not object on principle, but Gitel says that the Hebrew school tuition at the conservative shul costs more than they can afford. It is a very large and wealthy congregation, with many members from the South Shore neighborhood. Gitel is outraged at the discrimination against girls at the Hyde Park

Hebrew Center, so she reaches deeply into her *khutspe* (audacity) and goes to see the principal of the conservative shul. She tells him the problem, and asks if Ilana can have a scholarship even though their family are not members of the congregation. Gitel returns home jubilant. "My efforts succeeded! Ilana can transfer to the more egalitarian Rodfei Zedek for Hebrew school."

Shmuel says, "I cannot believe you had the *khutspe* to go ask that question. But I am glad you did!"

## 23

Gitel notices that Faye has a lot of dates with different boyfriends, although she never interferes with Faye's social life. Many of the dates try to get on Faye's good side by being nice to Ilana. Ilana pays a lot of attention to Faye's dates, and even sort of flirts with them in a child's way. She usually tries to talk to them and then later gives her opinion to Faye. Faye's boyfriends often bring little gifts to give to Ilana. Both Faye and Gitel enjoy watching Ilana's performances.

One of Faye's boyfriends gives Ilana a life-size stuffed panda! It is larger than she is. The Brookfield Zoo has acquired a panda from China, and all of Chicago is a bit panda-crazy. There are lots of pictures in the newspapers and talk of it on the radio news. Lots of kids have panda pictures or shirts with pandas on them. When Faye's friend brings the panda to her, he says that he had been stopped by the police on the way over. The life-size panda had been sitting in the front passenger seat of his car, and the policeman was not sure if it was real or stuffed. In any case, Ilana loves that panda. She cuddles up to it, leans on it, or just looks at it.

Gitel and Shmuel talk a lot about the Korean War, which had begun in 1950, as do Faye and her friends. Faye talks about various men she knows around her age or a little older who either were drafted or volunteered to serve in Korea. A few sometimes come to the house dressed in uniform.

Ilana listens carefully to the radio news, and is beginning to pick out words in the newspaper. When she overhears Shmuel and Gitel talking about the war, Ilana asks them what the word "Communism" means.

Shmuel tells her, "The US is fighting in Korea to prevent the north of the country, helped by China, from imposing Communism on the south of the country."

"But why would that be bad? And why does the US care about a country so far away?"

"Those are good questions. Mama and I, and the US government, think that countries should be able to choose their own form of government, not have it imposed by another country waging war on it. Communism has some good ideas about the equality of people and sharing wealth, but in practice it has harmed a lot of people."

Ilana says she is still puzzled. She sometimes tries to ask some of the soldiers who come to see Faye. Gitel tells her that she has to stop doing that. "Life is difficult enough for the soldiers without having to convince a child that they are doing the right thing."

Ilana complains to Gitel about school, especially when she enters first grade.

"I'm not learning anything in school. They never teach about anything important, like the war that is going on, or the presidential election that is about to happen. All the time in class is taken up with the children learning to read from a *Dick and Jane* reader. It is difficult for some of the students, and the whole class has to listen to them struggle to read out loud."

Gitel knows that Ilana has been reading books by herself for a while, and can even read the newspaper, asking the meaning of some of the harder words.

"I am incredibly bored in class," Ilana continues. "It is difficult for me to sit still. I don't want to get in trouble, but some days I just can't stand it."

Gitel frequently is called to the school to speak to Ilana's teacher about her behavior in class. She remembers how bored she herself was in school, but then as now there is not much that can be done about it. She suggests that the teacher find some enrichment activities for Ilana, but somehow that never happens. She thinks, *We have no choice but to leave her in the local public school, despite the fact that she seems so smart and advanced for her age—undoubtedly taking after Shmuel. I have heard that The University of Chicago runs a highly regarded private school. It is largely for the children of faculty, but it takes other children as well. But we certainly could not afford the very high private school tuition. I need to forget about that possibility. Instead, I will continue to nag the teacher and the administration at Bret Harte until they arrange some appropriate lessons or activities for Ilana. I have been doing a few things with the PTA. I wonder if I could run for a PTA office and thereby have some additional leverage over what is happening at the school—I will look into that.*

Shmuel and Gitel are excited about Adlai Stevenson's presidential campaign in 1952 against General Dwight Eisenhower. Stevenson is from Illinois, an intellectual and a liberal with whom they agree on most issues. Ilana pays attention to what they are talking about, and picks up on their enthusiasm, if not the details of its source.

"Kids at school are paying attention to the election," she tells Gitel. "On the playground at recess, the children hold hands in two lines opposite each other. One of the lines yells, 'Stevenson,' and the other yells, 'I like Ike.' I did a lot to organize the Stevenson line, because I was upset so many kids were using the 'I like Ike' slogan. When you and Dad were talking about the election, you sounded worried that it was such a catchy slogan."

"It is great that you and other six-year-olds are so involved and opinionated about politics. I'm proud of you. And it reflects well on the other children's parents. That is a good thing about living in Hyde Park, where so many people are activists. You should just remember, it is a good thing that people have different opinions. But you should also hold strong to your own opinions and act on them when you can. I see that you are on the way to doing that."

"I will," Ilana says. "I learned a lot from all the meetings you took me to. I understand how you lead people to what you want them to believe and do."

# 24

Gitel spends a lot of time with Sophie, as much as she can. Sometimes she takes Ilana and goes over there while Shmuel is at work in the evenings. But she also goes there while Ilana is in school, and she sees Sophie at various meetings. She values Sophie's opinions about a lot of issues, and often quotes them to Shmuel. For example, Sophie is very opposed to the US involvement in the Korean War. Being a member of the Communist Party, she does not share in the general panic among Americans about anything labeled Communist. She is not opposed to South Korea coming under Communist influence.

One day some men wearing suits and trench coats come to Gitel's apartment in the afternoon. They show her badges and cards that identify them as FBI agents, so she lets them in. One of them says, "We know you have a close friend Sophie who is a member of the Communist Party. We also know that you have other Communist friends, and that you regularly receive mail on suspicious subjects, such as the campaign to free Julius and Ethel Rosenberg. And you and your husband have a history of belonging to Socialist organizations. Your husband was an officer in the Young People's Socialist League, wasn't he?"

Gitel does not answer, so the FBI guy continues to talk. "You could be a great help to the US government. As you may have heard, there is an effort beginning in Congress to identify Communists and make sure they do not have jobs that could influence US policy. Senator Joe McCarthy is starting to hold hearings on the subject. You are well positioned to help us identify people who might be Communists. You would just have to tell us what your Communist or Socialist friends are saying about issues like the Korean War, relations with Russia, or any domestic issues such as the labor union movement."

"I think you need to leave," Gitel says. "There is no way I would ever spy on my friends. I am not a Communist, and neither is my husband. But I do think people are entitled to their opinions. I see no harm in people thinking that Communists and Socialists have some good ideas. And I see no harm in receiving mail and reading about any topic I am interested in. So please leave now! I will not help you."

Gitel is shaking after they leave. She calls Shmuel at the pharmacy and tells him what has happened. He is less worried. "I think that was just bluster that in the end will not come to anything. Just forget about their visit."

Gitel does not stop seeing Sophie, but she worries about what might happen—especially because Eisenhower has won the election and the Republicans have taken over Congress. She is aware that Congress is holding hearings and hunting for Communists. Luckily, neither she nor Shmuel have government jobs from which the Communist hunters could demand that they be fired, so there isn't much Congress could do about their sympathies and beliefs. That is also true for Sophie and her husband. *Maybe Shmuel is right*, she thinks. She tries to put the whole incident with the FBI agents out of her mind, but finds that impossible to do.

Around this time, the beginning of 1953, they buy a television. They watch the televised hearings about Communism, cheering when the people being questioned refuse to answer. Ilana is happy to have the television because she loves watching *Howdy Doody*, *The Lone Ranger*, and cartoons. She also watches some of the hearings with them, asking lots of questions and joining their cheers.

# 25

In 1953, a few days after Rosh Hashanah (the Jewish New Year) in mid-September, Gitel receives a phone call from her brother Nokhem. He tells her that Rayzel died in her sleep overnight. She starts crying. She has not been able to see much of her mother lately, but while she was alive there always was the possibility of seeing her. And they did talk on the phone frequently. Now she is gone. Ilana comes home as Gitel is sobbing quietly.

"What is wrong, Mama? Why are you crying?"

"Bobe has just died. It happened during the night. She just didn't wake up this morning."

"Is that because she was old?" Ilana asks.

"Yes, she was old. But still my mama. I will miss her terribly."

"Of course, Mama. I didn't mean to say that about her being old."

"That's okay," Gitel says. "We need to get organized immediately to go to South Bend. The funeral will be tomorrow morning. It will just be you and me. Dad can't get off work on such short notice. Faye does not want to miss her classes and also has to work."

"Okay, Mama. Tell me what you want me to do."

*Shmuel and Faye will have to manage on their own*, Gitel thinks. *Ilana and I have to plan to stay for the week of shiva [seven days of mourning]. And shiva won't end until Yom Kippur [the Day of Atonement], so we probably will have to stay until after that. I'll have*

*to explain Ilana's absence to her school. I have no choice but to bring*
*her with me.*

It is a long week. Ilana has nothing to do during the shiva. She
tries to help Tante in the kitchen, but, as usual, Tante wants to do
it all alone. Some of Gitel's sisters-in-law take Ilana to their houses
to play with their children, which is very helpful and Ilana enjoys
the visits. When the shiva ends and most of the family goes to the
Orthodox Taylor Street shul for Yom Kippur, neither Gitel nor Ilana
can figure out what is happening during the service. In the women's
balcony, none of the women are paying attention to what is happening in the men's section below. Some of the older women are praying
in a soft voice from Yiddish prayer books. Some of the women are
just sitting there, or talking to other women. One is passing around
a citron stuck with cloves, which apparently is supposed to revive
anyone who feels faint from fasting. On Yom Kippur, it is traditional
to refrain from food or drink for twenty-five hours. Gitel is reminded
of her youth, watching Rayzel pray from her women's prayer book in
Yiddish, peering down from the balcony at her father and brothers
in the men's service and hearing their communal singing in Hebrew,
but understanding none of it. She has a brief moment of anger at her
parents for withholding the teaching that might have made her comfortable in shul. Then she returns to wishing that the service would
just be over, or that she could find an excuse to take Ilana and go back
to the house. Eventually, Yom Kippur is over. Tante has prepared a
large evening meal for the traditional break-fast, to which the whole
family comes. The next morning, Gitel and Ilana return home to
Hyde Park on the train.

Gitel is concerned that Faye seems to be struggling in law school, which she started in the fall of 1952 when she was just nineteen years old. She is one of very few women in the class. She decided to go to the local, not very prestigious John Marshall Law School, even though she had been accepted to The University of Chicago. Her parents couldn't figure out a way to pay for U of C. Even John Marshall Law School was difficult to afford, between the tuition and the need to purchase expensive books. Faye keeps her job at the Board of Trade to earn enough to pay the tuition and other expenses. She seems tired all the time, and says she has difficulty keeping up with the readings and assignments because classes and the job take up most of her energy.

Gitel asks Faye, "Do you really want to be a lawyer? I see how hard you are working and how tired you always are. And will a degree from John Marshall lead to a decent job? Is it worth it?"

"My intention is to work locally in the field of juvenile justice. John Marshall will be fine for that; it is a good place to make contacts with the political class in Chicago."

"But it is true," Faye continues, "that part of me just wants to marry someone who will get me out of this cramped apartment and constant financial problems, who could support me so I could stop struggling. It is difficult to work and keep up with classes and homework, and it is difficult to find a place and the concentration to study in this apartment. It is hard to say which I want more—to become a lawyer or to get married."

In Faye's third year of law school, one of her friends suggests that she meet a man she knows who has just finished serving in the military for a few years. He is starting a practice as an obstetrician in a bedroom suburb south of the city. Faye goes out on a couple dates with this man, Joe, and comes home excited after the third date.

She tells Gitel, "Joe and I hit it off right away. I am sure you want to know if he is Jewish. He is, but not observant at all. He seems very healthy and is strong and muscular. Did you notice that when he came to our apartment to pick me up, he lifted Ilana and swung her around? He is already earning a pretty good living, and is likely to do even better in the future because the suburb is full of young couples having babies. I hate to say it, but he seems to be a welcome opposite to everything Dad is. He has asked me to marry him, and we want to get married right after I take the bar exam, in January 1955."

Gitel is thrilled with Faye's fiancé Joe. *I certainly want her to have an easier life than I have had, and Joe seems like just the ticket for that.*

A couple of weeks before the bar exam, Ilana comes down with chicken pox, which Faye had never had as a child. Faye catches it, and has a particularly serious case from which she is not fully recovered by the time of the exam. After she takes the exam, she tells Gitel, "I'm fairly sure that I failed. I hadn't finished studying before I got sick, and I couldn't concentrate during the exam. In addition, there was material on the exam that I had never studied. I should have taken a bar review course, which probably would have covered that material, but we had no money for that."

Gitel is worried when it turns out that Faye indeed did not pass the bar. She always feels that women should be able to earn their own living. One never knows what could happen in life, as her own life illustrates so well. But Joe seems so stable and competent. He is indeed everything Shmuel is not—although, looking back, Shmuel seemed quite different at the time he and Gitel got married.

She is more upbeat when she tries to comfort Faye about having failed the bar exam. "You can always take the exam again, Faye. I've heard that a lot of people who don't pass the first time take it again and go on to have a good career in the law. Maybe next time you will be able to afford to take a bar review course."

Gitel wants Faye to have a nice wedding, so she borrows some money from the bank. She thinks, *I usually am worried about taking on debt and reluctant to do so, but this is important. I don't want her to be embarrassed before her new in-laws.*

She books the ballroom at the Shoreland Hotel, near their apartment. The hotel is quite elegant, built in the 1920s as a luxury hotel and often visited by important people. But it is less expensive to rent the ballroom there than at most downtown hotels. The plan is for the wedding to be far less formal than the wedding Gitel herself had. Faye wants to have only one attendant, eight-year-old Ilana, as maid of honor. They have a special dress custom-made for her. It is pink satin, tailored and not frilly because that is what Ilana wants. They practice Ilana's role walking down the aisle and taking Faye's bouquet at the right time—over and over until she is comfortable with it.

One of Joe's good friends is a cantor, and he sings as the party walks down the aisle. Then he performs the marriage. There are about eighty guests, who are relatives and friends of the couple. The ceremony is followed by a dinner. Tante is still alive; Gitel's brothers bring her from South Bend to the wedding.

"Gitel," Tante says, "you have looked *shtralndik* through the entire *khasene*."

"Yes, I do feel as though I have been beaming through the entire wedding, as you say. It is a great milestone, Tante. Despite all the turmoil of our life since Faye was born, despite having to move her from place to place, despite her living through the deprivations during the Depression and the war, it seems like she is on the verge of a better life. I love Faye dearly. She seems so happy, and I am happy for her."

Even though Ilana is only eight—nearly nine—at the time of the wedding, Gitel feels as though she can glimpse a time in the future when she, too, will be going off on her own. And her hands-on mothering days would come to an end. She again begins to think, as she had before she became pregnant with Ilana, about what she wants to do with her life. *If I start college to become a teacher when Ilana starts high school, would it be too late? Probably. I'd be in my mid-fifties. But maybe I could find a job that I like as a bookkeeper. Especially if I lie about my age. I don't look as old as I am. I guess I shouldn't dwell on the future, because life has taught me that anything can happen. But I long for the freedom to do what I want to do, not what I have to do. And I long for the ability to do things that will make me happy, rather than try to make my daughters and husband as happy as possible, given our circumstances.*

Right after the wedding, Faye and Joe go on a honeymoon to Florida. Faye tells Gitel that she is excited about that. Ever since they moved back to Chicago, no one in their immediate family has gone anywhere but South Bend. Faye and Joe are gone for two weeks. After that they settle in Park Forest, a suburb south of the city. After all those years of Faye being so busy with school and work, she now is free during the day. They are living in a small rental apartment, so taking care of it is not such a big job, she tells Gitel. The only other thing she is doing is learning to drive. She is going to have her own car, as soon as she learns. There is no public transportation in Park Forest, so that is necessary.

Ilana really misses Faye, and keeps nagging Gitel to take her to Park Forest to see her. One day after Faye and Joe have been back a month or so from the honeymoon, Gitel says that they can take the IC commuter train and go to see her. "We'll take the train to the last stop, 211th Street, and then take a taxi to Faye's apartment," Gitel tells Ilana. "The train trip will take about forty-five minutes. Once

Faye learns to drive and Joe buys a car for her, she will be able to pick us up at the train station."

The taxi drops them off at what looks like a small house, with other houses attached on either side. It is different from how Gitel had imagined it when she learned that they were living in an apartment. It isn't an apartment building like those in Hyde Park; it is more like a very small house. They take a walk with Faye around the neighborhood. There is a large white cement building that Faye calls a 'mall.' She explains to Ilana, "A mall is a lot of different stores in one building. The biggest is a branch of Marshall Field's department store, but there are a lot of smaller stores as well. Park Forest does not allow neighborhood stores, so they all have to locate in the mall."

Gitel sees that there is a lot of construction going on near Faye's apartment. Whole blocks of single-story homes that look exactly the same as one another are being built. Ilana says that she has never seen anything like that, and in truth neither has Gitel. There are not many single-family houses in Hyde Park, but those that are there have individual character, not like their neighbors, and are all multistory. The same is true for South Bend. Faye says that they will probably move into one of those houses when they are finished. Gitel thinks, *They don't look appealing to me*, but she doesn't say anything.

Faye says, "It will be important to us to have our own house, and these will be affordable on our income." After their walk, Ilana and Gitel have lunch with Faye at her apartment, and go back to the train station to return home.

A couple months after the wedding, Faye tells the family that she is pregnant. Gitel is excited to have a grandchild, and Ilana is even more excited when her nephew is born in November 1955. They all go to Park Forest for his *bris*, his circumcision, where they name him Jay.

Ilana asks to hold him, and says that she wants to spend as much time with him as possible. Little does Gitel know how much opportunity and obligation Ilana will have to do so in the future.

# 26

Gitel thinks, *I am happy to see Faye with a baby, and she certainly seems happy. That is not a surprise, given how much she loved taking care of Ilana. But I'm also worried. Faye may be giving up what she has worked so hard to achieve. If she doesn't take the bar exam again and pass it, and do so soon, she will not have the option of practicing as a lawyer. For so many years, she has wanted to become a lawyer and worked hard to get through school even though Shmuel and I couldn't pay her tuition. I believe that women should be able to support themselves and not be dependent on their husbands for support, especially if they have children. They don't necessarily have to work when their children are young, although I would have been happy to do that, but no one ever knows what life will hold. A husband could get sick or die. And without their own career, women can be trapped in a bad marriage. I talked to Faye about all of this, but she says she wants to have several children with Joe and does not care anymore about being a lawyer. She wants to be a stay-at-home mom. I am worried for her, but there is nothing I can do. And part of me thinks that perhaps I am just projecting some of my own frustrations on her, and that I should keep quiet about my thoughts.*

About six months later, in the spring of 1956, the family has another all too real example of Gitel's concerns. One morning, just as Shmuel is getting ready to go to work, he becomes rigid and collapses.

Gitel calls an ambulance, which takes him to Michael Reese Hospital. When Gitel gets to the hospital, the doctors say that Shmuel has suffered a massive stroke. They explain, "The extent, if any, to which he might recover cannot be predicted. His legs are paralyzed, his hands and arms have some problems with movement, and we are worried about whether there are effects on his brain."

Gitel tries to absorb what the doctors are telling her. She feels dizzy, as if the walls and equipment in the room won't hold still. She sits on a chair and tries to gather her thoughts. *Shmuel has been sick before, of course. There was the lung problem when we were in New York. And a couple of years before this stroke, he had a bout of pneumonia that put him in the hospital for several days. But this is different. This feels like the end of everything, of our entire way of living. It certainly doesn't seem like he will ever be able to go back to work. And he might need care whenever they send him home from the hospital. I do not know what to do, but I need to do it quickly.*

Gitel begins by calling Lou, his boss. She truthfully tells Lou that Shmuel might never be able to come back to work. "If we are lucky, he might be well enough several months from now—but there is no way of knowing. I understand, Lou, that you will have to hire someone else to take Shmuel's place."

Lou says, "Oh no! I am so sad that this happened. And I'm sure this is just terrible for you. I will send you the pay Shmuel is owed, and add another two weeks' pay. I hope you understand that is the best that I can do."

Gitel thanks him and hangs up.

The extra two weeks' pay is not going to go very far. They have to pay rent and other expenses. Shmuel has good Blue Cross health insurance through an organization to which he belongs, the Chicago

Retail Druggists Association, but there are a few hospital charges that have to be paid out of pocket.

Gitel suddenly realizes that she needs a job, and soon. She abruptly sits down again and thinks. *I have been wanting to work, but not in these circumstances. Any job I could get would probably pay even less than Shmuel was making. Women always get paid less than men, and I haven't worked for so long. I can't see how we will manage. And Ilana is just in fifth grade. She still comes home for lunch every day.*

She calls one of her brothers, who agrees to organize the others to help. They will each chip in and plan to pay the rent for the next few months, until Gitel can figure out a plan. And she calls their rabbi, who says he will try to find some help for them.

As Gitel sits in the hospital staring at the unmoving Shmuel, her mind just circles around all the problems and obstacles—How can she find a job? What can she do about Ilana? How can they live on what she is likely to earn?—just trying to find a path forward.

# 27

On a beautiful, sunny spring day during her fifth-grade year, Ilana is walking home at lunchtime with Ruthie, a girl in her class who lives on Everett north of Fifty-Fifth Street, very near her apartment. They are not close friends, but Ruthie's family also belongs to the Hyde Park Hebrew Center. Ruthie normally is very quiet and shy, an only child. Ilana's parents have told her that Ruthie's parents were Holocaust survivors, and were themselves very withdrawn.

As they walk north on Everett and reach Fifty-Fifth Street, where Ilana would turn right and Ruthie continue straight ahead, there is a commotion taking place in front of Ilana's apartment building. They can see an ambulance and someone being lifted into it on a stretcher. Then Ilana notices one of her mother's friends who lives on Everett, Sibyl, walking toward her.

"Your father is very sick and being taken to the hospital. Your mother asked me to give you lunch at my apartment. Come with me now."

Ilana has trouble breathing. *Can the person on the stretcher really be my father? What will happen now?*

Ilana knows Sibyl but does not particularly like her. The woman never had children, and is rather blunt and not at all comforting.

Ruthie, who is still standing next to her, begins to hug Ilana. She says, "You should come to my apartment with me for lunch. My mother won't mind."

Ilana decides to do that. "I'm sorry, Sibyl, but I don't want to go with you. I will go with my friend Ruthie."

Sibyl replies, "Your mother's instructions were for you to come with me. She doesn't need to be worrying about you right now."

"No, I am going with Ruthie."

By this time, Ilana has started to cry and can't stop. *Is my father alive or dead? And what will happen to me if he is dead or sick for a really long time?*

She and Ruthie arrive at Ruthie's apartment, and Ruthie explains to her mother what happened. Ruthie's mother, who Ilana had never heard say anything, hugs her tightly. "Come in, *Liebchen*," she says. "I will give you a nice lunch, and you can stay here as long as you want. I will call the school and tell them that I will keep both of you here for the afternoon." Ilana thinks, *That is so helpful. I cannot imagine just going back to school.*

Ruthie's mother helps Ilana call her mother's friend who had tried to intercept her, so she knows that all is okay. Ilana asks her if she can call Faye, which is a more expensive toll call, and she agrees. Faye says that she has not yet heard from Mama, so Ilana tells her what happened. Faye says Mama will probably call her soon, and she will tell Mama where Ilana is now. With the new baby, there is little else Faye can do.

# 28

There is not much Gitel can do at the hospital. She calls Faye to tell her what happened and learns from her where Ilana is. That is fine with her, but she does not want to impose too much on Ruthie's family, since she doesn't know them all that well. Gitel leaves the hospital around 3:00 p.m., after she talks again to the doctors caring for Shmuel, and goes to get Ilana.

She is going to have to figure out something for Ilana to do at lunchtime and after school, so she can put her time and energy into being with Shmuel and perhaps looking for a job. She realizes that Ilana does not like the idea of going to Gitel's friends' apartments. And in any case, it would be difficult for her to ask them to do that every day. And there is after school to think about. On three afternoons a week Ilana goes directly from school to Hebrew school, so she is occupied until about five thirty. Gitel thinks, *I could get back from the hospital by then. Ilana could plan to go to one of her friends' houses the other two days. But that still leaves the weekends. And potentially some evenings that I need to be with Shmuel.*

Shmuel has difficulty asking for anything he needs, although he is beginning to be able to talk a bit and to push the call button—if it hasn't slipped away—to get a nurse. Some people pay to have private nurses stay with their loved ones who are in the hospital, but there is no way they can afford that. *I am so torn*, Gitel thinks. *I need to be with Ilana, and I worry that these makeshift plans are unfair to her. She is only ten years old. But I also worry that Shmuel won't get enough care if there is no one to stay with him.*

Gitel talks with Faye about the possibility of Ilana staying with her for a while. Faye and Joe and the baby have moved to one of the tract houses they saw being built in their Park Forest neighborhood. The house has three bedrooms and two bathrooms, so they have some extra room. Faye tells Gitel that she had anticipated that question and that she had talked with Joe. He is fine with the idea.

Gitel makes an appointment with Ilana's teacher and the principal at her school to see if they will agree to Ilana being homeschooled by Faye for at least a month and perhaps the remainder of the semester. "Faye graduated from law school, and her husband is a doctor. She doesn't have any teaching experience, but I am sure she can help Ilana with any of her assignments, if Ilana needs help."

Ilana's teacher agrees to mail assignments to Ilana and have her mail them back. In truth, Ilana probably doesn't need any help from Faye for her schoolwork, but Gitel thinks "homeschooling" sounds like something they would be more likely to accept. Gitel also talks to the principal of the Hebrew school, who agrees not to hold Ilana's absence against her moving to the next level in the fall.

When Gitel tells Ilana that she can go stay with Faye, Ilana smiles broadly and jumps up and down. "Yeah! I very much want to spend time with Faye and get to know my nephew. And as I repeatedly tell you, Mama, I am bored and not very happy at school. This will be great for me!"

The next weekend, Gitel takes Ilana on the train, and Faye—who has learned to drive by this time and has her own car—picks them up at the station with Jay in the car. Gitel helps Ilana get settled, spends a little time with Faye and Jay, and returns to Hyde Park the same afternoon. *I feel so relieved to not have to worry about Ilana*, she thinks.

With Ilana taken care of, Gitel turns her attention to their household finances. It certainly looks like Shmuel will be out of commission for a long time, if not permanently. She has to get a job. Her few private bookkeeping clients are not going to support them. She does not charge much. They have very little savings, having spent everything they had on Faye's wedding. After all these years of wanting to work and not being able to, Gitel now has to do it. But she is not sure how to start looking for a job. She is afraid that no one will want to hire a fifty-year-old woman who has not worked as a bookkeeper in an organization or company for the past nearly twenty-five years.

Gitel has heard from her AJC friends that the Jewish Federation of Chicago has a program for women who want to reenter the labor force. She calls and makes an appointment with a counselor there. At their meeting, the counselor agrees with her assessment that it would be difficult for her to get hired by a private sector company without any recent experience or recommendations. She says, "There is an opening for a bookkeeper at a facility owned and operated by the Federation, Resthaven Rehabilitation Hospital. It is in the North Lawndale neighborhood, at 1409 South California Avenue." Gitel thinks, *That isn't very convenient to Hyde Park. But this might be my only opportunity to get a foothold into the job market.* She agrees to go there for an interview.

When she checks the location on a city map, she finds that Resthaven is only about two miles from the apartment she and Shmuel had rented when they returned from New York. So at least the neighborhood is not completely unfamiliar to her. Getting there would involve taking two different buses that make local stops, or a bus and the "L"—each of which would take over an hour from home to there. Once school starts again for Ilana in the fall, Gitel would probably have to leave for work well before Ilana leaves for school, and she would get home pretty late for cooking dinner for the family. By the time she gets there for the interview, she isn't sure it is a good idea to work so far from home.

The person interviewing her, who oversees the accounting department, is nevertheless very encouraging. She says that she is impressed with Gitel's background, including her leadership roles in the PTA and American Jewish Congress and her initiative in finding private bookkeeping clients when she had to stay home. She is sure that Gitel will fit into the bookkeeping department and readily learn their systems. She mentions that Gitel would have to work part of the day on Sundays, because the families of the patients usually come to visit then and often have questions about billing and insurance. She would have to be on hand to answer their questions. That also gives her pause. She thinks, *What would Ilana do on Sundays while I am working? She does go to Hebrew school in the mornings, but I certainly would be away from home longer than she is in class.* Gitel must look uncertain, because the interviewer quickly says that they can offer her a competitive salary and benefits. She says they can offer her a salary of sixty dollars per week plus fully paid health insurance. Given what the Federation counselor had told her, she knows she can't expect to earn much more than that. But Shmuel had been earning a hundred dollars a week. She hesitates, and then accepts the job. She doesn't know how they are going to make ends meet, but she decides that some money coming in is better than nothing. The interviewer asks if she can start right away, and Gitel says she can be there the following Monday.

On the long bus ride home, she tries to think about how she can manage her life and the family going forward. Shmuel is likely to be in the hospital for some weeks longer, and she will no longer be able to sit with him or even see him very often. She goes through a mental list of various relatives who she might ask to help, but doesn't come up with anyone likely. They either have their own jobs or responsibilities during the day, or live too far away, or are not healthy enough to make the trip to Michael Reese Hospital. Gitel decides that she will try calling Shmuel's sister Zelda, who is living with her husband in Minnesota and does not have any children. Gitel doubts that she'll be willing to do anything, but she feels obligated to tell her what is going on anyway. As she predicted, Zelda says that she can't come to Chicago. She also implies that Shmuel had a stroke because she, Gitel, didn't take proper care of him—one of her favorite themes.

There is no help for it. Shmuel will just have to manage without Gitel at his side. The family needs money to pay for rent and other expenses.

# 29

Ilana and Faye talk about what has happened to their father. Faye tells Ilana, "I am sorry that our father is so sick, but the situation plays in my head like a broken record. My life with our parents has been repeatedly interrupted and affected by Dad's poor health—to say nothing of his bad luck in losing their drugstore and later having the fall at work that broke his back. Before you were born, Mama and I had to go live with Bobe in South Bend, then we had to move to New York, then we moved back to Chicago in Lawndale, then we moved to Hyde Park, and then we had to take care of Dad after he fell. I never felt secure for even a single day during all the time I was growing up. I feel bad for our mother, who tries so hard to make things right for us despite it all."

"I know that I have had it easier than you up until now," Ilana replies. "But going forward, who knows how we will manage. I am so happy that I can be here with you now."

"I really like having you here with me," Faye says. "It gets lonely taking care of a baby. Joe works so much and is always on call for a delivery. He is not home that much. You are good company."

Ilana tries to be as helpful as possible. She happily does laundry and other chores to give Faye some breaks. She spends long periods of time with Jay, playing with him and amusing him. When she is not helping with the chores or Jay, she does the schoolwork that her teacher at Bret Harte mails to her on her own. That absorbs only a few hours a week.

Ilana learns about Gitel's interview and new job from Faye, who has talked to her on the phone. Gitel would never tell her troubles to Ilana, but Faye treats Ilana as almost an adult and believes that Ilana has a right to know what is going on. The truth is always better than some story Ilana makes up in her mind, even if the truth is troubling.

"Our mother is worried that what she can earn will not be enough to support the three of you. She said that their rent alone is a hundred dollars a month, which is more than forty percent of what she would be taking home after taxes. But she says she realizes that she has to start somewhere to get back into the job market, so this is what she is going to do." Faye tells Ilana that she will do what she can to help financially. She would never want Ilana to miss out on something important because there is no money. She herself had experienced enough of that during the Depression and during their father's various health problems. "Joe deposits a generous sum into my checking account each month for household expenses and anything I might want for myself. I told Mom that I would try to give her what I could from that money. If necessary, I told her that I also could ask Joe if we could help more. But I would rather not do that if I do not have to."

"That is so good of you, Faye," Ilana says. "But I hope this doesn't become a big problem for you. I will try to not need anything that costs money for a while."

Ilana wants to learn as much as she can about baby care. She thinks, *With that skill I might be able to earn some money babysitting when I get back to Hyde Park. We are always short on money. But based on what Faye told me, we are likely to be shorter than usual because Mom won't earn as much as Dad did. It seems that Dad will not be going back to work, at least not anytime soon. Anyway, I love Jay. He is a fun baby to be with, because he seems to be very smart. He is only five months old, but already he is playing with toys and can put together some simple puzzles.*

"Are you interested in learning to cook?" Faye asks Ilana. She points out that Gitel will be coming home late from work after her long commute and will likely be tired. "It would be nice if sometimes you have dinner already made when she gets home." Ilana pays close attention while Faye is cooking dinner each night, and helps her to the extent she can. Faye mostly makes simple foods like hamburgers, steak, chicken, or fish. Ilana also learns how to make salads and various styles of potatoes. That is the kind of food their mom normally makes too. Ilana initially is nervous about putting on the oven and using the broiler, but it turns out to not be too hard. She just has to concentrate on what she is doing so she doesn't burn herself.

Ilana does not miss her school classes. It is a relief to not have to sit there and be bored. She does miss her classmates and friends, though. It is too expensive to call them, so she tries writing a few letters to them. This is not so satisfying, because her friends cannot understand what she is doing now at Faye's. It is a different world than a normal ten-year-old girl inhabits.

Luckily, there is a girl her age who lives a few houses down the block. Faye has met that family, and takes Ilana to introduce her to them. The girl, Donna, is very friendly. She, of course, is in school during the day, but they get together sometimes in the late afternoon. She has one older brother but no sisters, so she is happy to have Ilana living close by. It is possible to walk to the Park Forest shopping mall from their houses—a long walk but possible. They sometimes do that. Usually, they just hang out. When it becomes summer, Donna's parents bring Ilana along when they take Donna swimming in the community pool. It is a pretty good life. Ilana thinks, *I wonder if I could just stay in Park Forest and go to school here. I don't think Mama would like that, but I may have to ask her.*

# 30

Shmuel is improving a bit through the summer. Gitel gets a report from his doctors and therapists. They tell her, "He is able to get out of bed and walk a short distance. His right arm is usable in a limited way, although his left side is still stiff. He can talk, although it is a little hard to understand him. And he often is confused about what is going on. He remembers things from his childhood and long ago, and recognizes family members, but has trouble thinking through anything currently happening. He is receiving physical therapy at the hospital, but no one can say if his mental faculties will come back or not over time. There is not much we can do about that."

Gitel visits him at the hospital a few times a week on her way home from work. It makes for a very long day, but with Ilana at Faye's she does not have to rush home. She is grateful that they are still taking care of him at the hospital and that their insurance is paying for his extended care. She tries to spend most of each Saturday with him.

It is difficult for Gitel to get used to waking up, dressing, and eating breakfast early enough in the morning to get to work on time, and to work steadily all day. It certainly has been a long time since she has done that. But she likes the job. *It feels good to be using my bookkeeping skills,* she thinks, *and the people I work with are friendly and have helped me get used to the facility's systems. Working will be fine. It is the rest of my life that worries me—how to manage when*

*Shmuel comes home from the hospital and Ilana comes back from Faye's. I still have no idea of how I will be able to manage all that.*

At the beginning of August, the hospital calls Gitel to say that Shmuel is ready to go home. "There is not much else that we can do for him at the hospital," the doctor on the phone says.

"We live in a third-floor walk-up apartment," Gitel tells him. "I don't know how I can get him home."

"We will arrange medical transportation to take him home. You just need to be there to greet him."

"Thank you, Doctor."

Gitel tells her supervisor at work that she needs to take off the day that he is coming home, to get him settled.

The men from the medical transport carry Shmuel up the stairs on a stretcher with an inclined back, so he is sort of sitting up. They help him get from the stretcher to the easy chair he likes to sit in, and then they leave.

"I am so glad to be home," Shmuel says to Gitel.

"I'm glad too. Do you think you are able to get up from the chair on your own?"

"I think so."

Shmuel puts his hands on the arms of the chair and slowly pushes himself up, looking awkward and visibly shaking. He then walks, albeit unsteadily and occasionally touching a wall for balance, to the kitchen and to the bathroom to show Gitel that he will be okay on his own. He says, "I know that you have to go to work. I also know that we cannot afford anyone to come to the house to be with me. I am grateful that you are doing so much to support the family financially. I am sure it is not easy for you to be working so far away. I will try to be as independent as possible, so you do not have to worry about me too."

Despite Shmuel's protestations, Gitel is worried. He looks to her to be unsteady enough that he could fall. And if he falls, she is sure that he will not be able to get up on his own. As much as she does not want to, she decides that she has to ask Ilana to come home and be around to take care of him until school starts. And, after the summer, to come home at lunchtime and after school to check on him, and help him if he needs it. It is a lot to ask of a ten-year-old, but what choice does Gitel have? There is no one else.

Gitel calls Faye and tells her what she is thinking. Faye sighs. "Mama, I had hoped that Ilana's life would not revolve around our father's illnesses, as mine had to a great degree. It is so unfair. But I agree that there is no choice." Faye says she will ask Joe if he can drive Ilana home that evening or the next. "I will come along and bring Jay, so I can see you and Dad and both of you can see Jay."

# 31

Ilana doesn't want to leave Faye's house and go back home. She once again wonders why she can't just continue to live with Faye, Joe, and Jay and go to school in Park Forest. She went to school one day with Donna, and thinks the school is much nicer than Bret Harte.

Faye speaks gently to her. "I sympathize with you. It certainly is no fun having to take care of our father. I know that from my own experiences. But we are a family, and each of us has to do what we can to care for each other. And Mama is trying so hard to keep things together. You know I will miss having you here, and so will Jay. But there is no one else to take care of Dad, so you have to do it."

Gitel and Shmuel are happy to see Ilana when they arrive at the apartment. Faye and Joe, with Jay, stay less than an hour and then say they have to get back. Joe might get called to deliver a baby soon. After they leave, Mom asks Ilana to come into the kitchen with her. Shmuel is sitting in his chair in the living room with the television on high volume.

"Ilana, are you willing to stay in the apartment most of the time until school restarts? You may go out for a while, but not for too long. I'm worried that Dad might try to do too much and fall, or that he might need something he can't get for himself. You could invite your friends over to keep you company."

"Almost all my friends are away at summer camp." Ilana makes tight fists to try not to show her resentment. She thinks, *I had hoped to go to camp this summer too. I especially wanted to go to Camp Ramah in Wisconsin. There had been a presentation for Ramah at Hebrew school, and it looked great to me. I talked to Mom about it last winter. She said it was far too expensive for us to afford, but that she would look into it. She was able to get a promise of a half scholarship for me, and was trying to figure out if we could manage the rest. But after Dad's stroke, of course, all bets are off. There is no money.*

Aloud, Ilana says, "Yes, I will be at home most of the time and look after Dad." *What else could I say?* "I want to go to the Blackstone Library on Saturday. If I am just staying home, I need some books to read during the month until school starts." Gitel says that she will try to go with her to help her carry the books back.

Since Gitel leaves home around seven thirty in the morning to get to work on time, Ilana helps Shmuel get out of bed each weekday after Gitel leaves. She is able to fold up the Murphy bed so the living room is clear. She helps him put on his bathrobe, makes sure he doesn't fall as he walks to use the bathroom, and prepares some breakfast for him. He usually wants just coffee and a sweet roll, so that is easy for her. Then she helps him sit down in his chair and puts on the TV for him. He does not have the concentration to read a book, so there is not much else for him to do but watch TV. He mostly dozes in front of it anyway, unless there is a baseball game to watch. He is not interested in any other daytime programs. She usually makes a sandwich and drink for him at lunchtime, and they sit together to eat.

He says he is supposed to exercise to try to get stronger, so she helps him walk around the apartment and do some other exercises in the afternoon. In the later afternoon, she thinks about what they could have for dinner. They usually have some kind of chicken or meat, potatoes or bread, and a canned vegetable. Ilana sometimes helps by putting potatoes in the oven to bake or going to the corner deli to get rye bread if they are running out. Sometimes Gitel leaves money for her to get some deli meat for dinner. A little deli meat with scrambled eggs is a quick-to-make meal that they all like. She wants to make it as easy as possible for Gitel to make and serve dinner, because she always is tired when she comes home from work. Ilana usually does the dishes after dinner.

Shmuel is able to remember some things and not others. His religious studies from his youth are still in his head. Ilana will sit with him and ask him questions about the Torah. He usually is happy to give her extended answers to anything she asks. And often his answers reveal what he is worried about. When they are talking about the Israelites going through the desert after the exodus from Egypt, with an angel helping them destroy the various idol-worshipping tribes on their way to settling in the Promised Land, he quotes a passage from the book of Exodus (23:25). "God says, 'You shall serve/worship the Lord your God, and you shall bless your bread and your water. And I will remove sickness from your midst.'" Shmuel says that he remembers a commentary he learned about that verse from the famous twelfth-century Spanish rabbi Ibn Ezra, who said, "When a person sticks to the Holy One, blessed be he; sometimes their *mazel* changes for good." He wonders aloud if the reverse might be true. "If someone abandons worshipping or serving God properly, does his *mazel* turn bad? Certainly, there must be some explanation for my bad luck."

Ilana is silent. She does not know what to say.

Shmuel also tells her a lot about how he had studied Gemora, and explains what the Talmud is all about. Ilana finds all that interesting. And it makes the time pass for both of them. She is sure it is also good for his brain to try to remember things. She talks to him a lot and asks him questions about family members and things that had happened in his life; she wants him to keep thinking and remembering.

Sometimes Shmuel's friend from his shul, Mr. Goldblum, comes to visit. He is an older, retired man who had done well in business. When he comes, he always brings a gallon of milk and a box of food. He says it is from the shul, but Ilana thinks maybe it is from him personally. In any case, the rabbi and perhaps a few others at the shul must know that the family is struggling, and the milk and food are very welcome.

This September Ilana is more than ready to resume school and Hebrew school, even though school is always boring and Hebrew school sometimes is. Shmuel is steadily improving, and Gitel says that she feels better about leaving him alone during the day. But Gitel tells her, "I still want you to come home at lunchtime to check on him. And I also need you to come home after school on days that you don't have to go to Hebrew school."

"Coming home after school is just too much," Ilana replies. "I need time to go to my girlfriends' houses. If I can't be with my friends, I soon won't have any friends."

"Maybe your friends could come to our apartment?"

She tells Gitel, "I'm sort of embarrassed to invite people here. It might start gossip at school about Dad's condition, or about our shabby and untidy living conditions or our lack of food. We normally don't have cookies or pop to offer them, and we may or may not have milk on a particular day. I may have one or two friends who will understand and not start rumors. I'll think about what I want to do."

"You certainly are welcome to invite whoever you want to come over after school," Gitel replies. "But I do understand what you are saying, and I'm sorry about all that. You may do what you want so long as you are available to help your father."

# 32

When Ilana is alone with Shmuel, he often tells her what he is thinking. His brain does not have much of a filter about what is appropriate to say to his daughter.

"I feel terrible! What an awful turn of events. Your mother is working long hours and not even making enough money to support us. You have to take care of me instead of being with your friends. I need to recover and get back to work. I wish we did not live on the third floor. When I was recovering from my broken back and we lived in the building with an elevator, walking outside helped me recover."

Ilana helps Shmuel walk around the small apartment, around the dining room table and through the short hall toward the bathroom, into the living room, and back to the dining room. The therapists at the hospital also suggested that he try lifting some things around the house to regain strength in his left arm, so Ilana puts water in a pot and gives it to Shmuel to lift.

They sit down again, and Shmuel begins musing out loud. It is not clear to Ilana whether he realizes at the moment that she is listening.

Shmuel says in a soft voice, "I am again thinking about why this has happened to me, as I have after other setbacks. Is it something I am doing or not doing? Is it just random bad luck? What does bad luck mean? And why does it stick to me? Should I make a vow to change something in my life? Like going back to being observant? Would I be able to keep such a vow? Making a vow and not fulfilling it is the worst thing one can do. Our sages in the Talmud were suspicious of vows, and the majority opinion seemed to say that people should avoid making vows. Even those who fulfill their vows are regarded as doing something wrong. The Talmud even states in tractate Shabbas that the punishment for breaking a vow is the early death of one's children. While I know I should go back to being observant, I am not even sure I want to do that now. And there is probably no way to do that, given Gitel's views on keeping kosher and the mikveh. Vowing would just make the situation worse. Is there any other way to change my *mazel*?"

Ilana is silent, not knowing what to make of her father's words. She watches as he gets up and walks over to the dresser in the dining room where he keeps his clothes and opens the top drawer. He takes out his tefillin bag, opens it, and looks at the phylacteries. He resumes talking in a soft voice. "Could I go back to putting on the tefillin and praying every day? It feels impossible. I do not feel like blessing or praising God. I am angry at him. Why have I been sent all these problems and all this bad luck? Did I deserve it? I do not think so. I just wanted to have a family and support it, to do my work and enjoy my children. And I tried to be as good a Jew as I could be, given my work schedule and my wife's objections."

Ilana sees her father clench his fists and bring up his hands as he continues, "I definitely am angry. God—and life—have been unfair to me."

She is worried about what he might do, so she says, "I think you should put away the tefillin, close the drawer, and sit down. You are doing the best you can. We all are."

# 33

Gitel feels that she has to talk to somebody about everything that is happening, so she asks Ilana to stay home on a Saturday afternoon and goes to see Sophie. Gitel feels a little guilty because Ilana isn't able to see her own friends very much, but also feels that she might just stop functioning if she can't talk out what she is feeling. When Sophie asks how they are doing, she pours out her thoughts and feelings.

"We are managing. That is about all I can say," Gitel begins. "Shmuel is improving. He can walk around and even make himself a little something to eat in the kitchen. He still gets confused some of the time, but less and less frequently. I wish we could move to an apartment in a building with an elevator so he could get outside, but I don't see how that can happen. We can't really afford the apartment we are in, and certainly don't have money for moving expenses. Rent, utilities, and food take up everything I earn and then some.

"Ilana has been great," Gitel continues. "I know she doesn't want her life to revolve around taking care of her father, but she is doing it anyway. We are almost to the point where Shmuel can manage without her. That would be good.

"I do not have any time for myself. I'm home so little. I get home from work in time to eat dinner, clean up the house a little, and fall asleep so I can get up early the next morning. My only day off is

Saturday, because I need to go into work on Sunday morning. On Saturday I need to shop for groceries and take care of any other errands, pay bills, and do laundry. There is no time to do any of that during the week, so those chores occupy almost all my day off. Sometimes Ilana comes with me to my job on Sunday, because at least we have the travel time together. Otherwise, I rarely have time for her. When she does come with me, I try to teach her a bit of book-keeping. It might come in handy for her someday."

"I hear you," Sophie says while shaking her head. "That sounds so hard for you. It seems like you don't have any time to breathe properly."

"I do need to think about how to get my life a little more under control. I'm not sure I can keep up this pace forever. I think I need to find a different job, especially one that requires a shorter commuting time. And preferably one where I can work five days a week instead of six."

"That sounds like a good plan. Let's talk again soon, even if it is just on the telephone."

Sophie gives Gitel a long, hard hug, and Gitel leaves to go back home. She thinks, *Yes, getting a different job is what I have to do. Talking to Sophie made that clear to me.*

# 34

About a month later, when two years have passed since Shmuel's stroke, there is some good news. Shmuel has been walking down the stairs to go outside once a day and walk a bit around the neighborhood. The stiffness in his hands has gone away. And he says that his mind seems clear. He has been reading books again without any problem. He tells Gitel, "I feel like I could go back to work, but maybe not with such a difficult schedule and commute as I had working with Lou."

When Gitel gets home from work one evening, Shmuel seems excited and says he has some news for her. "As you know, the owner/manager of the drugstore directly across the street from us, Max, is a member of our shul. While out walking earlier today, I decided to stop in to say hello to him. He was very happy to see me out and about, and suggested we sit down and have some coffee together. Max asked me if I was ready to work as a pharmacist again. He said they could use someone who could work a part-time schedule. I would mostly have to fill prescriptions and answer customer questions about medications. Someone else would be available to sell over-the-counter items, liquor, and cigarettes. That sounded great to me, so I immediately said yes—without asking about the pay or hours. But Max was amused and mentioned a pay that seems fair. And I would mostly be working during the day and one evening a week."

"Wow! That is wonderful. Good for you! How many hours a week will you be working?"

"I think about twenty hours. We'll have to see how much they need and how much I can do."

"Of course. Did Max suggest an hourly rate of pay?"

"Yes. He suggested $3 an hour. If I worked full-time, that would be $120 per week—which is more than Lou was paying me. If I can work twenty hours, that will be $60 per week. Added to your pay, that will make us a little better off than we were before my stroke."

"I'm so relieved," Gitel says. "I have not yet told you, but I think I need to change jobs. Resthaven is just too far away. The commute added to the six-day workweek has left me exhausted. Your job will give me a bit more confidence to make a change."

"Maybe we finally are coming to the end of our problems, *kaynehora* [no evil eye]."

"I hope so."

Gitel is so relieved about Shmuel's new job. Ilana is already twelve years old, and her bat mitzvah will be next year. All her friends are having parties for theirs. Gitel would have hated to tell Ilana that they couldn't afford to have a party. Shmuel's earnings will provide a little breathing room to afford a few extras.

Gitel begins looking for a different job, and a possibility comes up quickly. She tells Shmuel about it.

"I have been offered a position at an advertising firm located on Wacker Drive just north of the Loop. I could get there a few different ways, including taking just one bus. It is a combination office manager and bookkeeping job, which pays $4,500 a year, $86 a week—significantly more than the $60 a week I have been making. And it would be a nine-to-five job, five days a week. It is a small company, and I know that advertising can be a fickle business because corporations change their advertising companies frequently. It might be less stable than working at Resthaven. But I would really like the additional pay, so I am planning on accepting the job."

Gitel changes jobs, and Shmuel is working. It no longer makes sense for Ilana to come home to an empty house at lunchtime, so she begins to buy her lunch at the Tannenbaum Pharmacy on Fifty-Fifth and Cornell. She tells Gitel, "I don't mind eating at Tannenbaum's. It is a much shorter walk from Bret Harte, which gives me more time to do what I want at lunchtime. I can socialize with a few other kids who also buy lunch there, read a book, or walk around outside. With the dollar a day for lunch that you give me, I buy a grilled cheese sandwich and a Coke or other drink, and it leaves me a little extra for a candy bar or whatever else I want."

Gitel says, "That's great." *One more problem solved*, she thinks.

Life is settling down. Gitel gets home in time most evenings to make dinner for the family, although sometimes they eat at Steinway's, which has a few booths as well as a counter and offers a few choices of dinner dishes each day. With Shmuel an employee, their food is discounted—and it is pretty good. Gitel is home on the weekends, although Shmuel sometimes has to work some weekend hours.

They begin to plan for Ilana's bat mitzvah, which will be at the beginning of March. At Rodfei Zedek, girls are allowed to chant the Haftorah—the selection from the Prophets—but are not allowed to read from the Torah itself or to say the blessings over the Torah, as the boys do. The girls' fathers usually recite the blessings in the girls' place, and Shmuel says that he will be able to do that. The rabbi emeritus at the shul is teaching Ilana the Haftorah, so all Gitel has to worry about is buying Ilana an appropriate dress and figuring out about the party. Many congregants of that shul pay for there to be a luncheon after the service for their guests. That is on top of paying for a light *kiddush* of wine and sweets for everyone who is at services, which is required of all bar/bat mitzvah families. The cost of a luncheon at the shul, however, is beyond what Gitel thinks they can afford. The combination of the cost of kosher food, the required staffing, and various add-ons make it impossible. Gitel decides that they will have a lunch after services for a small number of relatives at the Windermere Hotel, which has a much more reasonable per-person cost. Ilana wants to have an ice-skating party at a rink for her friends on Sunday afternoon, which is doable.

Ilana's bat mitzvah goes smoothly. Afterward, Ilana tells Gitel and Shmuel, "I am happy and grateful that the lunch and the party for my friends were possible. I know that if I had been bat mitzvah a year or so earlier, we wouldn't have been able to afford either one."

Shmuel tells Gitel that his job at Steinway's is working out well. "The owner had a cot put in a storeroom in the back, so I can rest if there is a lull in the need to fill prescriptions. I still do not have a lot of stamina."

Gitel replies, "I hope this better situation, with us both working, will last." She thinks, *By now, I certainly know never to count on anything.*

# 35

Ilana will soon be graduating from Bret Harte. Gitel goes shopping with her, and she chooses a tailored coral shirtwaist dress to wear under her robes. When they get home, she tries it on again and looks at herself in the full-length mirror that is on the door of the hall closet.

Ilana asks Gitel, "Do you think I am pretty? I've heard some people say that I am."

"You are indeed pretty. You are tall and thin. Your long curly hair is often messy, but it is shiny and healthy looking. And the features on your smallish face look just right. Your nose is small, your intelligence shines through in your eyes, and your lips are usually smiling."

"I definitely am tall. I'm already five feet, eight inches tall. I'm taller than your five feet for sure, and I'm also a couple of inches taller than Dad. At the graduation ceremony, we process down the aisle in pairs, one girl and one boy. I'm sure I'll be paired with the tallest boy in the class."

"You are blessed with being tall and beautiful," Gitel says. "You shouldn't think otherwise."

Ilana tells Gitel, "I am so glad to be almost done with elementary school. I have so much trouble sitting in classes, because I'm always bored."

Gitel is glad too. She had many consultations with Ilana's teachers over the years, because they often called her when Ilana's boredom led to unacceptable behavior in class. The teachers told Gitel that they could not cater to Ilana's intellectual needs, so they tried to arrange reasons for her to be out of class as much as possible. Ilana helped with the kindergarten class, giving the teacher a break. She also helped in the library, and sometimes in the office. But in the spring of Ilana's eighth grade, Gitel receives a very angry and distraught call from the school principal.

On most corners that the children have to cross to get to school, the school assigns seventh- and eighth-grade boys to act as crossing guards. They call them "Patrol Boys." They wear white sashes and are assigned to specific corners before school, at lunchtime, and after school. Because of their duties, they get to school late and leave early. The principal tells Gitel on the phone, "Ilana has admitted that she asked one of the boys if she could take his place as a crossing guard today. He agreed, and gave her his sash to wear. She got to his corner early before school, did the job, and arrived at school. I had seen that the boy already was at school, and asked him what had happened. He said that Ilana had taken his place. I was waiting for Ilana when she arrived wearing his sash."

On the phone with Gitel, he continues, "Our insurance only covers boys, not girls, acting as Patrol Boys. Ilana has no right to act as a crossing guard without permission—which certainly would not have been given. As a punishment, she will no longer be allowed to continue any of her out-of-class activities."

Gitel tries to intervene. She takes a couple of hours off the next morning and goes to school to confront the principal.

She says to him, "There is no difference in the ability of boys and girls to help younger students cross streets. It is just sex discrimination.

And taking away Ilana's out-of-class activities is just stupid, because it will invite her to be more disruptive in class. I know you are aware that she is extremely bored in class, which is the fault of the school because you have not found a way to engage her in the curriculum."

Gitel's efforts and arguments are futile. The principal remains hidden behind his insurance claim.

This is not the first time Gitel has had an unpleasant confrontation with the principal. When she was president of the Bret Harte PTA, before she had to take a paying job, they had lots of disagreements about how he was running the school. He seemed to have students he liked and favored, and those he didn't. Most of those he didn't favor were either Jewish or Negro.

Their biggest disagreement occurred when Ilana was in fourth grade. The entire school population had been given IQ tests. During a subsequent assembly, the principal said that most of the students did well on the tests. Then he told everyone that Ilana had the highest IQ score in the school, and that he had never before seen a score that high. Ilana came home furious, and began to yell and cry when Gitel got home from work.

Gitel told Ilana, "I understand that it was unfair to single you out that way. No student would want to be thought of as the 'brain.' I think he might have done it as payback to me, for opposing him on several fronts when I was PTA president. I will try to report him to his superiors in the citywide education office." But sometime later, Gitel told Ilana that his superiors refused to take any action.

In the current situation, Gitel tells Ilana that she is proud of her. "Protesting sex discrimination is not wrong; it is very brave. And the punishment he gave you is probably another instance of the principal's anti-Semitism that I have been fighting for years, since both you and the young man who let you take his place are Jewish."

Luckily, the semester is almost over and Ilana will soon graduate. Gitel appreciates that Ilana feels that graduation can't come soon enough.

# 36

Ilana finally is a freshman at Hyde Park High School, which she says she likes very much. That is a welcome change from her constant complaints about elementary school. And there is a cafeteria at the school where the students are supposed to eat lunch, ending the problem of where to go at lunchtime. Gitel and Shmuel are even able to send her to a YMCA camp, Camp Martin Johnson in Northern Michigan, for four weeks during the summer. It wasn't Ramah, which still is much too expensive for them to afford, but Ilana says that she had a good time. Gitel's job at the advertising agency is going well. Faye has had a second child, another boy, and is pregnant with a third. And Shmuel continues to work at Steinway's. Gitel is holding her breath. Could this continue?

While Gitel is ruminating on their circumstances during a break at work, she receives a call from Max saying that Shmuel has collapsed at the drugstore. They called an ambulance, which is on its way to Michael Reese Hospital. They think he probably had another stroke. Gitel leaves work and takes a taxi to the emergency room of the hospital. Sitting in the cab, she keeps thinking that she shouldn't have been counting their blessings, even just in her mind, without at least saying *kaynehora*. Did she tempt their bad luck to return? It is hard for her not to be superstitious about the workings of the "evil eye" in this situation. She was taught by Rayzel that as soon as someone has some good luck, the evil eye lurks and something has to be done to ward it off. Once it strikes, it is too late. For a couple of years, things were better. She was able to work, which she enjoys. They had her income and a significant supplement from Shmuel's part-time job. They could afford a few extras for Ilana. Now it is all going to come crashing down again.

By the time she gets to the hospital, Shmuel is surrounded by medical personnel, has an IV inserted and a mask on his face. She is told that he is intubated because he was having trouble breathing, so he can't talk. The doctors express a lot of concern about his future ability to talk and think, because he had been unconscious for several minutes before the ambulance arrived. The doctors also worry that he may have a bleed in his brain. They tell her that a repeat stroke often is more serious than the initial one.

Gitel feels like a deflated balloon. Everything they were working toward has just floated away into the air. She interprets what the doctors are telling her to mean that Shmuel probably will be an invalid, perhaps for some time or perhaps permanently, and will need care. She has no idea how they will manage that while she works and Ilana goes to school.

There does not seem to be anything she can usefully do at the hospital. Shmuel is not aware of his surroundings, so it doesn't matter if she is there or not. She decides to go home to call Faye and talk to Ilana. She knows Ilana, in particular, will be very upset. Faye is focused on her children, and Shmuel's incapacitation will not make any significant difference in her life.

Ilana is indeed upset when she comes home from school and Gitel tells her what has happened. Ilana doesn't say much, but Gitel guesses that Ilana is worried that she will lose some of her freedom, that she will once again be pressed into service to take care of her father. Gitel doesn't blame her. It is a bad situation, and unfair to her.

Gitel tells her, "We just will have to wait and see what happens. But at a minimum, you shouldn't expect that your father will be able to go back to work. That seems very unlikely, especially if there is a significant amount of brain damage. A pharmacist has to think clearly." Ilana does not respond. She just looks stricken—pale and a little shaky—and is silent.

Gitel continues going to work every day, but she leaves a little early to stop off at the hospital to see Shmuel. The owner of the advertising agency does not mind, so long as she gets her work done. Whenever there has been a push at the agency to get a presentation done in time or anything like that, she has always been willing to stay and help manage the various people working on it. So, her boss is willing to show her flexibility now. Ilana tries to have some dinner ready when Gitel gets home, tired and stressed.

This time Shmuel stays in the hospital for two months. There is not all that much that the physical therapy the hospital provides can do for him; he is not responding to it. His legs are very weak, and he cannot walk without help. His left arm is still stiff and partially paralyzed, so he cannot hold on to a walker very well to steady himself. And he becomes confused very easily. Sometimes he knows where he is and remembers things, and sometimes he does not. The hospital has to send him home because he is not getting any better, so once again they have the problem of Shmuel being alone for most of the day—and this time he is in even worse shape.

Gitel takes a morning off to go to the Social Security office to apply for disability benefits for him. She puts together all the documents from his hospital stay and letters she has requested from his doctors. Four years before, in 1956, Congress passed amendments establishing a disability benefit under Social Security for people aged fifty through sixty-four. Disability was defined as:

The inability to engage in any substantial gainful activity by reason of any medically determinable physical or mental impairment which can be expected to result in death or to be of long-continued and indefinite duration.

The clerk at Social Security accepts the application, and agrees to send a doctor to their apartment to examine him. Gitel says they will need notice of when the doctor is coming, because Shmuel can't necessarily get up to open the door. She can't imagine that any doctor they send could possibly find Shmuel able to work at any job. She hopes it will be an honest assessment. They really need that money; it would be equal to what would have been his retirement benefit. And she feels that Shmuel should be entitled to it; he has paid Social Security tax since the program began.

Once again Gitel has to ask Ilana to come home after school to check on Shmuel. Before work each day, she prepares a sandwich for him to eat at lunchtime and leaves it in the refrigerator. He is supposed to use a walker when he gets up from his chair to go to the kitchen or the bathroom, but Gitel knows that he often does not use it. He thinks he is steadier than he really is, and hates the idea of needing the walker. At least if Ilana comes home after school, she can fix any problems he might have had earlier in the day with food or other matters.

Ilana tells Gitel that she is not happy about losing her freedom to be with her friends after school. She is beginning to express her feelings rather vehemently. She has a lot of anger that she had been holding back until now. She says things like, "Other kids have fathers who take them places and do fun things with them. Why do I have a father who I have to take care of as if he were a child?" Or, "Other kids are free to hang out after school. Why do I have to be a nursemaid?" Gitel sympathizes with her, but has no way to make the situation any better. She tells Ilana, as she did the last time they were in this situation, that she is free to invite her friends over to their apartment after school. Ilana again seems reluctant to do that, given the way they live.

# 37

Ilana likes high school a lot more than she liked elementary school. She thinks that some of her teachers are pretty good, some less so. But the variety is helpful. The classes at Hyde Park High School are "tracked"; students are grouped by what the school thinks is their ability to learn. Ilana is in the double accelerated class, the highest track called "double X," which she thinks has many advantages and a few disadvantages. The advantages are obvious. Being grouped with other fast learners takes most of the boredom out of school. The disadvantage is that a high intelligence does not mean that she is equally good in all subjects. And double X students can only register for double X academic subjects. Homeroom, gym, music, and art classes are mixtures of all tracks.

For math, the double X students take three semesters in two. They have algebra 1 and 2 and advanced algebra in the first year. The teacher, who is old and can barely see through her bottle-glass spectacles, writes proofs on the board to a certain point, and then says, "The rest is obvious." But it often is not obvious to Ilana. There is a lot of algebra she never understands that year, which will come back to haunt her in college when she has to take calculus. She gets stymied when she has to simplify equations.

Ilana's social life is diverse. She has her friends from Bret Harte, and she gets to know lots of kids from the other elementary schools in the district. Hyde Park High draws from the Hyde Park and Kenwood neighborhoods to the north of the school, and also neighborhoods to the south, from Woodlawn to South Shore. The school is known as the only successfully integrated school in the city; the student body is about 80 percent Negro. Most of the students and faculty think they are in the vanguard of the nascent civil rights movement.

Ilana has met this Negro guy, Larry, whom she really likes. He is smart, funny, and good-looking. He is about as tall as she is and has a dark, somewhat shiny, complexion. His family situation is as complicated as hers, although in a different way. He is not one of the many Negro kids at school who are from well-off families, whose parents are doctors, lawyers, or teachers. Most of the time Larry lives with his mother, who works during the week as a domestic and spends a lot of time on weekends involved with her church. Sometimes he is with his father, who is, as they say, "on the streets." Ilana never learns exactly what his father is up to, but it certainly is not a nine-to-five job and it probably is not legal.

Larry and Ilana begin to hang out together whenever they can. Given her responsibilities to help Shmuel, there is not much time to be together. She often chooses to walk home, a distance of about a mile, so they can have about twenty minutes or so together during the walk. Ilana tells Gitel that she is saving money by not taking the city bus. But what she is really doing is postponing getting home. Sometimes Larry comes with her to her apartment. Unlike some of her white friends, Larry is not put off by the peeling wallpaper, less-than-clean carpets, and shabby furniture. When Ilana tries to apologize for the way they live, Larry says, "It is a whole lot better than the way a lot of people have to live. You shouldn't be ashamed at all."

He waits in her bedroom while she takes care of whatever her father needs, then they have some time together. Sometimes Shmuel notices him, and might even say something racist. Ilana explains to Larry, "That is my father's brain damage talking. He never was a racist before he had the stroke. He was a left-wing Socialist who believed in equality for all. Please forgive him." But mostly, Shmuel is too out of it to notice or care what is happening around him.

When it becomes spring with light lasting later in the day, Ilana finds more freedom. Most days Ilana makes some dinner, eats a little herself, and leaves the rest for Gitel and Shmuel. Then she goes out just before Gitel comes home. She meets Larry and several of their friends at the Point. There isn't much Gitel can do about that. Ilana suspects that Gitel might be happy not to have to deal with her after her long day at work. Ilana comes home when it gets dark and goes straight to her room to do her homework. Needing to study is a good excuse to avoid being with Gitel and Shmuel, who usually are sitting in the living room with the television on.

Ilana is looking forward to the summer, when she and Larry and other friends will have much more time to hang out. But just as school is about to let out for summer break, one more piece of bad luck lands on their family. Faye has come down with mononucleosis and is supposed to stay in bed for several weeks. At this point, she has three boys: Jay is four, Ben is two, and Ralph is eight months old. So how can she stay in bed? Ilana is once more drafted into the breach. It is decided for her that she will take care of Faye and her children for the summer. Although Ilana would rather have lazed around with her friends all summer, in truth she thinks, *I don't mind this so much. I prefer taking care of the children to taking care of my father. I will have to learn a great deal about childcare, cooking, and laundry, since I will have to do a lot of that alone. Quite a responsibility for fourteen-year-old me, but I think it also will be quite an education.*

Faye is supposed to stay in bed, but Ilana can go into her room to get advice if she needs it. In the late afternoon, Faye gets out of bed and sits in a chair in the kitchen to talk Ilana through dinner preparation. Ilana already can cook some things, but this expands her repertoire. Faye also teaches her how to prepare the special formula Ralph needs because he is allergic to cow's milk, and how to sterilize the baby bottles. Ilana cannot do the food shopping because she has no way to get to the supermarket, but she makes lists and gives them to Faye's neighbor to shop for them. Mostly, she plays with the children in the house and yard.

In the evenings, after the children are asleep, Ilana has some time to herself. If Joe is home, he and Faye often watch TV in their bedroom. Ilana doesn't want to intrude, so she has a lot of time to reflect on her life and her situation. She thinks, *I miss my friends a lot. But I would do anything for Faye. She took care of me when I was little, and has always been there if I needed someone to talk to. In truth, I feel that she is more important to me than Mom, with whom I am increasingly fighting. Mom disapproves of my boyfriend Larry. She won't admit that it is a racial thing, but instead says that I have to date only Jewish guys. I usually counter by saying that I am not getting married now, at age fourteen; I'm just having a good time with someone.*

*The bigger issue is the constraints imposed on me by the need to take care of my father. I need to be free to socialize after school and in the evening. It isn't okay with me to have to go to school, take care of Dad and cook dinner, do my homework, and then go to sleep and do it all over again the next day. I need some freedom. Mom keeps telling me that we are a family and that there are no other choices. Dad can't just be left alone until she comes back from work. I understand that. Sometimes when I get home after school, I find that Dad has fallen and is lying on the floor. And sometimes he is hungry or thirsty, unable to get up and go to the kitchen. And often he needs help to get to the bathroom. I see the need, but I can't help resenting it. And, as usual, Mom is worried about money. I want to do more babysitting in the neighborhood so I will have some spending money. Mom can't spare much, if anything, from our necessities budget to give me spending money. But my responsibilities for taking care of Dad get in the way of that too. On the weekends, I am reluctant to trade my rare free time to see friends in order to make some money. In a word, my life isn't much fun—and I think a teenager should be able to have fun. As I can see from Faye's life, responsibilities quickly accumulate after one's teenage years.*

With the summer drawing to an end, Faye is feeling much better and able to manage without Ilana. Ilana needs to go back to Hyde Park to begin her sophomore year in high school. She is excited about that, but far from happy about resuming her responsibilities for her father. It seems to her that he somehow managed during the summer while Mom was at work and she was at Faye's, so why does she still have to come home from school every day and see to him?

# 38

Faye tells Gitel that Ilana was incredibly helpful to her family over the summer. Faye says, "She never complained about doing anything, and the kids loved her being here." Now that Ilana is home, she and Gitel are back to their very tense relationship. If Gitel tries to ask her to do anything, she bristles and often doesn't do whatever she was asked. Gitel says to herself, *I seem to have no control over her behavior. She does come home after school to see about Shmuel. And most evenings dinner is prepared when I come home. But she leaves the apartment either just before I come home or immediately after I do. She doesn't say where she is going, just that she is meeting friends. She often doesn't come back until nine or ten in the evening, well after dark. If I ask her anything about where she has been or what she has been doing, she just gets angry. She says something like, "I'm just trying to live my life."*

Gitel doesn't have the energy to fight with Ilana. Sometimes she just gives up trying to parent her, and tries to feel grateful that Ilana does as much as she does for the family. Gitel thinks back and remembers when she was a teenager who wanted to hang out with her friends and play sports—and remembers arguing with her parents about how much freedom she could have. She does understand Ilana. She thinks, *It is just that our circumstances are so unfortunate. And the South Side of Chicago is nothing like South Bend, where I always felt safe. I worry about what kind of trouble she could get into.*

Gitel has worries on two other fronts. Social Security is taking a long time to decide whether Shmuel is entitled to disability benefits. She realizes that it is a relatively new program and that there might be kinks in administering it. But they really need that money. If they get it, they might be able to move to a building with an elevator. That would be much better for Shmuel. And maybe they could move to a nicer apartment where Ilana would be willing to invite her friends. Then she might not be out of the house so much.

Gitel's other problem is her job. Beginning in late 1960, there began to be some strange things happening at the company. She is pretty sure that the owner, who is married and has children, is having an affair with one of the secretaries. *That isn't my business,* she thinks, *but I credit my boss for having good taste. The secretary is certainly attractive.* The affair puts her in an awkward position. Toward the end of the workday, her boss often asks her to give him some money from the petty cash, saying that he needs to take a prospective client out to dinner. Gitel gives it to him, reminding him that he needs to bring back a receipt for what he spent. But she is pretty sure that the "client" at some or most of those dinners is the secretary. The names noted on the receipts as the client seem to be made-up. They never acquire clients with those names. And what happens to office funds is her business as the bookkeeper in charge. She thinks about her options. *I don't want to confront my boss or report the problem to anyone. I don't have the energy for that. I will just look for a different job!*

Gitel likes working for small companies where she can be in charge of the bookkeeping and the office management, rather than at a large company where she might be one bookkeeper among many and have to do just one repetitive type of bookkeeping, such as a portion of accounts payable. She starts paying attention to the help wanted ads in the *Sun-Times* and sees an ad for a bookkeeper/office manager at a real estate office on South Halsted Avenue. She calls and makes an appointment for an interview. She tells her current boss that she has a doctor's appointment and will be in to work late on the following Monday. Given the boss's lies, she doesn't feel guilty about lying in this situation.

The real estate office at Sixty-Ninth and Halsted, called Garnet Real Estate, is in a shabby single-story building in a low-to-moderate-income neighborhood. There is a used furniture store directly across the street. The office has a reception room with some plastic chairs for waiting customers and a Formica counter where customers come up to be helped. A short corridor leads to a few small, spartan offices behind the reception room. That is all. It is quite a contrast to the glitzy Wacker Drive office of the advertising company where she now works.

The owner of the real estate company is a middle-aged Jewish man named Morrie, short and a bit dumpy, whom she notes is wearing a flashy tie and blazer. He explains the business and job to her.

"The company has both a real estate and a construction arm. We buy single-family homes on the southwest side of the city that are old or run-down, and the construction part of the company remodels and fixes up the properties. Then we 'sell' the homes to people 'on contract.'"

Gitel wrinkles her forehead, not quite understanding what the owner is saying. He continues to explain.

"A land contract is a way that people who cannot come up with a down payment or qualify for a conventional mortgage can buy a home. Garnet Real Estate retains the title to the homes, and the 'buyers' pay Garnet a monthly amount, a portion of which goes to pay down the purchase price of the home. If the buyers continue to pay over a period of twenty or twenty-five years, depending on the terms of their contract, they will acquire the title to the home. But if they stop paying, the property reverts to Garnet and the buyer does not recover any equity from the payments."

"And what would my job be?" Gitel asks.

"Your job would be to keep track of all this for both the real estate and construction arms of the company. There is an assistant book-keeper who can help you, but she does not know how to do every-thing. And you would manage the office for matters such as procur-ing supplies and answering questions from clients."

At the end of the interview, the owner offers Gitel the job. Gitel is unsure of what she wants to do. She tells Morrie that she will let him know in a couple of days whether she will take the job.

*The pay is better than I am earning at the advertising company,* she thinks. *But I'm not sure what I think about the way they do business. Is it helpful to the low-income people who couldn't otherwise buy a home? I certainly have sympathy for people who don't earn enough to save for a down payment on a home. Our family is in that category. But I wonder if it is a bit of a scam, whether profits depend on a certain number of buyers defaulting and losing their investments.*

Gitel calls Faye to get her opinion on whether her concerns are valid. Faye does not have a strong opinion. "That is a difficult thing to decide without knowing more details. If most people eventually own their homes and few default, then the land contract system could be a good thing. If the opposite were true, then it might be more of a scam. My guess is that the boss is not going to tell you those details before you accept or decline the job. Have you made a list of all the pros and cons of the job?"

"You certainly are right about needing to know the details. I sup-pose that if I take the job, I will be able after a while to answer those questions. The pros revolve around the generous pay. Also, I think Morrie will be a good boss. And the atmosphere seems casual; he said that so long as I get the job done, he will not mind if I have to take time off for family matters."

"Those points seem important," Faye says.

'Yes," Gitel agrees, continuing. "One con is the location. I would have to take two buses to get there, one across Fifty-Fifth Street to Halsted and then transfer to go south to Sixty-Ninth Street. And I would have to work on Saturday, since that is when people who work during the week come into the office to make payments or check their accounts. In exchange, I would be off on Mondays."

"That is a hard decision to make. I do not really have any advice to give you."

"Of course. I just wanted to hear myself talk out the issues. Thank you for listening."

Over the next couple of days, Gitel convinces herself that selling houses on contract is helpful to low-income people. It certainly is more socially useful than advertising. And she feels that she has to get out of her current job before problems blow up there and catch her in the middle of a bad situation. She calls Morrie to accept the job, and puts in a two-week notice at the advertising firm.

Around that time, Social Security finally decides that Shmuel really is disabled. He begins receiving his benefits, and there also is a supplement for Ilana as his dependent. They receive a retroactive lump sum payment for the time since he applied, and then monthly payments begin. That relieves their budget quite a bit, especially combined with Gitel's higher salary at Garnet. She begins to look for a better apartment for the family.

As part of the urban renewal project in Hyde Park in the mid-1950s, two large, modern apartment buildings facing each other over a courtyard were built in the middle of Fifty-Fifth Street, stretching from just after Harper Street to just before Kenwood Street. To accommodate the buildings, Fifty-Fifth Street was rerouted around the perimeter of the buildings. The buildings are ten stories high, so there are elevators. The modern apartments seem ideal to Gitel, and she uses the extra money from the retroactive Social Security payments to rent a two-bedroom, two-bath apartment. She gives Ilana the large bedroom that has an attached bathroom at the back of the apartment, which provides her some privacy. Together, Gitel and Ilana go shopping for furniture, despite their strained relationship. They furnish Ilana's bedroom like a sitting room, with two couches that double as beds. Ilana tells Gitel that she is pleased with the choices, since they mean that she finally has a nice place to bring friends. She also appreciates the privacy that her new room affords her, something she's never had before.

# 39

Despite Ilana's gratitude for the new apartment, she is still deeply unhappy. A number of thoughts keep whirling through her mind. *Whenever I am at home, especially in the period after school when I am supposed to be taking care of my father, I feel a tightness in my chest. I have a burning feeling, as if something wants to burst out of me and scorch the world. What did I do to deserve this life? Always being poor, always having to take care of others, not being allowed to be a normal teenager. Why did Mom have to marry a loser? Why was I born to such a loser family? Mom says that Dad is a good person who has had bad luck all his life. I believe that, but it feels like he is giving his bad luck to me.*

Ilana watches the clock until it is time for Gitel to get home, which usually is around 6:00 p.m. As she has been doing for a while, she makes some dinner and helps herself to her share, keeping the rest warm for Gitel and Shmuel. Then she tries to head out five or ten minutes before Gitel is expected home. That way, Gitel can't ask her any questions about what she is doing or where she is going.

From the spring through the fall, she heads for the Point. She meets Larry and a number of other friends there. Sometimes they gather around one of the firepit areas and find fallen branches to build a fire to keep themselves warm. If the weather is hot, they might meet on the lowest level of the granite rocks where the breeze off the lake is strongest. They do not do much of anything there, mostly just talk. The police regularly come by wherever they are and look at the group with suspicion, undoubtedly because they are a young, mixed-race group of males and females. Most of the police in Chicago are not too enamored of integration. Ilana and her friends make up a song to sing—to the tune of *West Side Story*'s "Gee Officer Krupke," but with Chicago lyrics—to annoy the police whenever they come around. It goes like this: "*Dear Chicago policeman / you'll never understand / it's just our bringing up, see / that leads us to be friends. You go bother bad guys / and hit them on the head / Golly Moses, just leave us alone.*" There is not much the police can do about the singing, but they always remind the group that they have their eyes on them. And the police are very careful to make sure they leave the park by the 10:00 p.m. curfew for minors.

Even though none of them are even close to age twenty-one, the legal age for buying alcohol, someone in the group usually manages to bring some cheap wine or gin to share. Ilana never knows where they get the booze, but she is more than willing to drink a share. *While I am out*, she thinks, *I want to just forget about my unhappy life at home. Drinking is one way to do that. I think many of my friends have similar motives.* That is true of her boyfriend Larry.

He tells her, "My mother is always pestering me to be good, go to church with her, do all my homework, and hopefully go to college. She wants a better life for me, but her nagging just makes me angry and less likely to do what she wants. My father tells me that he can sponsor me as a junior member of his gang. He holds out the lure of easy money. My mother tries to forbid me from seeing my father, who does not live with us, but that makes hanging with my father even more tempting. I do not know which version of my future I really want! The stark choices eat at me."

"I certainly understand your dilemma," Ilana replies. "You do not have to decide now. There is time. The idea of you in a gang and possibly getting arrested scares me, but it is all for you to figure out. I hope to go to college, but I can see why discrimination may make that path harder for you. College is expensive, and you might have a harder time getting a scholarship than I would, even though you are just as smart."

In the winter, it is harder to find a place to meet up. But the group of friends do get together unless the weather is terrible. Sometimes the parents of someone in the group are away, and they go to that house or apartment. Sometimes they meet in a restaurant or café that is not that busy in the evenings, so the manager will not toss them out if they only order french fries and Cokes. Most of Ilana's friends want to be anywhere except at home with their parents.

# 40

Gitel sees that Ilana's grades are not as good as she is capable of earning. Gitel knows that she does not always do her homework, eat properly, or get enough sleep. What Gitel doesn't know is what to do about it. Sometimes a number of days go by without her even seeing Ilana or being able to talk to her. *I think that Ilana is purposely avoiding me*, Gitel thinks. When Ilana's grades come out, though, she has to ask Gitel to sign her "course book." The course book lists classes and grades for all four years of a person's high school career, and requires a parent's signature each time there is a new set of grades. But she isn't willing to listen about the importance of getting good grades for her future prospects of college and a job. It is as if she understands, but she does not care. She seems to be too consumed with anger—even after they moved to the better apartment.

Gitel has her own anger to suppress, and not much energy to spare for Ilana's nonsense. She takes two buses to get to work, five days a week, in all weather. When she finally gets home in the evenings sometime after 6:00 p.m., she never knows what will greet her when she opens the front door. Ilana may have made dinner, but she may not have. Shmuel may have spilled something on himself and may need a change of clothes that Ilana understandably wouldn't have wanted to do for him. Or—much worse—in the short time between when Ilana leaves and Gitel gets home, he may have fallen on the floor and been unable to get up. After a full day at work and dealing with the vagaries of public transportation, Gitel often walks into a world of need. On her days off, she still has to do laundry, shop for food, and do at least a little cleaning of the apartment. Ilana is no longer helping with anything other than staying with Shmuel after school and sometimes cooking dinner. She is acting as if anything else is not her problem.

Gitel's dilemma of what to do about Ilana is decided for her. When Ilana is fifteen years old, in January of her junior year in high school, she becomes very ill. She is spiking high fevers, and doesn't want to do anything other than lie in bed. She doesn't have the energy to go to school. Gitel hovers around Ilana's bed every morning. She feels reluctant to leave her to go to work, but her income is still most of what they live on. Gitel takes one morning off, and manages to get Ilana to their longtime pediatrician, Dr. Brown.

After examining Ilana, and questioning her and Gitel about what has been happening in Ilana's life, Dr. Brown says, "I cannot immediately say what is wrong with Ilana. However, it seems quite serious. I would like her to be hospitalized for tests. The tests will help determine what to do. I will put in the orders for her hospitalization at Michael Reese Hospital, and for the diagnostic tests she needs."

The next morning, Gitel takes Ilana by taxi to the hospital, as arranged by the doctor. Ilana is limp and only half-conscious, but she goes along with getting into the taxi and allowing Gitel to guide her into the hospital. Dr. Brown is there to meet them. Ilana is admitted into a semi-private room with an old woman who had a cataract operation in the other bed. Ilana lies down in the bed and goes to sleep, despite various nurses and technicians around her who are trying to take her blood, check her heart and lungs, and take her vital signs.

Gitel leaves Ilana there and goes to work. That is the only thing she can do. She isn't sure what the near future will hold in terms of Ilana's treatment, and she doesn't want to use up too much of Morrie's good will in allowing her flexible hours. She already is a few hours late for work for the second day in a row.

Gitel keeps in touch with the doctor, and calls Ilana each evening. It is too difficult to visit her after work, because she has to take care of Shmuel. Faye also calls Ilana most days. For the first two weeks, Ilana is mostly nonresponsive. She answers when Gitel calls the room phone, but isn't very coherent talking to her. Their conversations are very brief.

Dr. Brown tells Gitel, "Ilana mostly sleeps day and night, spiking high fevers during the night. I suspect that she has a bad case of mononucleosis, but I do not know how to bring her out of the state she is in. I am spending a lot of time in the laboratory at the hospital, trying to figure out what type of medicine might work for her. I have gotten some potentially useful results in the laboratory using steroids—which have not been used before to relieve symptoms of mononucleosis. We will have to see if those lab results transfer to human use."

Upon taking the steroids, Ilana does gradually begin to recover. She is still very tired and can't do much, but at least she can sit up and read a book for a little while. The doctor says that she is compliant with whatever he or the nurses ask her to do. When they ask her to try to get up and walk around, she tries her best to do that.

Gitel has some hope that the experience of being so ill and in the hospital for so long has taken some of the anger and oppositional fire out of Ilana, and that her improved temper might carry over to when she comes home. That remains to be seen.

Gitel is worried that the high school might not excuse Ilana's extended absence. They have a rule that calls for failing a student who is absent a certain number of days in the year. That is intended to avert truancy, but Gitel is concerned they might apply it in Ilana's case. She makes an appointment to talk to the principal and some of Ilana's teachers.

She tells the principal, "I can't predict when Ilana will be able to return to school, since the doctor told me that she will have to recuperate further at home after she is released from the hospital. I think she could do some of her schoolwork while she is resting at home, if her teachers are willing to send it to her."

"Of course, they can send the work home to her," the principal responds. "She should do it if she feels well enough. Neither you nor she should worry, though. We have no intention of holding Ilana back or making her repeat her junior year. We know how smart she is, and feel that she will easily catch up on what she has missed."

Gitel later tells Ilana what her teachers had said. Ilana says, "It is not that easy to catch up, particularly in math. In my double X track, the junior-year math has a unit on trigonometry in the spring semester, most of which I have already missed. By the time I go back to school, I'll probably have missed the whole trig unit. I don't know how I could learn that on my own."

Gitel replies, "Don't worry about that now. We'll figure out some way to catch you up."

Ilana is beginning to feel impatient to leave the hospital and come home. But the doctor thinks she needs at least another week in the hospital to be sure she will be able to manage on her own at home. He is aware that Gitel has to go to work every day, and that Shmuel could not be any help to her. She, in fact, will probably have to care for him.

# 41

When Gitel comes to visit Ilana at the hospital on Sunday, Ilana can see how tired she is. Ilana thinks about how difficult her mother's life is, working five days a week while trying to take care of her father. Since they received the Social Security money, her mother worries a little bit less about making ends meet for the family, but it still is a tight budget. Ilana realizes clearly for the first time that her mother never gets to do anything for herself. If she isn't working, she is cleaning the apartment, shopping, doing laundry, or cooking. Occasionally, she buys a *Redbook* magazine and sits down to read it. She never has time to see her old friends like Sophie; Ilana wonders if she even talks to her on the phone. Ilana knows that her mother has begun to make friends with the woman who lives in the apartment across the hall in the new building. But that probably will not be a deep type of friendship, the kind she has with Sophie, because her mother has so little time to devote to building a close relationship with a new friend. Ilana promises herself that she will try to be nicer to her mother, and—once she gets her strength back—try to be more of a help to her.

Finally, Dr. Brown comes to see Ilana and says that she can go home at the end of the week, but that she will still have to stay home and rest for a few more weeks. Ilana argues that she feels well enough to go back to school; she's worried about how much she is missing by being out of school. The doctor thinks about her concerns, and ultimately says that she will at least have to stay home and rest for one week. He will decide after that if she can go back to school full- or part-time.

On Monday, Gitel comes to take Ilana home. She helps her gather up her things, and then they take a taxi back to Hyde Park. Walking out of the hospital with her mother, Ilana realizes that she is still a bit weak and unsteady. Maybe she shouldn't go back to school so soon.

Resting at home after returning from the hospital, Ilana thinks about what happened to her. *I can't believe how sick I was. I don't remember a lot from the first two weeks I was in the hospital, but I do know that I felt awful. And scared. Sometimes a lot of doctors and nurses were around my bed in the middle of the night, taking my temperature, poking me for blood samples, and rubbing me down with alcohol. They just said that my temperature was very high, and they needed both to get it down and to analyze my blood at the time my fever went up. They never told me what the results were, but I assume they weren't good because I wasn't getting better.*

In the times when I was more coherent, I felt very lonely. There was another person in my room, but usually a curtain was drawn between the two beds. Even when the curtain was open, I didn't have much to say to the other person. Initially, the other person was someone I perceived to be an old woman, and she wasn't that friendly to a fifteen-year-old. After she left, there was a middle-aged woman who had some kind of pneumonia. She was a little more talkative, but again no one to whom I could relate. Mom only called me in the evenings, and sometimes I wasn't awake enough to talk to her. Faye also called me, but she couldn't stay on the phone that long because of the little kids. Larry did not come to visit me. I guessed he might be afraid to come to a hospital, or just not know what to do. He also did not call. I realized that just might signal the end of our relationship. I was, in any case, not sure I wanted to pick it up again when I recovered. One time, after I had been in the hospital nearly three weeks, one of the guys from our crowd, Mel, did come to visit me. He is a very large, dark-complected guy, and caused a bit of a stir among the staff. But I assured people that he was my friend and that I was happy to see him. He confirmed to me that Larry had pretty much moved on, and I told Mel that was fine with me.

*It felt weird not being in school. Like time had stopped or like I had fallen into some different universe where all the people and all the rules were different. I felt as though I was a little different as well. As I began to feel better with the steroid medicine that my doctor had discovered, I realized that the anger that was driving me before I got sick was no longer so strong.*

When Ilana gets home and goes into her bedroom, she looks at it with fresh eyes. She sees with appreciation everything Gitel has done for her. Ilana thinks, *I had forgotten how nice my room is.* The room is set up to give her a private place to entertain her friends. Given that Shmuel is always sitting in the living room, entertaining friends there is not an option—especially since he sometimes says inappropriate things to her friends without realizing that what he says is problematic.

Her large bedroom is set up with two modern couches with foam mattresses and bolsters that make it look like another living room. The couches can turn into beds with the addition of bedding at night; Ilana sleeps on one of them. There is a coffee table, a nice wooden dresser, and a large walk-in closet that makes it possible to store whatever needs storing to keep the room looking neat. There also is an attached bathroom, so that is private and separate from whatever problems her father might be having in the hallway bathroom. And Gitel has arranged for her to have a telephone with her own phone number. That is quite a luxury. She can talk privately to her friends for as long as she wants without inconveniencing her parents. She thinks, *Mom had taken me to buy all of this before I got sick, but I was so angry then that I didn't realize how lucky I am to have this setup.*

# 42

G itel breathes a sigh of relief to have Ilana back home. She no longer has to worry about her condition, nor does she have to *shlep* to the hospital to see her on her days off. She thinks, *By some miracle, Ilana's attitude has changed. She no longer seems to be angry at me. In fact, she expressed how grateful she is to me for setting up her room so nicely. Right now, she has to stay home to recover her strength. I am hoping that once she has fully recovered, she also will be finished with going out every evening to heaven knows where. While she is still resting at home, she has been taking care of Shmuel a bit, even fixing lunch for him. And she is beginning to cook some dinners again before I get home from work. I only hope all this lasts.*

Gitel never complains out loud to anyone. She only complains in her mind, to herself. But in truth, she is exhausted. Going to work, trying to take care of Shmuel, shopping for food and cooking, cleaning the apartment, and doing laundry is all too much for her. She is in her midfifties, and doesn't have the energy she once had. *I need to look at our budget again and see if I can at least get some help cleaning the apartment; that is the chore I dislike most. Not sure if we can afford to do that.*

It is almost the end of Ilana's junior year in high school, a little more than a year until she goes to college. Gitel initiates a conversation with Ilana about college.

Ilana says, "I want to go away somewhere for college, to experience being somewhere other than Chicago and South Bend."

"I hope you can do that," Gitel responds. "Of course, we don't have any money to pay for your college tuition and room and board, so that may not be possible."

"I hope I can get scholarships. I usually get very high scores on standardized tests, so maybe I can get an Illinois State Scholarship or even a National Merit. The latter is not as likely. And I can get a part-time job now that I am sixteen and can work legally, and I can also work during college. I'm hoping that my grades this semester, which will probably be low because of the time I missed, won't hurt my chances."

"I'll have to leave all that for you to figure out, Ilana. We don't have any experience in the family that helps. I hope your counselor at the high school can advise you properly."

Gitel thinks, *I hate to admit it, but I'm looking forward to her going off on her own. Even with her acting much better now, there is always some tension in our interactions. I'd be happy to live without that tension. And so long as she is living here, I feel responsible for her. If she is away at college, that responsibility as a mother will weigh on me a lot less.*

In the meantime, Shmuel's condition continues to deteriorate. Gitel sees that he can barely make it to the bathroom, even using a walker. And sometimes he doesn't make it. He falls frequently, and can't get up if no one is home to help him. The doctor says he now has diabetes on top of his other ailments, so Gitel has to find and prepare special foods for him. She knows that he is miserable, having to just sit and not do much of anything all day. He doesn't see well enough to read. And there is not much on television during the day, even if he could see it and understand it well enough to follow what is going on—which she suspects he can't. He can listen to music on the radio, but that is about all he can do. Shmuel sometimes talks to her about things that happened in the past, which he does seem to remember clearly. He has a lot of regrets, and brings up a lot of sadness. He also feels that life has been unfair to him, and Gitel agrees. Gitel, too, often thinks about how life has been unfair to both of them. For her, it began with her parents not allowing her to go to college and continued through the loss of their business in the Great Depression and all of Shmuel's illnesses and setbacks that made it impossible for him to earn a decent living. But unlike Shmuel, she is too busy to dwell on these thoughts. He has nothing but time on his hands. There is little if anything that she can do to make his life more tolerable now. She wishes there was something she could do.

The next year passes in much the same way. Ilana begins her senior year in high school. She does get a part-time job, working in a small dress shop on Fifty-Third Street on Thursday evenings and Saturdays. Gitel urges her to save as much of her small wages, twelve dollars a week, as she can, although Gitel acknowledges that a teenager should have some spending money.

Ilana also has a new boyfriend, a University of Chicago student who she met at a dorm party. She tells Gitel that she isn't interested in high school boys anymore, so she and a friend managed somehow to go to a party at Pierce Tower.

"At the party, I met Kevin, who is Jewish but not very observant," she tells Gitel a couple of weeks later, when Kevin is about to pick her up for a date.

Gitel thinks that Kevin is very polite when he comes to the apartment, although he seems unsure whether he should approach Shmuel, who is sitting in his usual chair. After hesitating, he does go over to

Shmuel and shakes his hand. *He seems nice enough to me*, she thinks, *the first suitable boyfriend Ilana has had since she began high school.*

A few weeks later, after Ilana has gone on a few more dates with Kevin, Gitel asks her if she is serious about him. Ilana says, "We enjoy each other's company, but he's definitely not a permanent boyfriend."

"That's fine. You have lots of time to find someone permanent."

Ilana begins the process of applying to colleges. She tells Gitel that she did win an Illinois State Scholarship as a result of taking the ACT test, which will pay about half her tuition if she goes to a private college—but it has to be a college in Illinois.

"I will still have to figure out how to pay the rest of the tuition, room and board, books, and travel costs," Ilana explains to Gitel. "If I go to a state school, the scholarship would probably pay all the tuition and perhaps some of the room and board. But the University of Illinois in Champaign is huge, and some of the classes have hundreds of students in them. I think I would get lost there. And I am not applying to any Ivy League schools. I don't think my grades are good enough, and they are unlikely to give me enough scholarship money to make going to one of them feasible. I would like to go to Brandeis University in Massachusetts, and am applying there. But it is such a new school that it may not have a lot of scholarship money."

"What about all the mail you are getting that seems to be from colleges? What is that?" Gitel asks.

"There are some schools that are sending me materials and inviting me to apply on the basis of my high ACT and SAT scores, but none are top-tier schools. They include Kerwin College in Midburg, Illinois, and Washington University in St. Louis. I wish I could visit some of these schools, but I know we can't afford that. That is just the way it is."

Kerwin College continues to woo her to attend there, and offers her a nearly full tuition and room and board scholarship for the amounts her Illinois State Scholarship wouldn't cover, with a requirement that she take a small government loan for the remainder. Neither Gitel nor Ilana has ever heard of Midburg, let alone Kerwin College. Central Illinois is a world away from Chicago. The only other place in Illinois that Gitel has been is the state capital, Springfield. Ilana had a class trip there in elementary school, for which Gitel volunteered to chaperone.

As the college acceptances begin to arrive, Ilana does get into her preferred school, Brandeis, but they don't offer her financial aid. Their letter confirms what she suspected—since they are a new school, they don't yet have the resources to offer the type of scholarship she would need.

Ilana tells Gitel that it seems to make sense for her to stay in Illinois and use the state scholarship. She reiterates that she doesn't want to go to a large state school. Gitel suggests that she take the train to Midburg to look at Kerwin, which is a relatively inexpensive trip. When Ilana returns, she tells Gitel, "It seems to have nice facilities for classes and a student union, with an old, historic dorm for freshman women. The dorm had been a stop on the Underground Railroad. The administration and students were nice enough to me during my visit, although it is hard to get a sense of how I would fit in. The campus is in the middle of several cornfields, which would be quite a different experience than Hyde Park. I did tell you that I wanted something different from what I have known."

Ilana tells Gitel that she has decided to accept Kerwin's offer. Gitel congratulates her, assuming that Ilana knows best what will be good for her.

# 43

Ilana gets ready to go to the senior prom. She and Gitel go shopping and find a long, turquoise strapless dress, on sale and not too expensive. It's a last-minute purchase, because Ilana did not think she would be going to the prom. She had broken up with Kevin about a month before, after they realized that they were not the right partners for each other. Since he was going to go back to Arizona for the summer and she was going away to college, they agreed that there was not any value in continuing to date. But surprisingly, he called her a couple of weeks later and suggested that they go to the prom together anyway. Ilana readily agreed and scrambled to get ready.

Gitel asked Ilana, "Would you like me to make a breakfast the morning after the prom for a few of your friends and their dates? I know many people stay up all night celebrating in one way or another after the prom, so breakfast could cap off the celebration."

"That would be really nice! Can we afford it?"

"I will make something simple. It will be the idea of getting together that counts, rather than the food itself."

Gitel buys some bagels, cream cheese, and lox spread, and makes scrambled eggs. She also serves orange juice and coffee and tea.

*I was proud to have Mom entertain my friends*, Ilana thinks. And everyone seemed to have a good time.

Ilana needs to earn some money over the summer, in order to have some spending money during the school year. She wants to do work that is challenging and socially useful, which is difficult to find at her age. She applies for a few different jobs, but she is especially interested in working as a counselor at a camp located in Kenwood, just north of Hyde Park, for mentally retarded children and adults. The camp is funded by the Kennedy Family Foundation, who are interested because a sister of John, Robert, and Edward Kennedy is retarded. Another sister, Eunice Kennedy Shriver, runs the foundation. The job announcement states that the camp wants to hire people going into their third or fourth year of college for senior counselors. It also is hiring junior counselors, for which Ilana qualifies by age, but these positions do not pay enough to meet her need for funds. Ilana is determined to get the senior counselor job, so she goes to the library and does a lot of research on mental retardation and social interaction, hoping to impress the camp leaders at her interview.

When Ilana is asked at the interview why she wants the job, she says, "I plan to major in sociology in college. I am very interested in assessing group dynamics, including tools such as sociograms, to figure out who is interacting with whom and whether anyone is routinely being left out and needs more attention from the adults to be able to fit in."

"And why do you think you are mature enough to take on this job?"

"When I was fourteen, my sister was sick. I took care of her three young children and her household for the entire summer, until she recovered," Ilana explains. "I also have taken care of my disabled father, starting when I was ten. My mother has to work to support us, so I have to come home after school and help my father with whatever he needs. He can't reliably walk to the kitchen or bathroom, and often falls. I usually also cook dinner for us, so my mother doesn't have to when she comes home tired from work and from commuting by bus. We don't have a car. And I have a scholarship for college in the fall, but I need money for other expenses such as transportation and incidentals. My mother makes just enough to keep us going. She can't afford to give me spending money."

"I must say," one of the interviewers comments, "you have had a lot of responsibility at a young age. I see why you think you can do the senior counselor job. We will let you know in about a week."

Ilana receives a phone call a few days after the interview. Her strategy worked. They hire her as a senior counselor.

When Ilana relates all this to Gitel after she gets the job, Gitel says, "I'm so impressed that you pulled that off. And I am impressed by the way you know what you want and go after it in a strategic way. I think that is a great skill that will help you throughout your life."

When the camp starts, Ilana, along with a junior counselor to help her, has a group of about a dozen of the youngest campers, ranging in age from four to eight. The kids need a lot of attention. Ilana often relates what happens at camp to Gitel over dinner.

One day she says, "Today I was able to get a very frightened girl to go into the swimming pool and began to teach her to float. I have been working gradually, for weeks, on making her feel comfortable near and then in the water. Today she finally was willing to go in."

Another day Ilana relates a funny tale to Gitel. "Today the whole camp went to the Natural History Museum, which is on the lakefront, and then had a picnic on the large lawn in front of the museum. This was also the day that Teddy Kennedy planned to visit us on behalf of the family. He chose my group to visit, and joined us sitting in a circle on the lawn as we ate lunch—hot dogs on buns. He was not eating, but one of my larger boys noticed that, got up, and forcefully shoved a hot dog toward his mouth. Kennedy did a backward somersault to avoid the onslaught, while I tried to pull the boy back. I was embarrassed, but luckily he took it all in good humor."

The summer ends. Ilana says goodbye to the campers, embracing and whispering something encouraging to each one. She also says goodbye to the senior staff who hired her, saying, "Thanks for taking a chance on me. This was a wonderful experience for me. The children taught me a lot. And I hope I gave them a wonderful experience as well."

"I think you did, indeed. You were a great counselor. Perhaps you will come back another year if the camp continues."

In the fall of 1963, Ilana leaves for Kerwin College with a heavy trunk stuffed full of clothes and books. While other students are driven to the college by their parents, she takes the train alone to Midburg and struggles to move the trunk the five or so blocks from the train station to the dorm, using a wheeled contraption for which it is too heavy. On arrival at the old, historic dorm, she meets her roommate. The roommate is also Jewish, which should have been a clue to her.

The dorm has a lot of rules. Men are allowed only in the formal parlor on the first floor. There is a curfew time by which all the residents have to be in the dorm. And it is necessary to sign out and in during the evenings. Ilana thinks that the school should be more trusting of its female students, and feels a bit insulted by these rules.

Ilana registers for her classes and looks for a job on campus to add to her small store of spending money. She notices that there is an old-fashioned plug switchboard at the reception desk to the student union. It intrigues her, because it is similar to the switchboard that she had learned to operate so many years ago when she went with her mother to her job at Resthaven. She asks for and gets the job working the switchboard on weekend evenings and a couple of other shifts. While working the switchboard, she shares the reception desk with another student, who sells the small convenience items and candy bars available at the desk.

There is a reason she is free to work on weekend evenings. Shortly after the semester started, so did pledging for the fraternities and sororities. It was explained to her by a Jewish student, Sue, who was already a junior.

"None of the sororities accept Jews. I tried to break the ban when I was a freshman, but was rebuffed. As you might have already noticed, almost all of the social life at the college is created by and happens through the fraternities and sororities. There are about five or six Jewish students and a similar number of Negro students. Both Jews and Negroes are excluded, and there is no way to challenge that. Apparently, the bigotry is accepted and normalized by the administration here, and it may even encourage the discrimination."

Ilana tells Sue, "I'm not sure I would join a sorority even if I could, because I generally disapprove of many of their practices. At my high school there was a Jewish sorority that drew from Hyde Park and South Shore High Schools, but I never was interested in joining it. They did stupid things like make pledges wear their blouses on backward for a week, without washing them." Ilana thinks, *In high school, there were plenty of other social opportunities. Kerwin is isolated, so it matters more here. I can pretend to scorn the Greeks or not care about the exclusion, but in reality I feel hurt.*

# 44

One evening when dinner is finished and Shmuel is settled in his chair, Gitel calls Sophie on the phone. She tells her, "I feel pretty much alone these days. I am both sad that Ilana is away at school and relieved that I don't have to worry about what she is doing day to day. I really miss my conversations with Ilana, and even our arguments."

"I can understand that," Sophie replies. "I know that Shmuel is not much company for you at this point. He is mostly someone who needs care."

"So true! I also realize that Ilana coming home from school most days a few hours before I get home from work made a difference in Shmuel's care. Now he often is in much worse shape when I get home than he had been when Ilana cared for him after school."

"Wasn't she also making dinner a lot of evenings? Are you having to cook now, on top of everything else you do?"

"I'm afraid so," Gitel says. "I really don't like to cook!"

"Have you thought about frozen TV dinners? I usually am lucky because my husband can sometimes bring food home from the restaurant where he works. But when he cannot, I pop one of the TV dinners that I keep in the freezer into the oven. You have a freezer part of your refrigerator, right? It is a quick way to have a decent meal. Not gourmet, but serviceable."

"I hadn't thought of that. I guess I'm not yet used to having a decent freezer. In our previous apartment, there just was enough room for an ice cube tray. I'll look in the freezer section in the supermarket next time I shop. Thanks for the idea."

"Glad to help!" Sophie tells her.

"It is always great to talk to you, Sophie. I hope we can get together sometime soon, although with Ilana gone there is no one to stay with Shmuel. Maybe you could come here?"

"Maybe. We should keep up by phone, at least."

Gitel is grateful that Ilana has found a way to pay for college, and also to earn her spending money. For the first time since Shmuel stopped working at Steinway's drugstore, she is able to save a little bit each month. That lowers her level of perpetual anxiety about finances, even if it is not enough to eliminate the worry.

They had agreed that Ilana would call home at least once every two weeks. Ilana has to go to a public pay phone to do that, so she has to call collect. They never stay on the phone very long, because those type of calls are expensive. Nevertheless, Gitel begins to hear some dissatisfaction with Kerwin in Ilana's comments, which grows more intensely negative over the course of the semester. She says that most of the students, who are from small towns in downstate Illinois, have never met a Jew before. One of them actually asked her if Jews really had horns on their heads. And Ilana explains to Gitel about being excluded from the sororities. After a while, she also has some complaints about her academic courses. She says that the teacher of a required English class doesn't like the style of her writing, which is essentially the University of Chicago style that is taught at Hyde Park High School. Ilana complains that she doesn't want to change the way she writes just for this teacher, who she feels is being arbitrary. In the past, she has always gotten kudos for her writing. She also says that a lot of her high school classes were better than those at Kerwin.

Gitel doesn't know what to say to her when she complains. She has no experience of college on which to draw. She calls Faye and asks what she thinks.

"I don't know," Faye replies. "I recall that I was so grateful to be able to go to college at all that complaining about fellow students or courses would never have occurred to me. But I have always admired Ilana's courage and ability to stand up for what she thinks is right, so maybe her complaints are a good thing—if she can figure out what to do about the situation."

Gitel thinks that Faye's take on Ilana's circumstances makes sense. Gitel decides that the next time Ilana calls, she will tell her that she will support anything Ilana decides to do about her situation.

When Gitel says that to Ilana on their next call, Ilana tells her that she does have a tentative plan. But Gitel would have to agree with it. Her plan is to try to transfer to The University of Chicago. She is going to try to make an appointment to talk to the admissions office at Chicago when she is home for Thanksgiving vacation. She asks Gitel, "How would you feel about my living at home again, since that would be the only way I could afford U of C? It wouldn't be ideal from a social perspective, because I wouldn't have that many opportunities to meet the other students who live in dorms. But at least the classes would be better, and I might be able to meet some students who are interested in the same things I am."

Gitel asks her how she will be able to pay the tuition. Ilana says that she will look for a part-time job during the school year that pays enough for her to manage the part that the Illinois State Scholarship doesn't cover.

Gitel takes a deep breath. *I would again feel responsible for Ilana if she lives at home. It might feel like one more burden. But it would be nice to have someone to talk with at home.* Out loud, Gitel tells her that she is welcome to live at home if all that works out.

# 45

Now that Ilana has a plan to escape Kerwin, even if she doesn't yet know if it will work, she decides to make the most of her time among the cornfields. Growing up in Hyde Park in an integrated milieu, she is very interested in civil rights. A large button from the Student Nonviolent Coordinating Committee proclaiming, "We Shall Overcome," is always attached to her purse. The button attracts many disapproving stares in Midburg, but Ilana has no intention of taking it off.

She thinks about what she could do that would be useful to the civil rights cause. She decides to do some organizing that will link some Kerwin students to the Negro community in Midburg. She starts by gathering a group of Kerwin students who might be interested in tutoring some Negro children. Like in most cities and towns, the schools in Midburg's Negro neighborhoods are substandard, and some enrichment from college kids could be welcome and helpful. Given her impression of the politically conservative student body, she is surprised that about twenty students come to the meeting at which she explains her idea. Then she contacts the pastors of the four Negro churches in town to ask if she might speak briefly during their Sunday morning services, to explain the opportunity to have children tutored. She is welcomed at the churches, and even enjoys going to the services and hearing the spirited singing of the hymns.

She also contacts the local chapter of the NAACP to speak there as well, and ends up joining the organization and attending their regular meetings. It all comes together well as she matches the children wanting tutoring with the Kerwin students. She even travels to Peoria with the NAACP to participate in a sit-in to integrate a lunch counter. When she tells Gitel about what she is doing, her mother says that she is proud of her.

Thanksgiving break arrives. Ilana takes the train back to Chicago and a bus back to Hyde Park. She has managed to make an appointment with The University of Chicago admissions office for the Friday after Thanksgiving. She is planning on bringing along her ACT and SAT test scores, and a transcript of her high school grades. And she thinks a lot about what she wants to tell them. She decides to tell them the truth about the anti-Semitism at Kerwin and her opinion about the quality of some of the professors and classes. That explains why she wants to transfer. But she also needs to make a case for why U of C should take her.

She decides to emphasize her political/social justice agenda and to focus on her activities. At the interview, she says, "I edited the Hyde Park High School yearbook to emphasize the theme of civil rights. Last summer I was a counselor in a Kennedy family–supported camp for mentally retarded children and adults. And I think I accomplished a lot in Midburg by setting up a tutoring program between Kerwin students and Negro children who go to substandard schools, as well as helping integrate a lunch counter in Peoria—working with both the Negro churches in town and the NAACP."

"That sounds pretty impressive for a first-year college student," the interviewer remarks. "Did you find time to study?"

"Of course. My grades are fine. None of the classes were difficult for me. And I would like to explain to you what Hyde Park means to me. I think it models what the world or at least the country should be like, and I so missed living in liberal Hyde Park while I was surrounded by nothing but cornfields and anti-Semitism in Midburg."

"Why did you end up at Kerwin in Midburg? Why didn't you apply here last year?"

"I didn't apply last year because I thought I was anxious to get away from my family's problems and my responsibilities for caring for my disabled father while living with my parents," Ilana explains. "But having gotten away for a year, I believe I will be fine living with them again. It is more important to me to get a high-quality college education."

# 46

*Ilana certainly knows how to take care of herself,* Gitel thinks. *She knows what she wants and figures out how to go after it. She is rarely passive if she thinks something is not right for herself, or even if something is not right in society.*

Gitel again tells her how proud she is of her, especially of her choosing to make a difference in Midburg and Peoria once she realized that Kerwin is not for her. Gitel has a cousin in Peoria, and Ilana stayed an extra day in Peoria to visit with the cousin while she was there. The cousin told Gitel all about the sit-in, which had received a lot of local media coverage and had indeed ignited a concerted local effort to force the integration of the lunch counter. Her cousin told Gitel that she also is proud of Ilana.

The admissions office at U of C sends a packet of materials for Ilana to fill out. She tells Gitel that they called her and told her that she would be accepted, but that she has to go through the application process. They also said that they couldn't give her any scholarship money for the first year she would be there. There is an agreement among some colleges, including U of C, to prevent them from buying students from each other. But for subsequent years, she could apply for a scholarship. Ilana has to think about how she can manage next year financially.

Gitel has an idea of how she could help Ilana, but first she has to talk to the owner of the real estate company where she works. She does not want to say anything to Ilana until she is sure it will work out. The woman who is her assistant bookkeeper and performs some clerical functions wants to cut back on her hours to spend more time with her young children. Gitel wonders if Ilana could do the assistant's work part-time and earn enough for her needs. She is sure that Ilana could quickly learn the job. She'd be happy to teach her the bookkeeping system in the office. She had already started teaching her the fundamentals of bookkeeping. Ilana isn't great at typing, but probably good enough. Gitel talks to her boss, and he is agreeable.

Then Gitel tells Ilana about the offer.

"Ilana, I talked to my boss at work. Beverly, my assistant bookkeeper, wants to cut back her hours to spend more time with her children. Morrie would be happy to have you work part-time with me. He would pay you two dollars an hour. What do you think about that?"

Gitel is not sure how Ilana will react, since she knows that Ilana likes to be independent and arrange her own life. She waits for Ilana's response.

"Thank you so much, Mom, for thinking of this and making it happen. I think I could work for eight hours on Fridays, assuming I can arrange my schedule to avoid having classes on Friday, and four hours on Saturday mornings. I would earn $24 a week, which is more than I could earn working in a shop or restaurant. When I worked at the dress shop, I only earned $1 an hour, and now the minimum wage is not much more, only $1.25 an hour. I would like the opportunity to work with you, and I will be glad to learn some additional bookkeeping skills. And if we take the bus together, we will have time to talk to each other."

Gitel continues to have some misgivings about her job, even though she values the flexibility Morrie gives her and his willingness to give Ilana a job. She isn't sure if they are helping low-income people buy their homes by selling on contract, as her boss repeatedly says they are. But every time they have to repossess a house because someone's monthly payments are too far behind, and the buyer has to leave without any equity in their house, she is bothered. The agency tries to work with people who get sick or lose their job, to take partial or no payments for some period of time, but there are people who just cannot catch up. At least repossessions are not frequent. For now, she just mulls over these issues in her mind. She doesn't anticipate making any job changes anytime soon.

Once Ilana is living at home for the summer and anticipating attending U of C in the fall, life becomes a little easier and a little more pleasant for Gitel. Her assistant decides to take advantage of Ilana's availability to take the whole summer off while her children are out of school, so Ilana is working with Gitel at the real estate agency five days a week; she isn't doing the Saturday shift in the summer. Taking the two buses to get to work is a bit nicer with Ilana's company. And teaching Ilana the bookkeeping is fun for Gitel. She has always wanted to be a teacher in a business school, and thinks she would be good at that if only she had the college credentials. Of course, not everyone would have been able to learn the process as quickly as Ilana does.

Since they get home together after work, they take turns making dinner while the other one looks after Shmuel. And Ilana will some-times cook something on the weekend that they could eat during the week. *Truth be told, Ilana is a better cook than I am. I think she must have learned from Faye during all those times she stayed with her. How Faye learned to cook so well is a mystery—definitely not from me. Faye's former next-door neighbor and good friend has a catering business, so perhaps Faye learned from her.* Ilana and Gitel often do the grocery shopping together when Gitel comes back from work on Saturday afternoons, so that they each can choose ingredients for what they want to cook. And they do take Sophie's suggestion to buy a few TV dinners for when they feel too tired to cook. And best of all, Gitel has someone to talk to at home.

Gitel occasionally thinks about the past tensions between her and Ilana, but they seem to have completely vanished. The hospital stay marked the end of her rebellious period, and most of the time now she is a pleasure to be around. That is quite unexpected but so, so welcome.

Gitel still is tired most of the time in the evenings and on the weekend. She wishes that she would have more time and energy to meet with her friends. She especially misses being with Sophie. Occasionally they have a short phone conversation on a weekday evening, but it has been a very long time since they have seen each other. Gitel wonders if she can take a taxi over to Sophie's place some evening when her husband is at work, while Ilana watches Shmuel. Ilana agrees and suggests it would be best to do that before school starts in the fall.

Gitel calls Sophie and arranges a time to visit her at her apartment on a Tuesday evening. Sophie now lives in what people call the "Indian Village," a collection of new high-rise apartment buildings built on the land that used to be occupied by the Fifth Army Headquarters during World War II and the Korean War. Each apartment tower is named after a Native American tribe. Sophie lives in the Algonquin, in a modern one-bedroom apartment that has its kitchen appliances arranged against one wall of the living room, hidden behind a folding door. Gitel thinks it is strange, but Sophie seems to like it. Clearly, she does not do a lot of cooking.

Sophie and Gitel are so glad to see each other that they hug for about five minutes when Gitel first arrives. Gitel thinks, *I always feel so good when we hug.* They sit on the couch taking turns talking nonstop for an hour and a half. When Gitel is talking, she often puts her hand on Sophie's arm as a way of connecting, and Sophie, when talking, puts her hand on Gitel's arm, shoulder, or thigh. Gitel feels so comfortable sitting with Sophie, catching up with what each of them has been doing. Sophie mostly talks about politics or books she has recently read. She reads constantly, something for which Gitel has no time or energy. Gitel mostly talks about work, Faye, and Ilana. Sophie is very fond of Ilana and proud of her activism.

Gitel asks Sophie what she thinks about her work dilemma. "Do you think selling houses on contract is moral?" Gitel knows that Sophie spends a lot of time thinking about improving the lives of the sort of blue-collar workers to whom they are selling, through the Communist Party as well as through other activities.

Sophie asks hard questions. "What are the demographic characteristics of the buyers?"

"Almost all Negroes. The houses are mostly in the Englewood neighborhood. My boss says that Englewood is 'redlined,' considered a high-risk area, so no mortgages are available there. And for the most part, Negroes can't get mortgages anywhere. That is why they need to buy on contract. At least that is what my boss says."

"What is the price at which the real estate agency sells the houses as compared to the price at which it buys them? How frequently have buyers lost their equity through inability to keep up with monthly payments?"

"We sell the houses for about seventy-five percent more than we pay for them, which is indeed a hefty markup," Gitel says. "Our related construction company does do substantial rehabbing of the houses, which often are in bad shape, before they are sold. But the markup still means a large profit on each sale. And despite my boss usually trying to work with buyers who are having financial problems, in recent years I'd estimate that about four or five percent of the contracts defaulted. My boss contends that the other ninety-five to ninety-six percent of buyers would have no way to eventually own a nice home were it not for the contract purchases. They probably would be renters all their lives."

Sophie replies that it is not the most socially responsible work that Gitel could do. "The profits the real estate agency is making are attributable to the fact that it is buying into and taking advantage of Chicago's segregation policies and the widespread racism in its power structure. But I also understand that you need that job right now. Perhaps you could make a long-term plan to find a better job when you can."

"I agree with your assessment. I will certainly try to move on when Ilana finishes college and is on her own. Or perhaps there will be an opportunity before then."

Gitel doesn't want to get home too late in the evening, so she calls a taxi from Sophie's apartment and prepares to leave. Again, they hug for a long time, and Gitel promises it won't be so long until they see each other again.

The summer is over, and Ilana begins attending The University of Chicago. She explains the system to Gitel.

"There is an orientation week for transfer students as well as first-year students, during which students have to take an extensive battery of tests. U of C has a common core of ten required courses, which is different from most schools. Most schools give choices of courses in specified areas. The purpose of the tests is to determine which of the core courses a student does not have to take because they already know the material well enough. This is particularly important for transfer students like me, because it would be hard to take all the core courses and sufficient courses for a major subject in three years. As a result of the testing, I placed out of the foreign language requirement because of my Russian studies in high school and at Kerwin, the philosophy course they call Humanities II because of a philosophy course I took at Kerwin, and the English writing course."

"Is that a good result?" Gitel asks.

"Yes, but I will have to carry a heavy load to graduate in three years."

Indeed, for the first month or so after first-quarter classes start, Ilana seems to spend every evening and many hours on the weekend studying in her room. Her door is closed, so it is hard for Gitel to know if she is studying or doing something else. But she says she is studying. What is clear is that Ilana has no social life at all. She isn't going out on dates or to parties as she had during high school, and she isn't bringing any friends home or going to friends' houses for visits. She says she is fine, but Gitel is concerned and does not quite believe her.

There is a Jewish woman neighbor on their floor of the apartment building that Gitel has met and knows slightly. They talk enough so that she knows that Ilana is back living in the apartment, and attending the U of C. She stops Gitel in the hallway one day and says that her nephew Drew has just started graduate school at the university. She wonders if it would be possible to fix him up with Ilana. Gitel says that he could try to call Ilana, but it would be up to her if she wants to go out with him; Ilana does not like anyone meddling in her social life. Gitel gives the neighbor Ilana's phone number to pass on to Drew.

A few weeks later, toward the end of November, Drew does call Ilana. Surprisingly, despite having never met him, she agrees to go with him to a party at the graduate student dorm where he lives. She tells Gitel that she is tired of having no social life, and going to a party can't be that bad—even if Drew turns out to be a dud.

# 47

The party to which Drew invited Ilana is scheduled to take place the next Saturday evening. Drew says in the phone call, "I will come to your apartment to pick you up at seven thirty. My residence is about four blocks from there. Would you mind walking? I do not have a car."

"That is fine with me. See you then. Thanks for the invitation."

When Saturday afternoon comes, Ilana is tired. She worked at the real estate office in the morning, and helped Gitel shop for groceries after they got home from work. Going to work means waiting for the bus to go west on Fifty-Fifth Street in the already cold weather, and then waiting to transfer to the bus to go south on Halsted. Coming home is a repeat in reverse. But the process is worse on Saturday, because the buses run less frequently. Shopping means carrying the groceries the three blocks from the co-op supermarket to home. By evening, Ilana is not much in the mood for going to a party. But she promised, so she starts to get dressed. She isn't sure of the proper dress for this kind of party; she's certain it is not the business clothes that she wears to work, and it probably is not the somewhat disreputable jeans that she wears to classes. She chooses a skirt over tights and a blouse and waits for Drew to arrive. As soon as she opens the door to him, he says, "Let's go. We are a little late." He does not greet either Gitel or Shmuel.

Drew and Ilana chat about not much of anything as they walk over to the dorm. Drew seems surprised that Ilana grew up in Hyde Park and went through public school. He seems somewhat leery of the neighborhood. He keeps looking behind them and to each side as they walk, as if he is frightened to be walking through the streets in the dark. He tenses up when a Negro man walking in the opposite direction passes them. Ilana smiles and says hello as the man walks by. Drew's behavior is a large mark against him in Ilana's mind. It suggests to her that he might be bigoted. He tells her, "I grew up in a mostly Jewish neighborhood in New Jersey. My high school was almost all Jewish students. In college, I did not mix with many non-Jews, although I am not particularly observant now."

*That he is not particularly observant is fine with me*, Ilana thinks. *But hanging out with only Jews is another mark against him. No wonder Hyde Park frightens him.*

They arrive at the residence, and Ilana looks around at the crowd of guys. Most are wearing slacks and blazers, so she is glad she has chosen a skirt. She thinks, *I must have inadvertently telegraphed some of my disapproval to Drew, because immediately after arriving he says he has to help with the food and leaves me on my own.* People are talking to each other in small groups scattered around the room. A lot of the guys must not have dates, because most of the people in the room are men.

A guy comes up to Ilana and says his name is Mitch. She introduces herself. He asks, "Are you a student at the university?"

"Yes, I am a second-year student in the college—an undergraduate. I transferred here from another school where I spent my first year and didn't like it at all. What are you studying?"

"I am a first-year graduate student in economics," Mitch explains.

They clearly are sizing each other up to determine whether

or not the other one is Jewish. Ilana decides that he probably is. Something about him seems interesting, so she decides to continue the conversation.

"I grew up here in Hyde Park and love the neighborhood. I hope that you will learn to enjoy it too."

"Would you be willing to show me around Hyde Park? I have not seen much of it yet. I just walk from the dorm to campus and back again."

"Perhaps, if there is a time when we are both free," Ilana replies. "I have a heavy course load and a part-time job, so I am very busy. Where are you from?"

"New York. I was born in the city but grew up in a Long Island suburb."

Ilana thinks, *I pretty much hate the suburban mentality, based on my observations in Park Forest. His growing up in a suburb gives me pause.* "Do you think suburbs are segregated and boring?" she asks.

"I rather agree with that. I went to college in the city of Baltimore, at Johns Hopkins University, and I appreciated the city atmosphere there."

Ilana thinks, *That makes me feel better.* She asks him, "Do you agree with Milton Friedman's economic theories?"

"Yes, I generally do. He is a brilliant man."

That answer gives Ilana some concern. *I'll let it go,* she thinks, *because he seems so pleasant. But I'm not sure of his politics. That is critical. I'd never go out with a conservative. What if he's a Goldwater supporter?*

Around that time, Drew returns to interrupt them. He asks if Ilana wants to dance with him. Ilana feels she should, since she had accepted the date. They have a decent time dancing and talking about not much of anything. Every few dances he excuses himself to take care of something, and each time Mitch quickly comes over to talk to her. He says that dancing isn't his thing. Eventually the party is over and Drew dutifully walks her back home. *And that is the end of that,* she thinks. *A pleasant enough evening, especially talking to Mitch. But I wouldn't accept another date with Drew. He doesn't seem to have much personality at all.*

Afterward, she realizes that she didn't ask for Mitch's last name, and she never told him hers. She thinks that she probably will not see him again.

# 48

Gitel is waiting up for Ilana when she comes home around ten thirty. She asks her what she thinks of Drew.

"I don't think much of him. He doesn't seem to have anything interesting to say. Something of a dud. Could you find a polite way to tell his aunt that we didn't hit it off?"

"No need to worry. His aunt will just be happy that you gave it a try."

"There was a nice guy at the party named Mitch," Ilana says. "I don't know his last name. I talked with him a bit. But I doubt I'll ever see him again."

Ilana continues her schedule of going to the university, going to work, and studying most evenings and through the weekend. But she seems to Gitel to be more lively and happier.

Gitel guesses what might be going on and asks her, "Have you seen Mitch around campus?"

"Yes, I have. We often eat lunch together."

Gitel just says that she is glad to hear that. She doesn't want to pry into Ilana's affairs for fear of upsetting something that seems good for her.

Shmuel's health continues to decline. He has difficulty getting up from his chair to go to the bathroom when he is alone during the day. He is supposed to use a walker for support, which they put in front of his chair before they leave for work and school. But sometimes he pushes it aside and chooses not to use it. When that happens, Ilana often finds him on the floor when she comes home after classes. She picks him up and settles him back down, taking care of what it is that he needs at the time—fresh clothes, water, or food. But it is not a good situation for him, and also not for Ilana. It is upsetting for everyone. And there is a concern that Shmuel could seriously hurt himself when he falls. The doctors have no solutions, other than placing Shmuel in a nursing home. But he is totally against that. In any case, there is no way they could afford to pay nursing home fees. That is not covered under his Blue Cross health insurance, and there are no government programs that would cover the cost either.

# 49

Mitch keeps appearing everywhere Ilana goes on campus. She is not sure how he manages that. She usually eats her lunch at the C-Shop located in Mandel Hall. Most days, she brings lunch from home and just buys a drink or chips. The hard part is finding a table at which to eat; C-Shop is usually jammed with students around lunchtime. About a week after meeting Mitch, she notices that he is standing at a two-person table trying to get her attention as she scans the room for a spot. She goes over to him; he says that he has saved a seat for her and asks if she would like to join him. Ilana is a bit dumbfounded, but grateful for the seat. This scene is repeated day after day. Mitch somehow arrives at the C-Shop early enough to snag a two-person table and then waits until she comes to invite her to sit with him.

At other times, Mitch must have been unobtrusively following her. Very often when she walks out of a campus building after class, he is waiting to say hello to her. If it is the end of her classes for the day, he offers to walk her home. If it is earlier, he will walk with her to the library, her next class, or wherever she is going. She begins to wonder if he is attending his own classes, but he assures her that he is.

They usually talk as they walk around or have lunch together. At first, Mitch tries to convince her that he is politically conservative, because he is studying with the well-known conservative economist

Milton Friedman. She tells him that she is very liberal, and recounts some of her experiences growing up in Hyde Park, especially her interracial experiences and friends. That does not provoke any negative reaction from him. Ilana wonders if he is saying that he is politically conservative just to be sufficiently controversial to be interesting to her. As they spend more time together, it seems like that indeed is the case. He tells her about his left-wing parents and uncle, and it seems that he, too, is quite liberal.

Mitch also tells Ilana about his family. "My mother died of cancer when I was in high school. I watched her get sicker and sicker, and then she died," he explains. "It was terrible. Then, long before I finished grieving, my father met this woman and decided to marry her. She and her two children moved into our house. She only cared about her own children, and found ways to isolate and ignore me. And my father, if he even noticed, was no help to me. I felt very lonely, and I was so glad to finish high school and go away to college."

Ilana tells Mitch the sad story of Shmuel. "I well understand what you are saying, and I'm so sorry it happened to you. I effectively lost my father when I was ten, when he had a major stroke. Most of the time, he was someone I had to take care of. Although there were a few better times, I watched him deteriorate. Right now, he can't do much other than sit all day staring into space. I don't think he has much longer to live, but who knows? It sounds as if both of us have had to overcome difficult family situations."

It is not long until Ilana learns Mitch's class schedule and waits for him after his classes. Mitch asks her why she's doing that.

"Because I feel lonely when we can't be together," she replies.

"I do too. Very lonely. I am so glad I met you. Maybe there will be a time when we do not have to be apart so much."

In addition to being together on campus as much as possible, they usually go out on dates on Saturday evenings and spend time together on Sundays, unless one of them has too much studying to do.

Around this time Ilana tells Gitel about Mitch, and how they feel about each other. "Mitch and I are getting closer and closer. We wait for each other after our classes, and we have lunch together. We both feel lonely if we are not together. I think I am in love with him. He is so thoughtful and kind. And very smart."

"I'm glad you have found each other," Gitel says. "Would you like to invite him to dinner on Sunday evening? That is when we would have time to shop for food and cook a decent meal."

"That is a great idea! I will invite him."

Mitch is happy to accept the invitation to eat dinner at their apartment and meet her parents. Ilana spends some time telling him more about the sad story of her father. "I hope you won't be put off by the way my father looks or eats."

"Of course not," Mitch replies. "I will not be upset. I understand how difficult it must be for you to live with that situation."

"I should also mention that my mother is not a great cook," Ilana adds.

"It undoubtedly will be a better dinner than what I would otherwise cook for myself in the kitchen of my dorm room. You should not worry. I am delighted by the invitation. All will be well."

Gitel and Ilana cook Gitel's signature baked chicken recipe, which Ilana thinks is pretty good. Gitel also makes a savory *kugel*, which Ilana loves and hopes Mitch will too. Gitel usually does not cook fresh vegetables, preferring to heat up the canned variety. While they are shopping, Ilana suggests that she could make a salad to go with the meal rather than a cooked vegetable.

"At Faye's house," she tells Gitel, "they eat salad with every dinner. I learned to make salad when I was taking care of the family."

"Sure. That is a good idea."

They buy vegetables for the salad and some bottled salad dressing. Gitel also chooses a chocolate cake for dessert.

"I served chocolate cake to Joe when he was courting Faye, and all indications are that it did the trick," Gitel says. "So, I want to serve it to Mitch as well. Not that I want you to get married yet, while you are still in college. But if you like Mitch enough to bring him home, he should have cake too."

The dinner comes off very well. Mitch is very cordial and friendly to Ilana's parents. He even tries to engage her father in conversation, with a little bit of success. Shmuel seems happy about the effort, because he is smiling. *It is pretty easy and almost natural for people who come to our apartment to just ignore Dad, as if he were an unmoving piece of furniture*, Ilana thinks. *But Mitch didn't do that. I love the fact that he treated Dad as a human being.*

# 50

Gitel is so thrilled with the Sunday dinner that she calls Sophie to tell her about it.

"I found Mitch to be charming. This is the first time Ilana has brought home someone I consider a suitable match for her, one who she says she might be serious about," Gitel explains. "Kevin, her boyfriend in her senior year of high school, might have been suitable, but she was clear that she was not in love with him. From the way Ilana talks about Mitch and how she looks at him, I can see that her relationship with Mitch is quite different."

"*Nu*, what is so suitable about him?"

"To start with, he is Jewish. His family is non-observant and he doesn't know much about Judaism, but nevertheless he's Jewish. If Ilana decides to care about that, which she doesn't right now, she can always teach him. He is a graduate student at U of C in economics. Despite that, he is politically liberal. And he is a nice guy. He even made an effort to talk to Shmuel and engage him. He gets a lot of credit for that."

"But Ilana is only in her second year of college. Do you think she might want to get married and drop out of school?" Sophie asks.

"I do worry about that. I can fully understand if she wants to leave behind all the problems of our family and create a different family situation and a different life. Marriage certainly could look attractive to her. But I think she is determined to get a college education. We'll have to see what happens."

Gitel suggests to Ilana that they invite Mitch to Sunday dinner every week. Gitel thinks, *It would be better for me to see firsthand how their relationship is developing.* Ilana says that she will talk to Mitch about that, agreeing that it's a wonderful idea.

Gitel decides to talk to Ilana about her concerns that she might not finish college.

"Ilana, you know what my life has been like, and my conviction that my life would have been so much easier and better if my parents had allowed me to go to college."

"I understand how frustrating that has been for you. I know that you are a smart person and are capable of doing much more important and interesting jobs than you can get without that education," Ilana replies. "And I assure you that I intend to finish college, even if I do get married—although marriage isn't really what I'm thinking about now. With everything that has happened to our family, I want to make sure that I can make a good living on my own. I never want to be dependent on any man for support. I'm actually worried that Faye is in that position now. Without having passed the bar exam, she probably cannot earn enough to support herself and the children if there were any reason to have to do so. If growing up in this family has taught me anything, it is that one never can know what might happen."

"I'm delighted and relieved to hear that you are thinking that way." *I promise myself that I will stop worrying about her. She really does have good sense,* Gitel thinks.

Gitel asks Ilana what she plans to do for the summer. She says that Mitch has to go back to New York to stay with his family during the summer, and to take up his usual summer job of house painting. He can't afford to stay in Chicago; his fellowship covers his tuition and some of his living expenses, but he needs to save the money he earns over the summer for his expenses in the next school year. His family is not helping him financially at all, even though he thinks they could. But his father had paid for his college years, so he says he doesn't have that much to complain about—especially in comparison to her situation. Ilana certainly understands his need to work and save money for the next school year. She says she hopes to do the same.

Ilana asks Gitel if she would be able to work at the real estate agency full-time this summer. Gitel says that she can. Her assistant again doesn't want to work much in the summer because her children are off from school. "I trust that you have learned enough of my job that I can take some vacation this summer. I'm entitled to two weeks of paid vacation each year, but I didn't take any last year. I'm hoping I will be able to take a little more than two weeks this summer, while you essentially do my job."

Gitel asks Ilana how she feels about being apart from Mitch for the summer. Ilana shrugs and says that she has no choice. "We've decided not to write a lot of letters back and forth, and just to think about one other. We'll see if we both feel the same about each other when summer ends."

# 51

The summer passes; Ilana begins college as a third-year student, and Mitch returns to town. After he returns, Gitel barely sees Ilana except at work. At all other times, she seems to be with Mitch. She does come home to sleep at night, but late, often after Gitel has gotten Shmuel in bed and gone to sleep herself. Gitel is anxious to know what is going to happen between Ilana and Mitch, but she keeps quiet and just waits.

In the meantime, Gitel sorely misses Ilana's help around the apartment and with Shmuel. Ilana no longer cooks dinners, except on Sunday when Mitch comes to eat with them. And she no longer comes home in the afternoon to check on Shmuel. Whatever he needs, he has to wait until Gitel comes home from work. That is hard on him. But Gitel feels that Ilana is finally entitled to her own life. She doesn't complain to her or even mention the issue, thinking that circumstances have already deprived Ilana of so much.

One evening in early October 1965, Ilana and Mitch come to the apartment in the early evening. They burst in smiling widely and giggling a bit.

"We are engaged! And we want to be married soon. We can't stand to be apart. What about Thanksgiving weekend?" they ask, tripping over each other's words. "We just want a small wedding, nothing fancy," they assure Gitel. "We will figure something out. You don't need to do a lot of planning or organizing for the wedding. We know that your plate is full with your job and Shmuel."

"*Mazel tov!* Have you told Faye?"

"We plan to call her just after talking to you."

"Faye might have some ideas for the wedding, and might even be happy to organize it," Gitel suggests. "You should tell your father, even though he may or may not understand."

"Of course." Ilana and Mitch go over to where Shmuel is sitting in his chair. "Daddy," Ilana says, "Mitch and I are engaged and hope to be married around the time of Thanksgiving."

"*Mazel tov.* Mitch, you seem like a nice guy. Be sure to take proper care of my daughter," Shmuel manages to say—surprising everyone.

Gitel talks to Faye after Ilana has delivered the news. Faye is very happy for Ilana. She and Joe have met Mitch, when Ilana and Mitch came to visit them on several weekends, and think that he is perfect for Ilana. "We offered them the option of getting married in our living room, with our Reform rabbi performing the ceremony," Faye says. "Ilana and Mitch accepted, saying that would be perfect. We also offered to finance a dinner for the guests at Mickelberry's Restaurant, the best one in Park Forest. They thanked us and said that would be lovely."

"I'm so pleased. That is so generous of you and Joe," Gitel replies. "Ilana and Mitch say they only intend to have about thirty-five guests at the wedding, but I would not be able to pay for the dinner. Thank you so much for taking that over."

Over the next few weeks, Gitel begins to think about what she will do after Ilana is married. She alerts the rental office of their building, saying that she and Shmuel would like to switch to a one-bedroom apartment. She can't see any value in keeping the room she had set up for Ilana. Ilana and Mitch will be getting their own apartment.

They had applied to the university for married student housing and were offered and accepted an affordable one-bedroom apartment on Fifty-Fourth Place near Greenwood. *If Shmuel and I move*, Gitel thinks, *we could allow Ilana to take the furniture from her room to their own apartment. That would be a major gift for them.*

The wedding is planned for the Saturday evening of Thanksgiving weekend. Faye has invited Mitch's parents—his father and step-mother—and his sister to Thanksgiving dinner on Thursday. Shmuel and Gitel and Mitch and Ilana also go to Faye and Joe's for the dinner. Mitch has rented a car for the weekend. He helps Shmuel get down to the car and drives to Park Forest for the Thanksgiving dinner and back to Hyde Park afterward, managing to get Shmuel back to the apartment and settled in. Mitch's family had rented a car from the airport, and went back to their downtown hotel after the dinner.

For the wedding, they are expecting Gitel's three brothers who still live in South Bend and their wives, a few cousins who live in the Chicago area, and some friends of Mitch and Ilana. But on Saturday morning, a massive blizzard begins dumping many inches of snow on the roads. Luckily, people who live in the Chicago area or South Bend are accustomed to driving in severe winter conditions, so most of the guests make it to the wedding.

At the wedding, Joe walks Ilana down the aisle; there is no way that Shmuel can do it. Faye is the matron of honor, and the best man is a close friend of Mitch's from college. Faye and Joe's youngest child, five-year-old Rose, is the flower girl. Ilana and Mitch had intended to use recorded music to play as they walk down the short aisle that is the length of Faye and Joe's living room. But Gitel insists that Ilana ask the mother of one of Ilana's friends, who is a professional pianist, if she would play at the wedding. Ilana and Mitch were skeptical of the idea, but it can be impossible to deny Gitel when she insists. The pianist agrees, but it all turns out to be a bit awkward. Faye and Joe's piano is in their basement recreation room, not in the living room. It certainly can be heard if the door is open, but Ilana has the sense that the pianist is insulted. In the end, the recorded music would have been better.

At the restaurant, Faye and Joe paid for a glass of champagne for everyone to toast the bride and groom, but not for an open bar. That makes Mitch's father uncomfortable, so he steps up to treat everyone to whatever they want to drink. There is no music or place to dance, but some guests decide to sing and dance around the tables. It is very informal and a lot of fun. Shmuel is not able to participate, but he looks happy just sitting and taking in the scene.

Gitel is able to give Ilana and Mitch fifty dollars to buy staples for the kitchen in their new apartment, such as spices and flour. They are very appreciative. "Thank you so much, Mama. Our food budget will be twelve dollars per week, from my earnings. It will be so helpful to have the basics already in our pantry," Ilana says. "We've given a lot of thought to our finances. Mitch's fellowship is not sufficient to pay a full year's rent, so he will teach a statistics course at the University of Illinois in Chicago to supplement our income. I think we will be able to manage very well."

Gitel and Shmuel move to a one-bedroom apartment in their building. But they do not stay there long, only about six months. Shmuel's condition continues to deteriorate. He is not able to walk to the bathroom during the day, or get anything from the kitchen. He can't even turn on a light or change the channel on the television. Gitel thinks, *It no longer is right or fair to leave him alone while I go to work.*

Gitel calls Faye to ask her opinion on what she should do.

Apparently, Faye had already been thinking about the problem. Faye says, "There is a small ranch-style house for sale a block away from our house. Joe and I would be willing to buy it and move you and Shmuel to that house. You would be close to me, so I could help you take care of Dad when I am not looking after the children. They are all in school during the day now, or in camp in the summer. You could quit your job and just look after Shmuel."

Gitel thinks about Faye's proposal. *If we don't have to pay rent, we could live on Shmuel's Social Security benefits. If I stop working, there would be a supplemental benefit for me. According to Faye, the people selling the house are willing to sell some of their existing furniture at a low price, particularly the items that were in the family room, and Faye said she and Joe could pay for that.*

Gitel says to Faye, "That is very generous of you and Joe. Once again! I don't see any other solution on the horizon, so I gratefully accept your proposal. I will give notice to my boss, and organize our stuff to move as soon as possible."

The house has both a living room and a family room behind the kitchen, with two bedrooms. Gitel just moves their living room and bedroom furniture, their pots and pans and dishes, and their personal possessions.

A month later, Gitel and Shmuel are settling in at the small house in Park Forest. There is nothing for Gitel to do while living there, except stare at Shmuel all day. She has never driven or owned a car, so she cannot even go shopping. There is nowhere interesting for her to walk, only streets with more houses. And almost no one walks around in the suburb. The sidewalks are usually empty. Having lived in lively neighborhoods in Chicago for so long, she finds it difficult to adjust to this new situation.

Gitel plays many games of solitaire, and she begins to watch the soap operas on daytime television. She has always made fun of women who watch the soaps, but now they are something of a lifeline for her. While she watches the trials and tribulations of the characters, she sometimes can forget how lonely and sad she is.

Faye repeatedly tells Gitel that she is willing to drive her wherever she wants to go, but there is no place in town to which Gitel is interested in going. Park Forest is a bedroom suburb in every sense. Nothing happens there during the day that she can see. Men go into the city to work, and women take care of their families, drive their children around to school and activities, cook, and garden. Faye's children are old enough to walk the block from their house to this one, but they rarely do. They have told Faye that they find it rather disconcerting to see Shmuel in his current state.

Ilana and Mitch, having bought a seventeen-year-old Cadillac limousine on a bit of a whim, often drive out on Sundays. They help get Shmuel into his wheelchair and push it to Faye's house, where they all have dinner. That gives Gitel a bit of a respite from her loneliness and isolation.

1966 slides into 1967, with nothing much changing. Faye takes Gitel to a meeting of the local chapter of the National Council of Jewish Women, a grassroots social justice organization in which she is active. Faye hopes Gitel might like to join the organization, or at least meet some women with whom she could be friends.

Gitel tells Faye after the meeting, "I approve of the group's mission and work. But I can't volunteer to do anything useful or even regularly attend meetings, given Shmuel's needs. It is nice to be out of the house for a little bit, but it isn't the solution to my problem." There is, in fact, no solution. Shmuel's health is not going to improve, and there is no one other than her to take care of him. So she has to endure, as she has done so many times in her lifetime. She thinks, *I hate to say it, but I wonder how long Shmuel could possibly live in his state. He has never explicitly said this, but I imagine that he would feel relief if he no longer had to live.*

As the year turns again to spring and then summer, life becomes a little more pleasant. There is a small patio and grassy area behind the house that can be accessed without navigating any steps. Gitel is able to move Shmuel outside in his wheelchair for periods of time when the weather is nice. That alleviates some of the shut-in feelings she is experiencing. There are no fences between the houses on this block, so sometimes neighbors wander over to talk a bit. From the patio, it is possible to see children playing outside the houses on this block and the one behind it, which is pleasant to watch.

In June, Ilana graduates from the college at The University of Chicago. Gitel goes to the ceremony. Faye drives her to the train to take her to Hyde Park, and she agrees to stay with Shmuel until Gitel gets back. Gitel is sure that Faye would have liked to be at the graduation as well, but Faye says it is more important that Ilana's mother be there. Mitch's parents come in from New York for the ceremony. Gitel thinks, *I am relieved that Ilana has finished. In the back of my mind, I had a fear that the pressure of being married and running a household, combined with the strain of their meager financial resources, would discourage Ilana from finishing, even though she insisted to me that she intended to graduate.* Ilana has already accepted a job with the federal government's Office of Economic Opportunity in a downtown Chicago office at a good salary, so she is all set. Mitch is planning on continuing in graduate school while Ilana works for a few years. She has not decided what kind of work she wants to do long-term, so she is happy to just earn some money for a while. Mitch needs to stay in school two more years, until he is twenty-six years old, to avoid being drafted for the Vietnam War.

The excitement having finished, Gitel's boredom returns. Faye's two oldest boys, who are ten and twelve, sometimes visit her after school but never stay very long. Faye sometimes comes over while her kids are in school, and Ilana and Mitch try to come out every other weekend or so. But all that is no substitute for having a job or regular volunteer work. There isn't much Gitel can do except stare at Shmuel, play endless games of solitaire, watch TV, or read. As the weather grows colder and they have to stay inside, her sense of confinement increases.

Faye and Joe take their children to the Reform temple to which they belong for Friday evening services most weeks. They think about trying to take Shmuel, but decide against it. It would be a big job to get him there, and he likely wouldn't even recognize what took place there as a prayer service. It bore little resemblance to an Orthodox service. They tried taking him to one service on Rosh Hashanah in September, but he didn't want to stay. They gave up on that idea.

Gitel is looking forward to Thanksgiving on November 23. The family plans to gather at Faye's house, including Ilana and Mitch and Joe's mother. They would celebrate Ilana and Mitch's second wedding anniversary a few days early. When Thanksgiving Day arrives, Shmuel seems to be a little sick with a runny nose and a mild cough. He insists that he is fine and wants to go to the dinner at Faye's. Gitel asks Faye to send a couple of her boys to help. They bundle Shmuel up against the cold, and wheel him up the street. All goes well at the dinner, with Faye's four children behaving themselves and paying a lot of attention to Gitel and Shmuel. Ilana and Mitch plan to stay overnight at Gitel and Shmuel's house, so there will be an extra day to visit with them.

Gitel tries to ask Ilana about her job, but she seems unwilling to say much about it. She does say a little. "I took a trip with the head of my office to visit some tribes in Northern Minnesota that are getting support from our programs. The tribal people were interesting, but I am not happy with my boss." She declines to say any more, which makes Gitel fidget a bit. Ilana does say that she is in the process of looking for a different job and has a few good leads. Gitel assumes that Ilana knows what she is doing, as she has in past situations. Gitel just says, "If you feel your job isn't right for you, it is good that you are looking for another one."

Shmuel continues to feel somewhat sick during the week after Thanksgiving. On the subsequent weekend, he seems to have trouble breathing. Gitel asks Joe to come take a look at him. Joe thinks he should be in the hospital. He contacts a friend of his who is an internal medicine doctor, who has seen Shmuel a couple of times. He arranges for Shmuel to be admitted to the hospital in nearby Chicago Heights where they both practice, late in the day on Saturday, December 3. Joe tells Gitel that she probably should ask Ilana and Mitch to meet them at the hospital. Shmuel seems quite sick to him.

When Gitel calls Ilana, Mitch answers. He says that Ilana has a bad cold or the flu, and is running a fever. Gitel says that they probably should meet her at the hospital anyway. The doctor thinks this might be the end for Shmuel.

When Ilana and Mitch arrive at the hospital at around 9:00 p.m., Shmuel seems more lucid than usual. For a little while, they think that is a good sign. He takes one look at Ilana and says, "You look green. You should go home and rest." Ilana tells him that she has a cold but will be all right. He then asks all of them to go home, says "goombye" (as he likes to jokingly do), and says that he loves everyone.

Gitel is a bit suspicious. Why did Shmuel seem to be in such a good mood? He rarely talks at all, but tonight he had a lot to say. The doctors are sure that he has pneumonia, so why doesn't he feel bad? She wonders if he has made an agreement with the doctors to not treat the pneumonia, to not take any antibiotics or other medications. Gitel wonders if he has decided that he's had enough of his constrained life. Could the prospect of his life ending make him act upbeat? She would never know for sure.

They do leave the hospital. Ilana and Mitch go back to Gitel's house to stay overnight, and Joe returns home. Faye had stayed back with their children. They all fall asleep and are still in bed when the phone rings at Gitel's house at 6:00 a.m. It is a nurse telling them that Shmuel has passed away during the night. She says that they should make arrangements to have his body picked up, preferably sometime this morning.

Gitel tells Ilana and Mitch, but it isn't up to them to make arrangements. She is reluctant to wake Faye that early, so she waits an hour before she calls her. Faye says that she or Joe will talk to their rabbi and contact whatever funeral home he recommends. They will also ask him if he would officiate at the funeral. Gitel is pretty sure that he is not the kind of rabbi that Shmuel would have wanted, but there is nothing else to do except to follow Faye's lead. Gitel doesn't know whether there are any different resources in the area that she could tap.

Faye arranges for the funeral home to take Shmuel's body from the hospital. She picks Gitel up and they go to the funeral home together to choose a casket. Gitel knows that Shmuel would have wanted a plain pine box, which is the standard for Jewish burials. But the funeral home is not able to provide that kind of casket, so they settle on the least expensive wooden casket that is available. Faye says that she and Joe will take care of the cost of the casket and the services provided by funeral home, including a room to have a service before the burial. They also will arrange for a burial plot in the cemetery that their temple uses. It is called Beverly Cemetery, far south on South Kedzie Avenue in the town of Blue Island. The service and burial would take place the next day, on Monday, December 5.

Ilana and Mitch have to make a quick trip home so they can pick up some suitable clothes to wear to the funeral. Ilana is planning to stay with Gitel for the subsequent week of the shiva, so she needs to bring back clothes and toiletries. Mitch drops her off at Gitel's house in the late afternoon, after the funeral, and then returns to Hyde Park for classes and teaching obligations. Ilana tells Gitel that she left a message at her office, saying that her father had died and that she couldn't come to work for the next week. The boss's secretary is Jewish, so she will understand and explain to others.

Gitel isn't sure how she feels about Shmuel's death. She thinks, *I above all people understand how bad his quality of life has been these past few years. I can easily believe that he wanted to end the struggle. I remember that some years ago he explained to me that Jewish law was somewhat ambiguous and complicated about whether a patient could refuse certain treatments for an illness. He felt that in some situations, refusal could be permitted. I wasn't paying that much attention as he explained the points of view of various authorities. My eyes usually glazed over and my attention wandered whenever he tried to explain Jewish law, and that time was no different. But looking back, I can imagine why he was trying to explain all that to me.*

The funeral happens. The immediate family, Gitel's brother Aisik and his wife, and a few of Faye's friends come to the funeral home. Gitel's brothers Hirsh and Nokhem had several years before moved to California. They couldn't come on short notice, so they sent telegrams, as did a few other family members. Shmuel had no longer been in contact with any of his friends or colleagues. The rabbi doesn't know much about Shmuel, so he gives a largely anodyne eulogy. Neither Ilana nor Faye is willing to speak at the funeral. Gitel speaks a bit about how they met and just a little about their lives together—avoiding difficult issues. Afterward they travel to the cemetery and bury him there. The family says the mourner's kaddish and fills dirt into the grave on top of the casket, as is the tradition. Then they all go back to Faye's where her friend has prepared a traditional meal of consolation for the immediate family, and they prepare to begin the shiva period, the seven days of mourning.

# 52

Ilana is still pretty sick at the time of the funeral, so most of it goes by her in a blur. She has never been to a funeral before, so she has no idea if things are being done well or not. Ilana observes that Gitel seems unhappy with the rabbi's eulogy. She thinks, *It is too bad that someone who knew my father better couldn't have officiated, such as his rabbi at Hyde Park Hebrew Center, but I guess that was impossible for them to arrange.*

The shiva week is difficult for Ilana. Since it is at Faye's house, it isn't possible for her own friends to come; it is just too far. Even if they took the train, someone would have to pick them up at the train station and drive them to the house. Ilana had recently learned to drive, but doesn't feel confident driving around in the winter. And it wouldn't be appropriate for her, as a mourner, to go pick them up anyway. Thus, everyone who comes is a friend or acquaintance of Faye's. Ilana suspects that Gitel feels as excluded as she does, but they don't talk about it.

Ilana also is concerned and distracted because she has been looking for a new job and had planned to leave her current one at the end of December. She has a few different potential jobs she has been pursuing, but she can't follow up during the shiva because that would be inappropriate. A mourner is just supposed to mourn. It also is going to be awkward to return to her current job and soon after tell them she is leaving.

Ilana thinks, *I don't feel as sad as I think I should feel. I feel like I had mostly lost my father ten years ago, and then again when he had his second stroke. It has been so clear for the past few years that he is unhappy with his situation and limitations. I feel that I am glad for him, that his struggle is over. But I have to go through the ritual mourning nevertheless.*

# 53

Shiva is over, Ilana has returned to the city, and Gitel is alone in this house, which in her view is in the middle of nowhere. *I certainly don't want to stay here much longer,* Gitel thinks. *It is nice to be close to my grandchildren, but they have school, lots of activities, and generally busy lives. I don't see them much more than I did when we were living in Hyde Park. And I miss working. There is nothing like a boss telling me that I have done a really good job. And, if I say so myself, I always do a good job at work.*

As Gitel thinks, she realizes that for the first time in her life, she is free. She was under a tight rein as she was growing up; she couldn't do many of the things that she most wanted to do, including going to college. Even though she worked for a while before she got married, she still lived in her parents' house and needed to abide by their rules and preferences. Could she have made choices that gave her more freedom back then? Could she have been more like Ilana? Could she have been confident about what she wanted to do and figured out how to achieve her goals? What if she had insisted to her parents about going to college, and not let them say no to her? What if she had tried to get a scholarship to a college, succeeded, and moved away from home to attend? Would lightning have struck her?

And what about her choice to marry Shmuel? She knew about his mother dying when he was born and his early malnutrition. She knew about how a serious case of meningitis had postponed pharmacy school for him. Should she have taken those as a clue to his future *shlekht mazel*, his persistent bad luck? Was she too dazzled by his intelligence and knowledge, his activism and care for the poor, to see or think clearly? To say nothing of his good looks!

Once she married and soon after had Faye, of course, her life was linked to the welfare of Shmuel and Faye. And later there was Ilana. She thinks, *I love my family, but I felt anything but free. Now I am free! Shmuel is gone, and Faye and Ilana are married and living their own lives. I can make any decisions I want to about my life. I just have to get used to that situation, and act on it.*

Gitel is sixty years old. Her mother Rayzel lived to be close to eighty. She might have at least twenty years to live, so she feels it would be stupid to sit still and do nothing. She thinks, *I need a plan! I need to decide on a plan and make it happen!* Right now, she is entitled to continue receiving Shmuel's monthly Social Security payment if she is not working, but she doesn't have any resources beyond that. Their savings were used up long ago. If she wants to move back to the city, she needs to first find a job and work long enough to afford the security deposit on an apartment. *Or*, she thinks, *maybe Faye would loan me the money for a security deposit so I wouldn't have to commute to a job from here for long. Affording taxis to and from the train station and the train tickets could be difficult initially.*

Gitel begins looking at the help wanted ads in the *Sun-Times* newspaper that is delivered to her each day. After a couple of weeks, she sees one that looks very appealing. It is for a person to manage the bookkeeping department at a large food-service organization, the kind that has concessions to run cafeterias and other types of food service in museums, public buildings, institutions, and corporations. She calls the number listed in the ad and speaks to someone briefly about her qualifications. The person suggests an appointment for her to come to the office for an interview, and she readily accepts.

She needs to type out a résumé but doesn't have a typewriter. She asks Faye, who says they have an old manual typewriter she can use, and Faye brings it over to Gitel's house. Thinking about how to do the résumé, she decides to list her birthdate as 1912, so they would think that she is only fifty-five years old. She knows that there is no good way they can check; she has neither a birth certificate nor a driver's license. If by any chance they write to Social Security to check her age, she would just claim that it got recorded incorrectly when she naturalized and that she had never gone to the bother of fixing it. But she is sure that they would have no reason to check.

The office is located on Michigan Avenue in the Loop, so it is not difficult to get there for the interview. She meets with a few different people there, and can tell they are impressed with her knowledge of bookkeeping and her overall attitude. They tell her that there are several young women working in the bookkeeping department to enter data, and they are looking for someone mature to run the department and insure its stability. That is a good sign.

Gitel asks about the pay and benefits, noting that she would need health insurance. The pay, at $9,000 a year, is more than she had been earning at the real estate job, and there are adequate benefits. She leaves the interviews feeling pretty good. They promise they will call her within the next two weeks.

While she is in the city, she decides to look around for an apartment to rent. There are a lot of choices she could make. She could move back to Hyde Park where she knows people and could be close to Sophie. But Hyde Park also holds a lot of sad and upsetting memories for her, among them the day in 1956 when Shmuel had his first stroke, the visit from the FBI, and her largely unsuccessful battle against Bret Harte's anti-Semitic principal.

She thought a lot about Sophie while she was in "suburban exile" with Shmuel. If she is going to move back to Hyde Park, she considers whether she might want to try to get an apartment in the Algonquin, where Sophie lives. But maybe that would be too close. She doesn't fully understand her feelings and reactions—often intense—when she is with Sophie. She thinks, *I find being with Sophie both wonderful and frightening. It is frightening because my feelings seem wrong in some incomprehensible way. I'd like to talk to Sophie about my feelings, but I'm afraid I'd lose her as a friend. I certainly want to keep seeing her, but maybe some distance would be a good idea.*

Gitel always has imagined that it would be nice to live in one of the high-rise buildings on North Lake Shore Drive, in an apartment with a view of the lake. Especially one that is not too far north, so it would be relatively quick to take the bus to the Loop. She takes a bus up Lake Shore Drive for a few stops, then gets off and goes in and out of the apartment buildings, asking whether they have small apartments for rent. She thinks she would be fine living in a studio apartment, as she doesn't need or want anything larger just for herself, especially since she will be out of the apartment working all day. She also knows that these apartments are unlikely to be advertised. Many buildings depend on people asking in person as a form of silent discrimination. Gitel isn't happy about taking advantage of that phenomenon, but she doesn't see any alternative.

Three of the buildings she visits do have vacancies for studio apartments. The rents are around $150 per month. She thinks that is a lot for a studio, because just a couple years ago, before moving to Park Forest, they had paid $175 for a large two-bedroom apartment. She guesses that is the difference between Hyde Park and the

Gold Coast—as the strip of housing along North Lake Shore Drive is called. Nevertheless, she thinks it will be affordable if she gets the job at the food-service company. She has calculated that after taxes, she would have take-home pay of about $550 a month. Gitel tells the rental agents at the buildings that she is not yet ready to commit, but hopes she will be soon. Then she takes a bus back to the Randolph Street train station and returns to Park Forest, taking a taxi from the 211th Street station to her sad little house.

Two days later, the company calls to offer her the job. She accepts.

She asks Faye, "Do you think you and Joe could lend me the money to start my new life? I need three hundred dollars for a security deposit and first month's rent, money to pay movers, and enough to live on until I get my first paycheck."

"I will talk to Joe and let you know," Faye says. "I think we can probably do that, but I don't want to be definite until I have a chance to ask him about it."

Gitel plans to sell some of the furniture she no longer needs and use that money to buy some pieces more suited to a studio apartment. She has in mind to buy two living room chairs that open out into single beds, rather than moving one of the twin beds. She is sure she will not mind opening it to sleep on each night, as she did all those years that she and Shmuel slept on pull-down Murphy beds. When Faye asks her how the arrangements are going, she says, "I prefer the one-room studio apartment to look like a living room so I will be comfortable having guests. I have a couch, a coffee table, and an end table to put between the chairs that I will move. Other than those pieces, I just will need to move my clothes, a dresser, and kitchen things. I have never liked cleaning apartments, so I am happy to live simply."

Now that she knows that she can afford the apartment, she decides to rent one at 1350-60 North Lake Shore Drive. The buildings are modern twin towers, built in the 1950s. Faye and Joe are willing to lend her the money she needs to get started, so she again takes the train downtown and the short bus ride to the apartment to close the deal. She has agreed to start work in two weeks to give herself time to make the move, so she rents the apartment, starting in ten days. Then she goes back to Park Forest to arrange for movers and figure out how to sell the furniture.

Gitel is practically jumping up and down when her moving day arrives. She bustles about checking every box that is to be moved several times. She thinks, *I am about to start my life as a free person.*

Her new life is indeed working out well for her. Since the company manages cafeterias, they have one in their building for employees to eat lunch. She can have her substantial meal of the day there and then just needs a light dinner after work—meaning she rarely, if ever, has to cook. And it is nice to sit with some of her coworkers at lunch and get to know them.

Working in the Loop, she has many choices of what to do after work. There are many inexpensive restaurants for dinner or a snack if she decides to stay downtown to go to a movie, a play, or a dance performance. Sometimes Sophie will join her for dinner or entertainment if her husband is working the dinner shift. Sometimes they will go together to volunteer at the downtown offices of the IVI or AJC. There's always something important needing doing at one or the other of the organizations.

Gitel has time on weekends to visit Faye's family, or see Ilana and Mitch, or to catch up with several different cousins who live in the city. For the last ten years that Shmuel was sick, there was not time to visit anyone.

Gitel also finds a foursome for playing bridge in her apartment building, which she loves to do but hasn't done for many years, and she has met other tenants. She tells Sophie during one of the times they get together, "This is the life I always have wanted. A good job, a good friend, and interesting acquaintances, free time, and few obligations."

Sophie replies, "You deserve it."

Gitel thinks, *I hope this isn't too good to be true. I hope Shmuel's bad luck has died with him, and hasn't transferred to me. In truth, I do feel like I deserve some good luck after all the years and problems I have endured. I think back on how strong I was through it all. How I had the* khutspe *to ask for Ilana's Hebrew school scholarship, even though we weren't members of that* shul. *And how I successfully insisted that Pharmall make up the difference between the Workmen's Compensation and Shmuel's pay. And how I figured out how to get a job after all those years of not working and managed the job and the household. I also think back on all the successful leadership, programming, and fundraising I did for the AJC before I went back to work, and to all the improvements I made happen at Bret Harte when I was PTA president. I think Ilana learned how to go after what she wants and needs from my example, at least in part. I promise myself now, if I really want something in my new life, I will find a way to get it!*

# Author's Note

This book is based on my family's experience, but it is fiction. Portions of the text are based on actual happenings; other portions reflect my imagination of family events and the characters' reactions to those events. I attempted to be accurate about world and national historical events through which the characters lived. In two cases, however, I felt that I needed to change the names of locations to avoid giving a negative present-day impression of those places based on events that happened very long ago. Thus, the chain pharmacy at which Shmuel periodically worked, and the college in downstate Illinois that Ilana attended for one year, have fictitious names in the book.

Some of the characters are presented with their actual names, particularly Gitel's and Shmuel's parents and grandparents. Some others are given fictitious names, in part because they or their children are still alive.

There are several people who helped me as this book developed and evolved. My friend and neighbor Diana Zurer provided invaluable help with the Yiddish words and phrases. I grew up hearing a lot of Yiddish around me and, like the Ilana character, had to sort out my Yiddish from my English when I started school, but I never actually learned to speak it. Diana is fluent in Yiddish; I cannot thank her enough for her help. She also read and provided comments on a very early, somewhat different, version of this novel. Any mistakes in the Yiddish are undoubtedly my fault rather than Diana's. Thanks also goes to the Hyde Park Historical Society for helping me find bits of historical information. Genealogical research on my mother's family by Florence Minkow and on my father's family by Emily Lopatin also provided some background information.

Two editors gave me important feedback on this novel, both of whom were suggested to me by She Writes Press. After I wrote the first draft, which had more characters and points of view than the final novel, I received great advice on how to hone down the text in an editorial assessment by Jodi Fodor. A very helpful copy editing was subsequently done by Sheila Trask.

Several readers of early and near-final drafts gave great feedback. In addition to Diana Zurer, they include Aaron Lav, Heather Blair, Jonathan Warren, Michael and Michal Schneider, Rabbi Ethan Seidel, Jessica Weissman, and my husband Michael Lav. My husband and children Aaron, Daniel, and Jen have been unfailingly encouraging throughout this process.

I also thank all the wonderful folks at She Writes Press, especially the ever-encouraging publisher Brooke Warner and my editorial project manager Shannon Green.

# Resources

Several books and numerous websites were helpful during the writing process in refreshing my memories and providing additional information. They include:

Irving Cutler, *Chicago's Jewish West Side* (Arcadia Publishing, 2009)

Irving Cutler, *Jewish Chicago: A Pictorial History* (Arcadia Publishing, 2000)

Orlando Figes, *A People's Tragedy: The Russian Revolution 1891–1924* (Penguin, 1997)

David M. Kennedy, *The American People in the Great Depression: Freedom from Fear Part One* (Oxford University Press, 1999)

Bea Kraus and Norman D. Schwartz, *A Walk to Shul: Chicago Synagogues of Lawndale and Stops on the Way* (Priscilla Press, 2003)

Peter Martin, *The Landsmen*, ed. Matthew J. Bruccoli (Southern Illinois University Press, 1977)

Ida Maze, *Dineh: An Autobiographical Novel*, translated by Yermiyahu Ahron Taub (White Goat Press, 2022)

Todd Tucker, *Notre Dame vs. The Klan: How the Fighting Irish Defeated the Ku Klux Klan* (Loyola Press, 2004)

Michael Wex, *Born to Kvetch: Yiddish Language and Culture in All of Its Moods* (Harper Perennial, 2006)


## Selection of websites consulted:

Various articles on JewishGen.org

The YIVO Encyclopedia of Jews in Eastern Europe, https://yivoencyclopedia.org/article.aspx/Military_Service_in_Russia

https://www.britannica.com/summary/Great-Depression-Timeline

https://www.federalreservehistory.org/essays/bank-holiday-of-1933

https://www.history.com/topics/great-depression/works-progress-administration

https://www.theholocaustexplained.org/events-in-the-history-of-the-holocaust-1933-to-1939/

https://history.state.gov/milestones/1937-1945/american-isolationism#:~:text=Isolationists%20advocated%20non%2Dinvolvement%20in,its%20interests%20in%20Latin%20America

https://encyclopedia.ushmm.org/content/en/article/american-jewish-congress

https://www.history.com/topics/cold-war/huac

https://www.theatlantic.com/health/archive/2020/03/tuberculosis-sanatoriums-were-quarantine-experiment/608335/

https://economicarchitectureproject.org/rethinking-land-contracts/

## Glossary

*a dank* – thank you

*a groysn dank* – thank you very much

*antshuldik mir* – I am sorry, excuse me

*aufruf* – the Saturday before the wedding when the groom is called to
the Torah reading and the couple receives a blessing

*bagrisung tsu ir* – welcome

*bima* – Hebrew word; typically a raised area in the front of the synagogue where the reading table and pulpit are found

*bobe* – grandmother

*bris* – ritual circumcision

*daven* – to pray the prescribed prayers. Observant Jews pray three
times a day: first thing in the morning, in the afternoon, and in
the evening after sunset.

*der mentsh trakht un got lakht* – man plans and God laughs

*der shvakhinker* – the weakling

*dibuk* – demon, or soul of a dead person that has taken over the body
of a living person

*dos volt zeyn vunderlekh* – that would be wonderful

*farshteyt?* – do you understand?

*frum* – a word that describes Jews who are religiously observant, pious

*fun dayn moyel tzu gots oyer* – from your mouth to God's ears

*ganif* – thief

*Gemora* – an extensive set of commentaries created by sages and rabbis between the years 200 and 400 of the Common Era that through discussion and argument develop Jewish law. They are written in Hebrew and Aramaic and are especially difficult to decipher and study. Also referred to as Talmud.

*gey veys!* – go figure!

*gotenyu* – dear God

*Gott's dank* – thank God

*goyim* – Hebrew word for non-Jews

*gut morgn* – good morning

*gut shabbes* – good Sabbath. The traditional greeting before and during the Sabbath.

*halacha* – Hebrew word for Jewish law

*ikh vintsh dir ales gut* – I wish you everything good

*ilui* – a young Torah and Talmudic prodigy or genius

*kaddish* – the Aramaic memorial prayer said for a period of time after a close relative's death, and on the anniversary of their death *kaddish yatom* – mourner's prayer

*kashrus* – the process of keeping the kosher laws

*kaynehora* – no evil eye. Said to prevent a demon from being attracted to a person because of good fortune or good looks.

*khasene* – wedding

*kheder* – school for boys that taught Hebrew, the Bible, and Jewish ritual. In Belorussia, it was the only education most boys received. As the word continued to be used by immigrants in the United States, it most often referred to the supplemental Jewish education boys attended in addition to public school.

*kholile* – God forbid

*khutspe* – audacity. Often spelled *chutzpah* in English.

*kiddush* – the prayer said over wine, but widely used to denote the food served at a *shul* after the service

*kiddushin* – sanctification. A name for the wedding ceremony.

*kreplakh* – dumplings

*kugel* – a baked casserole that may be savory or sweet, usually made of noodles, potatoes, or vegetables

*Liebchen* – German word; used as a term of endearment

*lokshen* – noodles

*loshn hora* – literally, evil speech. It refers to gossip, which is a sin in Jewish law.

*mazel* – luck, but the literal meaning is constellation, referring to the stars controlling destiny.

*mazel tov* – traditional way to express congratulations

*mentsh* – literally, a man or human being. Used to describe a person of integrity, morality, dignity, with a sense of what is right and responsible.

*mikveh* – a ritual bath or bathing place for purification in accordance with Jewish law

*Mincha* – Hebrew word for the afternoon prayer service

*Modah Ani* – Hebrew; I am thankful, grateful. A reference to a prayer said immediately on waking up in the morning.

*nu* – so

*oy gevalt!* – oh violence! Used to express shock or amazement, or concern that there could have been a negative outcome. Similar to good grief, oh dear me, oh my gosh.

*oy, vey iz mir!* – oh, woe is to me!

*rakhmones* – mercy, compassion

*shabbes* – the Jewish Sabbath lasting from Friday at sunset to just after Saturday at sunset. Observant Jews refrain from any type of work on the Sabbath.

*shamus* – a person who takes care of a synagogue. The duties of a *shamus* vary from place to place.

*shed* – invisible Jewish demon said to prey on prosperous Jews

*She'ma* – Hebrew word; a shorthand reference to an important prayer that observant Jews say twice each day

*sheva brochos* – the seven blessings recited to a bride and groom after dinner for seven days after the day of the marriage. It is customary for seven different households to host the seven dinners.

*shiva* – the seven days of intense mourning following the death of a parent, spouse, sibling, or child. The mourners stay in the house, and people come to visit and pray with them.

*shlekht mazel* – bad luck

*shlep* – to drag; to go or move reluctantly with effort

*shlimazel* – someone to whom bad luck clings, a ne'er-do-well

*shmekel* – one of several words for penis in Yiddish

*shoykhet* – a person trained to slaughter poultry and meat in the ritually prescribed way

*shtralndik* – beaming (with happiness), radiant, jubilant

*shul* – synagogue

*tante* – aunt

*tefillin* – Hebrew word for phylacteries; two small boxes containing text that are placed on the arm and forehead for the morning prayer service

*Torah* – Hebrew word; literally the five books of Moses, but often used to refer to the whole Hebrew scriptures or even to Jewish law as a whole *treyf* – food that is not kosher

*tsuris* – trouble, distress, aggravation

*tukhes* – rear end, buttocks

*tzedakah* – Hebrew word for charity, with allusions to doing social justice

*tzedek* – Hebrew word for justice, righteousness

*ver veyst?* – who knows?

*vilde khaye* – literally wild animal, or a person acting with freedom against the culture

*vos a relief!* – what a relief!

*vos makhstu?* – how are you?

*yichud* – privacy. Used to describe a short period of time immediately after a wedding ceremony when the bride and groom have time alone together.

*zay gezunt* – be well

*zay shtil* – be quiet

*zemiros* – songs, particularly ones sung at a *shabbes* table

*zeyde* – grandfather

# About the Author

**I**ris **Mitlin Lav** grew up in the liberal Hyde Park neighborhood of Chicago, Illinois. She went on to earn an MBA from George Washington University and an AB from The University of Chicago, and to enjoy a long career of public policy analysis and management, with an emphasis on improving policies for low- and moderate-income families. She also taught public finance at Johns Hopkins University and George Mason University, and in 1999 received the Steven D. Gold award for contributions to state and local fiscal policy, an award jointly given by the Association for Public Policy Analysis and Management, the National Conference of State Legislatures, and the National Tax Association. *Gitel's Freedom* is her second novel; her first, *A Wife in Bangkok*, was published in 2020 by She Writes Press. Lav and her husband now live in Chevy Chase, Maryland, with Mango, their goldendoodle, and grandchildren nearby.

## Looking for your next great read?

We can help!

Visit www.shewritespress.com/next-read
or scan the QR code below for a list
of our recommended titles.

She Writes Press is an award-winning
independent publishing company founded to
serve women writers everywhere.